USA TODAY BESTSELLING AUTHOR

JENNIFER
ST. GILES

KAYLEE'S
JUSTICE

Case File #1

ISBN: 978-1-530858-27-9 (Print version)
ISBN: 978-1-9444785-13-0 (Digital version)

Cover Design and Interior Formatting by Day Agency
Editing by Ivy D. Truitt

KAYLEE'S JUSTICE

PROLOGUE

Golden Gate Bridge State Park
San Francisco
November 3rd
Friday, 10 PM

THE WIND COMING OFF the choppy, black bay had Adam Frasier by the short hairs. He shivered with a bone deep chill as cold as the crime scene. Ten years of Washington D.C. winters had yet to beat the need for warmth out of his Southern hide. He watched Matt Hessler, a Bay area homicide detective, walk from the cordoned off area. Matt's only concessions to the cold drizzle were an Oakland A's baseball cap and a zipped windbreaker. Adam had the collar of his trench coat turned up against the November rain and a fedora planted on his head; he either wasn't as stupid or as tough as Hessler.

"Makes your skin crawl, don't it, Frasier?"

"Teri McClutcheon's murder?" Adam studied Hessler's expression as the cop exhaled smoke then snuffed his cigarette against a bear-proof trashcan before dumping the butt. Any evidence had already been collected from the can. Not that there'd be any viable clues in it. The state park had seen a hell of a lot of traffic over the past four years.

The Artist of Death had yet to be wrong. Adam didn't doubt Teri had been a victim of the Route 101 Butcher, which meant the son-of-a-bitch had killed her and buried her here four years ago, *before* being caught and convicted for the murders of three women up in Eureka.

"Hell no, bones like these are easy." Hessler nodded toward the crime scene scattered about twenty feet along the hillside. She'd been buried in pieces. "It's the flesh and blood crime scenes that are hard to take. I'm talking about the Artist of Death. How does he know this shit? We get a mailed envelope with a drawing of Teri's face, the 101 Butcher's mug, and dead-on coordinates where we find her buried, undisturbed bones. She's been in the ground for something like four years. Logic demands that this Artist of Death witnessed the murder, but it's impossible for him to have seen all the murders he reports. How many does this make?"

Adam clenched his teeth. "Twenty-six." He'd been searching for this Artist of Death for five years. Once the mystery of the Artist of Death's work grabbed the FBI's attention, Adam obtained special permission to head up the investigation. So far, the Artist had sent to various police departments across the country, accurate sketches of twenty-six victims, their killers, and the GPS of the remains. At first, Adam theorized the Artist had gleaned his information from the dark web, where killers bragged about their deeds in detail. Then the Artist sent in information for Alice Bell, a sixteen-year-old girl who'd disappeared from Layton, Utah in July of 1975. She, along with two other teens from the town, went missing that summer. All had been never found victims Ted Bundy confessed to killing. So, how had—decades after Bundy's execution—the Artist of Death known Bell's remains were buried in a Wasatch Mountain picnic area not far from Layton? Unless Bundy had secretly told another person, or left behind an unknown map to Bell's body, there weren't many ways for the Artist to have known.

"It's a mystery," Adam muttered.

"That's all you can say? I mean how in the hell does this Artist know where all these people are buried?"

Adam shrugged. "Your guess is as good as mine." He sounded nonchalant, but he was far from it.

Adam had left his position in the FBI's Critical Incident Response Group to focus on finding the Artist of Death. He had to know how the man knew the things he did. So far the Artist had left nothing behind to identify him. He never used the same paper twice, never used the same pencil twice, never left DNA, a finger print, or any consistent fibers. Hell, he never even mailed his pictures from the same city. There were no patterns to follow—only a trail of locating victims and exposing their killers.

Hessler's grim mouth curved to a smirk. "You suits don't know any more than we do, do you? What the hell is the government paying you guys for?"

Adam was immune to local resentment. He expected it whenever he nosed uninvited into a breaking case. Being on the trail of the Artist of Death trumped any protocols or niceties. He always caught the first plane out as soon as reports of the Artist came in. Adam fruitlessly hoped that by being on scene as soon as he could, he'd find a clue. "You got any theories, Hessler? I'm all ears."

Hessler pulled out another cigarette, lit it, took a drag, and puffed into the rain. "None that I can believe in," he finally conceded.

Adam sat in the same boat. He gazed out over the bay for a long moment, frowning. Fog blanketed the Golden Gate Bridge in a ghostly mist as if all of the spirits haunting him had converged here to cry for justice. The one that cried the loudest, his sister Jenna, had been with him twenty-eight of his thirty-two years. All professional duty and morbid curiosity aside, deep down it was because of her he wanted to find the Artist of Death. He was obsessed. He knew it. He also knew how self-destructive obsessions were. "I'll let you know when I figure it out."

Inhaling the damp, salt air, Adam gave Teri's crime scene one last glance.

The Route 101 Butcher had hunted the west coast from California to Washington State, plucking young women right from the arms of their happy towns. From the beginning the bastard had refused to give up any information on his other victims or where they were buried. He sat on death row with a smug smile at the secrets he kept. Psychologists were still piecing together when and where the Butcher began killing, so it was anybody's guess how many of the hundreds of women missing from California this man had killed.

Adam should take comfort that the Artist of Death had made it possible for one more family to bring a loved one home for closure. He didn't, though. He needed answers and wouldn't stop until he had them.

The drizzling rain and depressing fog made the evening piss-ass miserable and as chilly as a morgue. Turning, he left the craggy area where Teri's body had been spread. Cars crept along the nearby Golden Gate Bridge, lights marking the passage of people going about their lives, oblivious to the stalking monsters among them. Hunching in his overcoat, Adam braced for another lonely hotel bed and the memories he could never seem to escape no matter how far he ran.

DAY 1
SATURDAY, MAY 10TH

1:00 P.M.

EVA ST. CLAIRE HUNG up the phone. Mason T. Smith had just
made her day.

"From that smile you'd think you'd made a date with a four-star general
instead of a serial killer."

Eva looked up to see live-in housekeeper, Lannie Andrews, shaking her head as
she brandished a Swiffer dust broom over the marble floor. Her sprayed-in-place,
iron-gray hair was as stiff as her starched uniform. They stood in the foyer of the
St. Claire's ancestral home, an old Victorian built in 1860. The ex-army nurse with
her crew of two cleaning women, Shirley and Elena, and Larry the handyman kept
the historic house in tip-top shape.

After Eva's parents died, free-spirited but loving Aunt Zena moved in to take
care of the St. Claire orphans. Long story short, disaster ensued. Though no Mary
Poppins, Lannie had stepped into the fray and immediately became indispensable.
The semblance of order and normalcy she brought had been, and still were, lifesavers
for Eva, her brother Devin, and her sister Iris.

Lannie, along with Paddy their father-like chauffeur, kept the St. Claire's
grounded—something essential given their cursed gifts and the constant battle to
keep them hidden. Before their deaths, their parents had drilled deeply into their
minds that keeping the St. Claire's psychic abilities secret was essential to their

survival. Apart from family, only Lannie and Paddy knew.

"I've been trying to see Smith for months."

"And once you do will that be the end of it then? You're as haunted and pale as a victim."

Eva shook her head. "Considering what Smith did to his victims haunted and pale would be a picture of health. But to answer your question, no, it won't be the end of it. Not until he gets the death penalty he deserves."

Lannie sighed. "You need to live, laugh, and love a bit. Or this work *will* be the death of you. Your aunt agrees with me on that. She'll be here in two weeks."

Eva had forgotten her aunt's impending arrival. Having Lannie and Aunt Zena in cahoots on anything spelled trouble. She patted her hip and grinned. "What's doing me in is your irresistible cuisine. After your lobster Eggs Benedict this morning I'll be eating oatmeal or toast for a month."

"Avoiding the subject—"

"I know. I know. Won't change the problem." Lannie never let anything slide. "I promise I will think about it. Where are Devin and Iris?"

She expected her brother and sister to be chomping at the bit to leave. As usual, she'd made them all late. At least Sheriff Doug and Trisha Kendrick, who were in charge of the charity auction today would forgive Eva anything, whether she deserved it or not.

"Iris and Devin are already in the car. Your migraines are worse after every vision, Eva. You're past the thinking stage."

Eva winced, truth was a bitch. "I promise I'll do something then. Yoga is good for stress."

Lannie rolled her eyes. "Make it naked in a sauna with a man, and it would be a start."

"Later, Lannie." Eva shook her head as she hurried out the doors and down the double staircase to the waiting car. Opening the sedan's door, she stuck her head in, surprised to find Iris at the wheel instead of Paddy.

Barely creasing his gray suit Devin sat stiffly in the back, impatiently tapping his fingers on his cane, a heavy frown visible above his dark glasses.

Eva set her gaze on Iris and tightened her grip on her purse. She'd been about to drive separately to the charity auction so she could get to the penitentiary faster after the event. Now that Smith had finally agreed to see her, she wanted to get there before he changed his mind. Tomorrow he'd be transported several hours away to maximum security at Georgia State Prison near Reidsville.

Instead of asking Iris if she was ready for this step Eva bit her tongue and got into the car, buckling her seatbelt. At some point, they all had to get back to the way things were before her sister's breakdown. They never had, and never would, have a normal life, but at least before then, every moment hadn't been balanced on a broken eggshell.

Leaving the house, Iris rounded the gray marble fountain of a blindfolded Lady Justice with her sword in her right hand. She stood dead center of the circular driveway. Unlike her counterparts, this Lady Justice held unbalanced scales in her left hand where a broken heart was outweighed by a lounging, horned demon. Not even the sparkling water at the statue's feet nor the bright yellow pansies at the fountain's base, could alleviate her grim presence.

Eva hated the daily reminder of the St. Claire's curse. She used to believe that she, Iris, and Devin would escape their dark fates, but they hadn't.

Their ancestors' circumstances and stories of fighting evil might differ, but the end results were too similar to ignore. Blindness, brokenness, and a fruitless battle for justice that always ended in tragedy.

"You both need to say something before you explode. I won't shatter." Iris's teasing tone didn't match her white-knuckle grip on the steering wheel. Iris was sunshine and bohemian compared to Eva and Devin's dark coloring and conservative style. She had long, blond hair, bright blue eyes, and wore silk T-shirts over stone-washed jeans—everywhere. Her concession to dress up for an occasion was to wear killer shoes and a blazer. Today's jacket gleamed a bright jade; her shoes, zebra striped platforms.

Eva wore a navy suit and matching flats.

Devin snorted. "As if anything we said could make a difference. You will do as your impulsive heart leads you to do. But if you're fishing for a premonition, I haven't had one of us dying in a fiery crash. So, we may be good to go."

"Great," Iris said, dryly.

Eva dug in her purse for her sunglasses. With a headache already edging closer, she needed shielding. The bright Georgia sun stabbed shards of blinding light between the live oaks lining the equestrian estate's driveway. She also wanted to hide her doubt and fear from her sister.

A lot of ground lay between "good to go" and a "fiery crash," so Devin's answer didn't help matters much. He'd be the first to admit that sometimes his allegorical premonitions were as "tunneled" as his vision. Every year, Retinitis Pigmentosa stole a little more of his sight while his psychic gift carved out another chunk of his soul.

"I'm surprised Paddy stepped aside to let you drive," Eva said, searching for a gentle way to address her worry without causing Iris to doubt herself even more. The transplanted Irishman had been more than the family's driver for twenty-five years, he'd stood in for the father they wished they'd never had.

"We've been practicing on the commute to Dimensions for the past few weeks." Before turning onto the main road, Iris met Eva's gaze. "I—we—uh, even rode MARTA the other day."

Eva searched her sister's expression. "You should have told me. I would have come with you."

"You were up at that horrible cabin, and had enough to deal with investigating Kaylee's murder. Dr. Caro rode with me and Paddy. She asked about you, Devin." Iris glanced into the rear view mirror.

Before Dr. Caroline Ward became Iris's psychiatrist, she'd dated Devin for a few months. He'd yet to say why he'd broken off the relationship.

"You told her I was never better, I hope," Devin said.

"I told her you were a stubborn ass in desperate need of her attention."

Devin leaned forward in the seat, mouth open to start a World War with Iris. Eva held up her hand. "She's jerking your chain to change the subject, Dev." She glared at Iris. "You're not getting off that easy, missy. What happened on the ride?"

Iris exhaled. "Nothing really. Just the normal bombardment of random thoughts from the people around me. Heard one guy thinking over and over again the 'all work and no play makes Jack a dull boy.' I keep thinking about that, but otherwise I'm fine."

Eva froze then blinked with shock. Was it happening again? Had a killer linked to Iris's mind? Thanks to Stephen King's *The Shining*, the "all work and no play" phrase would be forever connected to horror as would the possession of a man's mind by evil spirits.

Devin broke into laughter. "Now she's jerking your chain, Eva. Even I can see that's too coincidental to be believable."

Iris giggled. "I only said what she was *dying* to hear."

Eva practically collapsed in the seat with relief and laughed, too. "You, brat. That wasn't funny."

"Then why are you laughing."

"Because…because I need to." Eva wiped a tear from the corner of her eye. Everything from her head to her toes seemed less tense than it had seconds ago.

"Exactly. And FYI, the Marta ride went without a hitch. I'm back in control."

For now, Eva couldn't help but think. Her sister wouldn't be in the clear until they found the bodies of the murdered women and caught their killer, whose mind had trapped Iris's. Why the killer's thoughts had suddenly bonded so strongly to Iris during a month-long killing spree that she couldn't shut them out was a mystery. Somewhere, five women had disappeared during that month. Given that proximity usually factored into Iris's telepathic abilities, Eva and Devin had done as much under the radar investigating as they could in the surrounding area, but had come up empty handed. No stories of five missing women had appeared in the media. Were the victims homeless? Or prostitutes? Or runaways? Crimes against those that mattered least, rarely made the news.

To Eva, every person mattered. Even though she only saw things after it was too late to save the victim, she didn't let that stop her from doing what she could to give the victims justice and their families' closure, no matter the cost.

Iris helped Eva in her mission, and Eva wondered if by doing that, Iris had become more susceptible to being overwhelmed by the killer's thoughts. The horror for Iris had stopped as suddenly as it had begun and none of them, with all of their abilities, had been able to help.

Eva refused to consider the killings had only been in Iris's imagination. Though that's what they'd led Dr. Caro to believe, so Iris could get help. It had been an easy enough deception to call Iris's readings of the killer's thoughts "nightmares" and to blame the "nightmares" on a childhood trauma she'd suffered. That they had all suffered, really—and had all purposely buried in the past.

Their shared trauma was likely why none of them had ever sustained a relation-ship with a significant other for any length of time. God only knew what role their parents' psychic gifts had played in their deaths. Their father had been telepathic as well as a medium to the spirit world. Eva didn't know which of their father's psychic curses had led him to kill their mother and then himself. She only knew the inescapable reality, that the St. Claire's history of tragedy would repeat itself.

"I am back in control," Iris said again, this time more forcefully. "And I'm giving you both fair warning. I'm going to expose and stop the son-of-a-bitch. He has to be close by. Somewhere in my routine I connected with his mind and I will find him."

Eva caught her breath. *Damn. Iris did not need to be actively trolling the minds of the populace for a killer who had come close to destroying her psyche.*

"Anger is good," Devin said. "There is strength in anger."

Eva glared at him. "There are also rash decisions and reckless actions in that foolhardy direction as well." She bit her lip and searched for reason. "Iris, you need to give your mind time to heal—"

"What? Are you the only one allowed to pick up the St. Claire sword for justice?"

"No, but—"

"Then stop trying to shelter me from the realities of our lives. I need to carry my load instead of spending all my time painting rose gardens and riding horses."

Iris could out-ride her and Devin, and had gained fame for the beautiful gardens of light she painted. She was known as the Thomas Kinkade of the flower world. Her art demanded a high price, which was why they were on their way to do a benefit for the National Victim's Assistance Program. Among a number of other items from local talent, Sheriff Doug Grant and Trisha Kendrick, who ran the NVAP in Atlanta, had arranged for Iris's art and Eva's signed True Crime books to be auctioned.

"You do a lot to help, Iris," Eva said, trying to reassure her sister. "You draw what I see. Twenty-six victims have found justice and their killers exposed because of your skill."

Iris shook her head. "That's your fight and your gift. I just help out. Something I am more than grateful to do, but it's not enough."

Eva clenched her jaw and pressed her fingertips to her aching temple. "Then we'll talk and figure out a solution, but give me a few days. I'm overloaded right now."

"Are you going to tell us about it before your head explodes?" Devin asked. "You've been nuclear ever since taking on Kaylee Waters' story."

She bit her lip. Trying to put into words her disjointed visions of Mason Smith's torture and murder of the girl no one seemed to care about. "I don't know what to tell you. Something about my visions in the cabin are off. Everything is a doubled blur. I am seeing things from Kaylee's pain-hazed perspective. What Mason Smith did to her was so horrific that... it's hard to get through." She shuddered. Eva never knew if she would see a crime from the victim's point of view or from the killer's. Both were bad.

"You should have taken a break after writing *Hayden's Hell*," Devin said. "Smith is in prison and yesterday they sentenced him to life without parole for Angel Banning's kidnapping and rape. Why are you putting yourself through this? Why continue with Kaylee's book?"

"People need to know about cold-blooded monsters like Smith. He's lived off the grid for twenty years and is refusing to tell investigators anything about his life. There are more victims, but until we know where he's been, finding them will be hard. Putting his mug and MO in the hands of people everywhere, might bring in valuable information. More importantly, Kaylee deserves justice. Even the death penalty doesn't make up for what he did to her. The DA thinks Smith's DNA on Kaylee's clothes and her forensic report is enough to fry him, but I'm not willing to just sit back and see. If I can get Smith to talk about himself, about Kaylee, about anything, it might help. And if I see him in person, maybe then I can figure out what's bothering me about my visions of him."

"I'll come with you," Iris said. "I can get into his head and tell you everything—"

"No!" Eva shouted in unison with Devin.

Iris pulled to the roadside, hit the brakes then glared at her and Devin. "This is exactly what I am talking about. Either let me carry my load or...or I'll move out on my own."

Eva shook her head. She knew Iris was grandstanding. Her sister wouldn't last a week without the stained glass turret where she painted and her beloved horses she rode every day. Eva and Devin each kept one horse to ride. Iris had four. "I'll see you moved to Timbuktu before subjecting you to Smith. Seriously, Iris, it was bad. To do what he did, he is evil to the bone. There's no point in you suffering, too. We'll find a way for you to help, but there're some hells I just can't take you to. Please, can you understand that?"

Iris sighed and put the car back in motion. "Maybe. There were things from that guy's thoughts last month that were so twisted...I couldn't tell either of you about them. Some things are better left in the dark."

"And you're deliberately going to hunt him down, Iris?" Devin asked incredulous.

"That's crazy," Eva said.

"You're no better, Eva," Devin said. "Subjecting yourself over and over again to Kaylee's torture when her killer is already behind bars for life, is just as crazy. Unfortunately, the price for justice will be greater than any of us can imagine."

"What's that supposed to mean?" Eva demanded, wanting to snatch off Devin's dark glasses to see his expression. "Did you have a premonition?"

Devin shrugged. "Nothing I can speak about yet. Aunt Zena will arrive early for her visit, and I did see round circles dripping with chocolate."

"Krispy Kreme donuts await us? When?" Iris cried, eyes wide at the mention of her biggest weakness.

Eva inwardly groaned. The last things she needed right now were Aunt Zena and donuts.

Devin only smiled. "You just missed the exit for the auction, Iris."

1:30 P.M.

A DAM EXITED THE ATLANTA Hartsfield-Jackson airport and reveled a moment in the humid heat that instantly went bone deep. He usually welcomed any excuse to duck home for the weekend, but this time, he dreaded the decisions he had to make. Seeing his father's souped-up "Batmobile" illegally parked and his flushed father arguing with a traffic cop told him the old man's blood pressure was up, and the day was off to a bad start.

He hurried over, praying he could defuse the situation before his father ended up in jail. An irritating but lovable mix of Colombo and Oscar from the Odd Couple, Vince Frasier just didn't get that the old school philosophy of we're-on-the-same-team-so-let-the-little-things-slide didn't exist anymore. Political correctness and righteous high horses ruled the day. Besides, being retired from the Georgia Bureau of Investigation (GBI) didn't give a man the right to park where he wanted, roll through neighborhood stop signs, or burn rubber doing donuts in an empty parking lot. His father had racked up twelve points on his driver's license in the year since "fixing up" his beloved Mustang. Three more points and the courts would suspend his ass.

The cop pulled out his ticket pad and Adam's father rolled his eyes heavenward then broke into a relieved grin the moment he saw Adam. "There he is Officer.

Like I said, he's FBI and we're on an important case. Show the man your badge, Adam. We've only thirty minutes to make the meeting."

Doing his best to keep his temper, Adam glanced at the cop's name tag then met his glare. "Is there a problem, I can help with, Officer Robb?"

"You FBI?"

"Yes. Just off the plane from D.C." Adam gritted his teeth as he reached for his badge. He hated being put into this position.

Officer Robb snapped his ticket booklet closed. "Don't do this again. You won't like what happens next time." He abruptly turned away and motioned for cars to keep moving in the loading and unloading zone.

Adam snatched the keys from his father's hand. "Get in," he said, opening the driver's door and tossing his carry-on onto the backseat.

For once, his father didn't argue; he piled in shotgun and buckled his seatbelt. "You need to step on it. We have to be there in thirty minutes." Adam settled behind the wheel and eased into traffic. "You didn't tell me we had a hard appointment, Pops. Is it with Mom's doctor or Magnolia Place's director?" He'd scheduled this last minute trip because his mother managed to not only rack up a thousand dollars to a 1-900-psychic number on a cell phone she'd borrowed from a fellow patient, but she'd also escaped her care facility and had been getting into a "psychic's" car up at the main highway when she'd been caught yesterday.

Twenty-eight years ago his sister Jenna had been taken. The obsession to find her had eventually stolen his mother's sanity and she'd been placed in a home with early onset dementia the year he'd graduated high school. Both tragedies were Adam's fault.

"No. We don't meet with them about your mother until this evening."

"Then what's the hurry?"

"We need to make an auction before it starts. St. Claire is supposed to be there and I have to see her."

"Auction for what? And who is St. Claire? How can that be more important than Mom's situation right now?"

Adam winced at his father's curse and the quiet defeat in his voice as he whispered. "If there were anything I could do for Linda. Any way I could save her. Any way I could change the past, you know I'd die to do it."

"I know." Adam squeezed his father's shoulder. "I didn't mean that the way it sounded. It's just I expected to go see Mom immediately."

"They've got her on high security and the nurse you hired is with her. God willing, what happened yesterday won't happen again. We'll get into all of her stuff later. Right now, there's a killer to be caught."

Adam gripped the steering wheel. If he hadn't been flying down the interstate toward Atlanta, he might have hit the brakes, too. "What the hell are you into, Pops? You're *retired*. What killer? And why am I just now hearing about this?"

"Oh, you've already heard about it. More times than either of us can count." His father held up a hardback book from a bestselling True Crime writer. Adam hadn't made the name connection at first. He did now. On the red cover was the picture of a blood spattered Top Secret File with crime scene tape across it. *HAYDEN'S HELL* BY EVA ST. CLAIRE. "I couldn't sleep last night, so I read. The book just came out this week. Not only does St. Claire question Carlan's guilt, but she had to have interviewed the Haydens's *real* killer. It's the only way she could have known."

Adam wanted to bang his head on the dash, but bit back his frustrated reply. He understood all too well how survivor's guilt never allowed a person to let go of the past…or rest. Tony Hayden, his father's best friend and fellow GBI agent, had been slaughtered on his rural farm along with his wife and two young daughters fifteen years ago.

Tony had called Vince an hour before, asking him to come to the farm; he'd figured out something scarier than hell about an investigation. Vince's cell died before anything else could be said. Vince had forgotten to charge it, as usual, lost his back up battery—somewhere—as usual, *and* he'd left his charger at the office, as usual.

Vince had hurried from the nursing home where he'd been eating dinner with Linda and raced to Tony's farm. As soon as the car charger juiced enough bars to connect, Vince called Tony back. Tony never answered. Vince was the first one to the scene of the bloodbath.

Three days later, John Carlan, a serial killer terrorizing the east coast, was killed in a standoff with the GBI. Evidence found in Carlan's apartment linked him to the Hayden murders, but Adam's father had never accepted it. His constant harping on the case likely led to him being pushed into an early retirement a few years ago.

Adam had always humored his father's need to play "what if" on the Hayden murders. But maybe that had been a mistake. "Now, Pops—"

"St. Claire asks the same questions. Carlan's MO was to hold a family for hours, sometimes days, but he kills the Haydens in less than an hour? He also targeted families with teenage girls. Megan and Melissa were six and four."

"I get that, Pops. But hard evidence says Carlan deviated from his pattern for some reason. Maybe he was just desperate to kill and the Haydens were there. He picked his victims from BuyMart chain stores and Mary Hayden had been at the local store that morning. The axe with the Haydens' blood still on it was found in Carlan's apartment. You just can't accept the facts because you feel guilty. Even if your phone hadn't died, it wouldn't have changed what happened."

"You don't know that. Tony was onto something and had called to tell me about it. Tony was a seasoned agent, yet he and his whole family were killed and Carlan got off unscathed? No bruises anywhere? Why were the house alarms turned off? Why were the security cameras disabled? I've always had doubts about the case. Now, thanks to St. Claire, I have proof." Vince slapped the book with his palm.

"What proof? And why go to an auction to see St. Claire. Why not just set up a meeting to ask her questions?"

"According to her website, she doesn't do interviews and has no public appearances scheduled any time soon. She is, however, attending an auction for the National Victim's Assistance Program today. So I thought we could bid on her books, meet her, and ask a question or two about who she interviewed for the book. Quietly, you know. Don't want to let anyone know we're onto them."

"Onto *who*? The killer? You still haven't said what this proof is."

Vince sighed. "You have to understand. I'd just found my best friend and his whole family butchered. It was surreal. I couldn't believe what I was seeing. Blood everywhere. Faces frozen in horror. Mary in the kitchen. Meagan nearby at her tea table. Tony in his office. But Melissa was nowhere. After I searched the house, I found her in the garden. He'd posed her with a flower on her chest and her arms and legs spread like a snow angel. About two feet away, he'd done the same with her doll. I fell to my knees in the dirt, wondering if she'd been violated. The horror overwhelmed me. I'm, uh, sorry, I wasn't thinking clearly. I had to do something, anything. I reached over and put Melissa's doll in her arms."

Adam sucked in air and blinked back the burning in his eyes. His father had never before revealed so much about finding the Haydens' murdered. Adam knew it had been bad. He'd read the file and knew the details, but hearing the torment in his father's voice, wrenched Adam's gut.

"As soon as I did it, I realized I'd altered the crime scene. Still, I just left it that way and never told a soul. At the time, it mattered more than anything else for Melissa to have her doll close."

Adam thought he might have done the same thing in his father's shoes. "It's okay, Pops. I understand why you did it. But you should have reported what you did at the time. If you go back and tell everyone now, it will put every case you worked in jeopardy. They'll say if he fudged here, where else did he do it?"

Vince didn't seem to hear, he kept on talking, gaze fixed on the book in his hands. "Ironic that one act is going to help me find out who killed them and why."

Adam shoved his lecture to the back burner. "I still don't get how that is proof Carlan didn't do it."

Vince opened the book. "St. Claire describes the crime scene in the garden with the doll placed a few feet away from Melissa, posed like Melissa with a flower on her chest. Only two people know that.

"You, and the killer." Adam's mind scrambled through the implications. No one had ever been able to question Carlan about the Hayden murders. As far as Adam remembered, Carlan hadn't confided in anyone before he died, so it was slim that anyone else knew that detail. "Damn. That would mean…" If his father was right and Carlan hadn't killed the Haydens… "That would mean the axe found in Carlan's apartment had been planted."

Vince inhaled hard. "Yes."

"That would mean one of the agents working the case or close to the case planted the evidence…maybe even made sure Carlan didn't survive the standoff with the GBI."

"Yes."

"Hell."

"Exactly. Someone Tony knew did a sloppy job copycatting and framing a serial killer because they wanted to shut Tony up. Whatever Tony wanted to tell me about an investigation he was into got him and his family killed."

"I believe you, but it's not like we have hard proof. We need to keep this between the two of us and you need to let me call the shots until we figure out who did it. Or somebody could get themselves killed."

Vince surprisingly agreed.

They made it to the Egyptian Room at the Fox Theater in downtown Atlanta in time. The next two hours passed in a harried blur as surreal as finding rich, middle-eastern décor in a southern landmark. He'd grown up in Atlanta, but had never been to the Fox. Tragedy and the resulting battle to survive had consumed so much of life he hadn't had the time nor the opportunity for plays or concerts.

He'd have to come back to the Fox someday, but under more pleasant circumstances. The auction had ended. He'd paid for and received eight books signed by St. Claire and that was it. He was five thousand dollars poorer with little hope of making a connection to Eva St. Claire. Either afraid of crowds or a diva too lofty to mingle, she sat in a cordoned off VIP section with bodyguard-like ushers as gate keepers.

Now that the auction was over, the dozen or so other people seated in the VIP section had moved to mingle with the crowd. Only Eva, and her siblings—a well-dressed man holding a cane and a quirky woman with zebra striped stilettos from which you could high dive—remained. They sat, talking amongst themselves, their expressions obscured behind dark-tinted glasses.

Worse yet, the determined edge to his father's expression told Adam that Vince Frasier would leap over the barriers and march up to his target in any second. Adam grabbed his father's arm, and dragged him over to the woman running the show, the local spokesperson for the National Victim's Assistance Program. She'd just stepped away from a group. and appeared to be leaving the high-columned room. Adam caught up with her.

"Ms. Kendrick, my father and I have a favor to ask."

She turned with a frown then smiled. "Mr. uh, Frasier, right?" She shook hands with Adam then Vince.

Adam nodded to his father. "He's Mr. Frasier. I'm just Adam."

She laughed. "Adam then. We appreciate your contribution today."

Adam shrugged. "Considering your mission and the resources needed to help, it's not nearly enough. I'm a firm believer in your cause. What I wanted to know is if Eva St. Claire would personalize these books to my father here. He's a fan and it would mean a lot to him."

Her frown returned and she directed her gaze to where Eva sat. "I don't know. Let me see if the author is able to now. If not, we can have them personalized at a later date and ship them to you free of cost."

It was all Adam could do to keep from rolling his eyes. He'd just paid an arm and a leg. The author was present, so what was the big deal? The response should have been a resounding "*absolutely*." "We'd appreciate you seeing if she could."

"Of course. Hold on a moment." Kendrick headed to Eva.

Adam stood with the gift bag of books at the front of the room, feeling like a pauper petitioning the queen...or make that the royal family. There'd been about a hundred people who'd come to the auction. Some of the bidding had been fierce, especially for the flower garden paintings by Iris St. Claire. He'd been impressed with her work and had bid on one but had lost. It was just as well. The empty swing in the garden would have been too much of a reminder of Jenna. Still, each of Iris's paintings had a magical light with a vibrancy that drew him in.

The sisters were intriguing with their creative works; polar opposites of each other. Eva wrote about death, murder, and mayhem, while Iris's art conveyed tranquility and...hope.

Eva shifted her head in their direction as Kendrick spoke to her. Even across the room, Adam could see the author take a bracing breath before nodding. Kendrick waved them over to the St. Claires.

"You're a genius," Vince muttered.

"Glad you've finally realized it. So leave this to me. We might not get to ask questions today, but I promise we will soon." Considering the gun-shy signs, even a single question now might lock and close all future windows and doors. The ushers let them pass and Kendrick introduced them to the St. Claire's—Eva, Iris, and Devin. Though they smiled and had firm, welcoming handshakes, their tinted glasses still made an unbreachable barrier.

Adam handed Eva the bag of books. "We appreciate this. Vince, my father is-"

"An admiring fan," Vince interjected. "An envious one, too. I've always wanted to write."

Adam blinked. That had been Adam's line. And a true one. Adam had hundreds of pages full of his late night ramblings stuffed in the bottom drawer of his bedside table. He hadn't known his father wanted to write as well.

Eva smiled and pulled out the books. "A page a day will give you a book a year. Make these out to Vince then?"

Vince nodded.

Adam quickly went for Plan B and turned to Iris. No point in putting all their eggs in one basket. "To my dismay, I missed out on one of your paintings. Do you have a local venue for your work?"

Iris nodded. "My studio in Buckhead, Dimensions. Which painting did you bid on?"

"The one with the swing set. It seems to be just waiting for a little girl to come out and... play." Adam's voice caught and he quickly cleared his throat to cover the emotion that started to rise.

Iris surprisingly lowered her glasses to meet his gaze. Clear blue eyes combined with golden hair, she appeared as idyllic and pure as her paintings and much younger than he'd thought, given her degree of success. "That painting is part of a series. Stop by the gallery and maybe you'll find what you're looking for."

"I'll do that—"

Devin St. Claire stood and leaned their way. "No one ever finds what they are truly looking for. Just what they think they want, until they realize they don't."

Scowling, Iris snapped her glasses back up. "Pessimism is my brother's strong suit."

"Just realistic," Devin said. "Nothing in life is what it seems. *Or who.*"

Adam tensed, unable to ignore Devin's pointed suspicion. Even though Adam's interest in Iris's paintings was sincere, Devin seemed to know he was there for a different reason.

"Which is why you fail to recognize happiness when she's standing in front of your face," Iris said. "You'll have to forgive, Devin. Now, where were we? You were about to say you'd come by the gallery, right?"

From Devin's furrowed brow and clenched jaw, Adam could see Iris gave as good as she got.

Adam nodded. "I'm only here for the weekend. Are you open on Sundays?"

"Yes, from noon until five." Iris suddenly swung around, gazed across the room then turned back. "I'll see you tomorrow then." She elbowed her brother. "Dr. Caro is here. I'm bringing her over and you had better be nice." Iris adeptly leveraged over the rope in her heels and hurried away.

Devin muttered a curse. Reaching into his breast pocket, he pulled out a slim business card holder and handed over a card. "Only wolves need wool, Adam. Give Eva your card."

Adam winced. The embossed card simply had Devin's name and contact information. Nothing else. Adam watched as Devin used his cane to navigate his way from the room. The man had some degree of blindness but he'd seen right through Adam's ploy. The last thing Adam wanted to do was give Eva his card. He didn't think alerting her to his employment with the FBI right off the bat would open any doors. The entire encounter had been odd. He could see from Iris's trajectory, with a stunning redhead in tow, that Devin would not make the clean escape he sought. *Interesting.*

Returning his attention to the remaining St. Claire, Adam discovered Eva had removed her tinted glasses to sign. She opened the last book, clearly listening to his father ramble very convincingly about an Andy Griffith-like bounty hunter story. Either his father was serious, or it was a Colombo-worthy distraction, deserving of an Emmy. After finishing, Eva laughed lightly and looked up. "Very Interesting, Mr. Frasier."

"So how do you go about researching everything? I just read your newest book, *Hayden's Hell*. You're very good."

Adam saw Eva tense and stepped into the situation. "I'm sure Ms. St. Claire doesn't have time—" She met Adam's gaze and he froze. Her haunting gray gaze sucked the air out of the room. Thickly lashed, her eyes teemed with dark mystery. Adam's body clenched as if he were poised on the edge of a cliff.

Eva's eyes widened with awareness before she looked away, snapped the book closed, and smiled at Vince. "It's no trouble. Hearing your enthusiasm for your story is refreshing, Mr. Frasier. In fiction, very little of the research an author does actually ends up in detail in the book. It flavors your story, though. You want your *facts* accurate, but the conflict and your characters are the backbone of the book. Whereas, with true crime writing, the facts are the backbone of the story. They have to be as accurate, and sometimes as detailed, as possible. I research through interviews, articles, case files, or anywhere else information about the subject can be found. Like today, I hope to shed more light on a young girl's tragic death. I'll be interviewing her killer who got a life sentence yesterday for another crime."

"Who?" Adam found himself asking before he could stop.

She startled and blinked, as if suddenly waking. Her cool reserve fell like a curtain. "I really shouldn't say at this point." She handed Vince the signed books.

"Forgive me," Adam replied quickly. "I didn't mean to pry but were I to take a guess, you're seeing Mason Smith. His sentencing was yesterday. Stopping predators and making sure they never see the light of day is my job." He went ahead and handed Eva his card. "Your brother asked me to give this to you."

She didn't confirm or deny his guess, and until he told her that her brother had made the request, Adam was sure Eva had been about to reject his card.

Though his father would whine for the next thirty years for not coming close to talking about the Haydens, Adam decided to cut their losses and ride this horse another day. "Thank you for signing the books." He offered Eva his hand. Her grip was firm but brief, her smile fleeting.

"You're welcome. And you had better write that book, Mr. Frasier. Don't forget, a page a day will give you a book in a year."

Vince nodded. "I will. You've been great. I hope to see you at your next signing. Do you know when that will be?"

"Not for a while. I'm in the middle of a book. But you can sign up for my newsletter on my website and that will keep you posted."

"I'll do that," Vince said.

"Be careful," Adam told Eva. "Mason T. Smith is one sick son-of-a-bitch." Adam had taken particular interest in Smith's trial. Any killer who preyed on young girls, caught his attention. He couldn't bring Jenna home, but he could make sure justice was served.

"I'm always careful," Eva replied. Rather than assuring, her tone sounded more like a warning…to him.

"Good," Adam said, urging his father away.

Outside the theater, news vans lined Peachtree Street. Several reporters and their camera crews milled around the exit looking like predators ready to pounce on trapped prey. Adam recognized one woman who always wore red, as being a crime reporter for a popular news and radio station, WGGS. Grace DuMond had built a career on sharp, and sometimes controversial questions.

Crossing the street to the parking garage, Adam looked back at a sudden commotion behind him. Eva and her siblings had just exited the theater with two of the burly security men who'd been manning the auction. The barrage of shouted questions completely drowned out the sounds of traffic and everyday life on the busy street corner. Reporters surrounded the St. Claires like sharks in a feeding frenzy.

Now Adam understood the siblings' dark glasses and Eva's "no interview" policy. A hefty woman dressed in black from cap to boots, and dreadlocks bouncing, hurried across the street with a video camera glued to her pale face. She shoved Adam aside in her haste to film the St. Claire's exit from the theater.

"Pardon me," Adam shouted at the woman's back.

The woman shot him a left-handed bird that looked particularly obscene from her fingerless gloves.

"Did you see her?" Adam muttered to his father.

"What can you expect from the press?"

"True." Adam laughed, letting go of his anger. If he allowed the actions of idiots rule him, he'd be a slave for life.

"I've seen her before. She wears all black and works with the shark in blood red. Never did like that reporter," his father muttered as they entered the parking garage.

"DuMond?" Adam asked.

"That'd be her. Nobody at the GBI liked her. She gets in your face and sensationalizes tragedy under the guise of 'the public has a right to know.'"

They reached his father's wannabe Batmobile. "How is she any different than Eva St. Claire? Don't the two do the same thing? Sensationalize crime for profit?" Adam asked.

His father shook his head. "Not even in the same universe. Besides, you never see St. Claire deliberately in the public eye hounding a victim for a story. That reminds me. I *had* her in the palm of my hand. Why'd you stick your nose into the conversation?"

"'Had her'? Come on, Pops. St. Claire wouldn't even tell us whom she planned to interview today. Do you honestly think she would have discussed her research on the Haydens right then and there?"

Vince frowned, climbed into the car, and shut the door hard. "No, *damn it*. No. It didn't play out like I thought it would. And why in the hell did you let the cat out of the bag? Seems like a brick wall went up the second she knew you were FBI."

"With her, I think that wall is always up. Her brother pegged us and requested I leave my card with his sister. For someone who walks with a cane, he sees pretty damn well."

"Tunnel vision. I read up on the whole family. Originally from Scotland, with a string of tragedies that goes way back through their ancestors, Retinitis Pigmentosa runs in the genes. He'll eventually go completely blind. He graduated Harvard Law at the top of his class, but never went into practice. Plays the piano instead."

"In night clubs?"

"With symphonies. That classical stuff your mom always played."

A smile tugged Adam's lips as a whisper of a memory washed over him. Whenever his dad blasted country music in the garage or out at the barbeque grill, his mother would either play Bach or Beethoven on the piano or amp up opera on the stereo inside the house. Adam didn't know whether to twang or to trill. "What sort of tragedy?"

Vince grunted. "Their father killed their mother then himself twenty years ago. The youngest was home at the time, but too little to call for help. The older two found their little sister in the parents' room covered in blood when they returned home from school. As I recall, that story was DuMond's big break into crime reporting. You couldn't turn on the news back then without her going on and on about the murder and suicide in one of Georgia's wealthiest families. Now that I think of it, Sheriff Doug Grant, the man you outbid for Eva's books, was one of the first responders to that crime scene."

"The man with the Elvis-like toupee?" Adam frowned. He would have been twelve then. He didn't remember hearing about the St. Claire's tragedy, but then his own situation with his sister missing and his mother losing touch with reality had pretty much consumed Adam's head. "No wonder they all seem…haunted." Especially Eva, he thought. If he hadn't gone to the auction intent on seeing her, once he'd seen her striking gray gaze, he'd have singled her out of the crowd anyway.

He'd been to Scotland once in an attempt to connect to his Frasier roots. He remembered two things from the ageless homeland, pub hangovers and the ghostly gray mists blanketing the lakes and glens in the early mornings. From the Highland crags and moors to the sea, he'd loved the place, but he'd never been back. He didn't deserve it.

5:00 P.M.

THE QUESTIONS FROM THE reporters outside the Fox Theater continued to hound Eva during her drive to the prison. After all these years, she should be immune to them—especially Grace DuMond's abrasive voice. It grated like sandpaper. The reporter, and her in-your-face camerawoman, never failed to bring up the past and set Eva's nerves on edge.

As she drove, nightmarish memories of her parents' death intermingled with Kaylee's cries for help and the lingering questions about the slaughter of Tony Hayden's family pounded her to the point her head throbbed with almost dizzying pain. She barely saw the burly, bald guard who'd escorted her to the visitation room or realized he'd complimented her several times on her books.

"Can I get your signature, Eva?" the guard asked as she sat at the visitor's booth. "You don't mind if I call you Eva, do you? I've read your books so many times, I feel as if I know you." He set a black pen and the back of a store receipt in front of her. Eva blinked at the "Repent or Perish" slogan on the pen with a chewed-on end. Forcing her mind to focus on the guard, she studied him a moment. Aside from a squirrely beard, he looked like a regular, tooth-pick chewing Joe who'd just met his all-time idol.

Though her stomach churned and her hands shook, Eva managed a smile and signed her name. The man held the signature and the chewed pen in his left hand, practically dancing a jig as he left her. She thought it a bit odd, but dug hand sanitizer from her purse and set her thoughts on the task of cracking Smith's silence.

Relentless research, tireless Kaylee investigation, and extensive interviews always consumed her whenever she wrote a victim's story. But usually by the time she finished the rough draft, she had enough data to back up her visions from the crime scene and could let the tragedy fade to the nightmares hidden deep inside her mind. This time, she couldn't let the story go. From the very beginning, Kaylee Waters had gotten lost in the system—a great injustice.

Her disappearance from a downtown housing project three weeks before Angel Banning's kidnapping, had barely been a blip in the local evening news. Though her mother insisted differently, law enforcement thought the twelve-year-old had run away on the heels of arguing with her mother about babysitting her younger siblings after school that day.

By contrast, Angel Banning's abduction from an upscale neighborhood near the Governor's mansion had received national coverage from the beginning. Part of it was that Angel's kidnapping had been caught on a high-tech surveillance camera monitored by an expensive home security company. Driving a white, carpet cleaning van, Smith had been seen snatching Angel off her scooter and knocking her out, before dumping her in his vehicle. The Amber alert and APB went out almost immediately.

Even then, Smith evaded detection until the next day. He made the mistake of stopping for gas near the location he held Angel captive in the North Georgia Mountains. Receiving the tip, local police, State Troopers, and a SWAT team quickly canvassed the area, found the van, and Angel, still alive. Had Smith stuck to the economically depressed suburbs where high-tech security systems didn't exist, he'd probably still be killing.

Smith had yet to talk, refusing to reveal information about his life, or about other victims, but everyone knew Angel had not been his first. She just happened to be the one who lived because he got caught. Pinpointing other possible victims was difficult because in the Atlanta sex trafficking trade there was hot market for girls around that age.

Watching Smith sitting smugly at his trial had angered Eva and sent her hunting for his victims. Following his rural cabin MO, she had doggedly visited dozens of cabins in and around the area he'd been captured in. That's how she'd found Kaylee's crime scene.

Revealing the girl's murder to the authorities, while keeping her psychic secrets, had been tricky. Eva had Paddy rent the cabin for a weekend and use Blue, their adopted Irish Wolfhound, to find Kaylee's grave. Paddy then reported the discovery of Kaylee's remains and the police took it from there, thankfully finding Smith's DNA on Kaylee's tattered clothes.

So far, no one had considered it too suspicious that Paddy, a person close to a true crime writer, had discovered another of Smith's victims.

She'd eventually find more of Smith's victims. Exposing them would be difficult, but she and Iris would cross that bridge another day. Thus far, she and her sister had been able to stay anonymous while sending portraits of victims, mugs of killers, and the GPS of the crime scenes, but she had no delusions that they could go undiscovered forever.

Right now, only Kaylee mattered.

Even though DNA tied Smith to Kaylee's murder, the information had come too late to be presented during Smith's trial for the kidnapping and the sexual assault of Angel Banning. The DA now planned to prosecute Smith for Kaylee's torture and murder and Eva hoped to push Smith into talking. Most killers craved fame, to be written about in a book. She hoped to tempt him with that carrot, or at least trick him into saying something that would crack his silence.

Unless he talked, she'd have to leave out a lot of details from Kaylee's story. The forensic report revealed part of what Smith had done to Kaylee, but not enough to give a true picture of the monster he was. *Smith had to pay.*

It took fifteen minutes for Smith to appear at the plexi-glass barrier of the visitor's booth.

She just stared at him for a few moments. In Kaylee's visions, Smith had no hair. Now he had thin brown hair, balding on top. It came out during Angel Banning's trial that Smith had shaved his entire body before kidnapping the girl, less chance of leaving any nuclear DNA behind. He looked so arrogant. She wanted to mop the floor with his face in a new trial—this time to get Kaylee justice.

Eva needed for that to happen.

The longer she stared at Smith, the bigger his smile became. He leered at her through the plexi-glass and her stomach churned. At first glance, his thinning hair, pinched nose, and bifocals presented a hefty, mild-mannered, unremarkable man. As much of a regular Joe as the prison guard, until she looked closer and saw the evil gleaming in his brown eyes.

"You got the hots for a con?" Smith finally asked, fleshy lips settling in a twisted smile. "You write books so's you can get all cozy with us?"

"I want to talk about Kaylee Waters. The girl you kidnapped three weeks before Angel. You took her to a cabin off Greenbriar Road." It had been Green Forrest Road.

Smith blinked at the discrepancy, but ignored the question and made a crude gesture with his right hand. "I am the god of fuck. I can give it to you harder and better than you've ever had it. Then maybe I'll talk."

Tamping down on her anger and revulsion, Eva clenched her toes and forced a smile. "Surely you remember Kaylee Waters. The red-haired girl you tortured and killed?"

Smith shook his head, his smiling growing bigger. Kaylee had been blond. "Your ass as tight as that uppity suit?"

Eva switched tactics. "Do you want to tell the public something? Now is your chance to be heard and understood."

He paused a beat then leered grotesquely, his tongue snaking out like a whip. "I like it young and tight, but you'll do. As I said, you dish then...maybe I'll tell you something."

This was the mastermind killer who'd escaped detection for years? He seemed to have a one-track mind that really didn't move all that fast. Eva gritted her teeth, determined to shake him up. Who knew when, or if, she'd get another interview? She'd waited months for this. She lowered her voice and threw caution out the door. "I don't need you to *tell* me anything, Smith. I know *exactly* what you did to Kaylee Waters, and when the world reads the details, or even an inmate or two, you're dead. Child rapists and killers don't fare too well in prison...so I hear."

Mason laughed. "You don't know shit."

"I know *everything*," she said softly. "How she begged and pleaded for you not to hurt her, but you twisted and broke her fingers anyway."

He scoffed. "Good guess."

"I know she promised to be a good girl and do anything you wanted, if you wouldn't hurt her again. And when she did as she promised, you tied her up and violated her with the barrel of a pistol."

Mason's eyes narrowed and he slammed his right fist into the plexi-glass. "Who the fuck are you?" Guards rushed over to grab him.

"I know she cried for God and you laughed as you cut her. What did you say? Not even God can help you now. There's a special place in hell for you, Smith, and I'm making sure you get there and burn. You're going to suffer like Kaylee did for an eternity."

Mason rammed his ample body against the plexi-glass. "We're coming for you, bitch!" He screamed, his face twisting with purpling rage. Frothy spittle hit the plexi-glass as he wildly fought the mounting guards.

Eva smiled at Smith then turned. Mouth agape and eyes wide, the guard who'd escorted her in, approached, losing his toothpick. "What did you say to Smith to put the fear of God in him?"

"That he couldn't escape justice," Eva said.

"I tell these sons-of-bitches that every day, but none of them listen. Most of them don't care about what they've done or who they've hurt. They sit in here all smug, enjoying a free ride, like pigs in slop. People on the outside don't realize that."

The guard had Eva wondering if justice was ever truly served in this world. Smith had sat through his trial unfazed and seemed on cloud nine with a life sentence and no chance of parole. She shouldn't have lost her cool and needled him as deeply as she just had. She usually left enough ambiguity in revelations from her visions to make a killer wonder where she'd learned things. Tonight, she'd wanted to annihilate Smith's smile. She'd done it and she hoped visions of his own torture hounded him.

"You should write a book about that," the guard said.

Eva focused on the guard again. "About what exactly?"

"About how big a crime it is that evil has such a cushy life. It makes working here hell," he said with passion.

She blinked, regular Joe wasn't as mild-mannered as he seemed. "I'll keep that in mind, but as I hear it prison is far from a bed of roses."

"You don't see the real picture here. I'd be honored to tell you like it is and help write that book in anyway. My name's Hatchett, Tom Hatchett."

They reached the check-point and Eva picked up her pace to exit through the scanner. "Uh, thank you, Officer Hatchett."

He stood watching as she collected her cell phone and purse then gave her a left-handed wave as she exited the building. She learned long ago that most conversations with strangers usually led to suggestions of what she should write next. She never gave them a moment's thought, but Hatchett's words comparing evil in prison to pigs in slop, stuck.

She hurried to her car, feeling naked as she dug for her keys. Even though she had to pass through a maned gate to enter the restricted parking lot, she still glanced apprehensively about.

She never left any building for her car without her keys and mace in hand, but had forgotten the mace in her haste to leave. With Smith's threat still ringing in her ears, her vulnerability slapped her hard.

Reaching her car, she hurriedly shut and locked the door, regretting that she'd left her Glock at home today. She should have at least put it in her car. She backed out, moved forward two feet, and slammed on her brakes, sending her purse and cell phone flying to the passenger's side floorboard. A man stood at her driver's side window. The shine on his bald head from the security lights brought a flashback from one of Kaylee's visions.

Eva caught her breath and blinked hard. She opened her eyes to see Officer Hatchett holding out a piece of paper. If every shiny, bald-headed man became Smith, then she had to be losing her grip. Still, she only slightly cracked her window open, ready to hit the gas, if needed.

"Here's my number. I really want to help you write that book," he said, sliding the paper through the narrow slot.

Eva took the paper. "As I said, I'll think about what you said. But in all honesty, I'm working on several stories right now. It will be sometime before I can even give the idea any serious thought. You should write the book." She put the number in the cup holder.

Hatchett shook his head. "Never was much good at writing."

"Then tape-record your story, Officer Hatchett, and hire someone to write it. If you've got the will, then there is a way. I wish you great success."

He shook his head again, but less adamantly this time. She didn't give him time to argue. She rolled up her window, and he stepped away from the car. She waited until she exited the guarded gate before she stopped to get her phone and stuff her things back into her purse. She found Frasier's card in the process.

Adam D. Frasier, Special Agent, Federal Bureau of Investigation. His warning that Smith was a sick son-of-a-bitch, didn't quite cover the bastard. Unhinged, unbalanced, and purely evil was more accurate. She put the card back in her purse. Before she threw it out, she wanted to ask Devin why he'd specifically asked Frasier for it. Devin always had a reason. He did nothing on a whim or by chance and sometimes that really scared her.

Aside from keeping in touch with Sheriff Doug Grant, one of the first policemen on scene to their parents' deaths, the three of them tried to stay away from law enforcement's radar. Her one aberration to that rule had been writing *Hayden's Hell*. The crime, fifteen years ago had haunted her at the time. It had been called the second most heinous crime in Georgia. The first being the 1973 massacre of the Alday family in Donalsonville, Georgia.

Eva had been thirteen when the Hayden's were murdered. She'd just begun exploring her gift and had wanted to do something to help. She and Aunt Zena had argued at length about it. But in the end, she had to accept that doing anything then would have risked exposing herself and her siblings. Then Carlan had been caught, killed and blamed for the murders.

Despite Carlan's demise, Eva continued to lose sleep for months afterwards. Much like the Haydens and the Aldays, she and her siblings lived on a rural estate, and even though the St. Claire's had security, the murders still made Eva feel horribly vulnerable.

School and family events had consumed Eva's life and she'd forgotten about the Hayden's until she'd stumbled on an Internet time trap citing America's most vicious serial killers. John Carlan had been on the list, with the Hayden's as his last known victims, before his shootout with the GBI. She then carved out time to investigate the local story. After that, she had to write the book. The facts about the case didn't add up and she had serious doubts that Carlan had been the killer.

Were her visions off? Was she losing her balance between the past and the present?

She rubbed her temple, hoping to ease the ache that never seemed to go away—at least with these last two books. The Hayden's story had been as hard to write as Kaylee's, but for a different reason. When she'd entered the farmhouse in rural Georgia, she'd seen the crime through the eyes of the killer. It was as if she were the one slaughtering Tony in his office, Mary in the kitchen, Meagan at the tea table, and then running into the garden after Melissa, who stood crying and hugging her soft doll. She'd *seen* the victims' surprised reactions, *heard* their screams and pleas.

Eva shuddered then blinked at headlights coming right at her. She swerved hard and ran off the road, bumping over rocks and ruts before she could get back to the shoulder. Once there, she came to a stop, heart thundering so hard that her chest hurt. She gasped for air, wondering what had just happened.

Had she crossed the center line or had someone come into her lane? She'd been so distracted with her thoughts that she had no idea. She felt as if the darkness of the rural area was swallowing her alive. That she could disappear in a heartbeat and no one would ever be able to find her. In her rearview mirror, she saw headlights coming and hit the gas, spinning in the dirt before gaining traction and flying down the road.

She didn't slow down until she hit city lights and traffic.

She didn't think she'd overreacted either. Something had her spooked.

For the rest of the trip home, she did her best to focus on her surroundings rather than the mayhem in her mind. Nothing more happened. By the time she waved to Hank at the estate's security gate, she'd decided she'd let stress get the better of her. She'd leapt to a sinister explanation rather than admit her own distracted state.

The full moon hanging low in the night sky bathed the St. Claire homestead in romantic shades of gray. She often thought gargoyles and black stone would have been more in keeping with the St. Claire's curse rather than pristine white paint, peacock blue shutters, wraparound porches, and a turret with windows of stained glass butterflies.

Inside the house, she found Devin pounding the keyboard in the music room and Iris completely engrossed in a *Game of Thrones* episode. Lannie had left a note that she and Paddy were playing cards. Though barely eight o'clock, Eva opted to call it a night.

She skipped Lannie's extra cheese lasagna, made a half-sandwich on sprouted grain bread then indulged in a relaxing bath before feeding her puzzle addiction. It didn't matter what kind—crossword, logic, jigsaw, Sudoku—anything in which she could distract her mind, she consumed.

With puzzles, there was no evil to battle, no tragic endings, it was just about putting the pieces together and getting perfection in the end. She thought she'd shut out the world, then a crossword question brought it all racing back.

Name Kelsey Grammer's long running series: Frasier.

She'd done her best to ignore the FBI agent's appeal, but his sharp green gaze, commanding jaw, and five-o'clock scruff had captured her interest from across the auction room today and continued to gnaw at her.

His persistence in bidding for her books against Sheriff Doug had surprised her. Five thousand was the most her books had ever brought a charity.

Besides the amount Adam spent, it was the manner in which he'd bid that surprised her the most. He'd seemed like a soldier on a mission, determined to win. Then he'd sought her out after the auction and even warned her about Smith—

Eva suddenly sat upright, tumbling her crossword book and pen to the floor. "We," she cried aloud. Mason Smith had said, "We're coming for you."

Not, "I'm coming for you."

Did Smith have someone on the outside to help him? A partner maybe? And how long had he had a partner?

Eva called the head of her home security team, Zeb, alerting him to a possible threat. Ex-military, the five-foot-nine man packed a *Die Hard* punch. He reassured Eva that he'd pair up the men on duty and change the perimeter patrol to every hour.

After that, she Googled Adam Frasier before going back to bed, looking to make sure the man was legit. She surprisingly didn't find that much out there on Adam. He didn't appear to be active on social media. No Facebook nor Twitter accounts.

She did find him listed as a "notable alumni" from the University of Georgia. He'd been a keynote speaker at a Critical Incident Response Group (CIRG) Safety conference last year. Five years ago, his stern picture appeared in an article about a CIRG agent who'd died in the line of duty while rescuing a small girl from a hostage situation in Washington, D.C. Adam had given the eulogy at the man's funeral. CIRG agents were like the special forces of the FBI. The elite, trained to handle crisis situations.

Why had Devin singled Adam out?

Before logging off, Eva had the misfortune to catch a video clip of Grace DuMond hounding her outside of the Fox Theater. After showing Grace, dynamic in red and holding out a microphone as she rapid-fired questions at Eva, the camerawoman had zoomed in on Eva's face. Thank *God* for sunglasses. They'd be the only thing keeping Eva from being a murder suspect should the reporter end up dead. DuMond had been a nightmare in Eva's life since Eva's father killed her mother.

Eva, Devin, and Iris all learned long ago to paste on stoic expressions and keep walking no matter what verbal crap from the media hit their faces or their souls. This morning had been no different.

DuMond had shoved her microphone in Eva's face. "Ms. St. Claire! I saw you at Mason Smith's trial. Does that mean you're writing Angel Banning's story? She'll be your first living victim, right? Will you ever write your mother's story? Doesn't she deserve her own book?"

As the camerawoman zoomed out for a full body shot of plump Eva next to a thin Iris and a fit Devin, Eva saw Iris reach out and grab Devin's arm just as her brother fisted his hand. Apparently he had wanted to punch DuMond as much as Eva had.

With that clip on her mind Eva spent a restless night. Her thoughts bounced between facts about Smith's life, DuMond's questions, and Frasier's intrusion into her already stressed-to-the-max life. Somewhere in her dreams, a steamy sauna popped up and she hadn't been alone either.

9:00 P.M.

AFTER MEETING WITH HIS mother's doctors and the nursing home's director, Adam dropped his father off at home before returning to spend time with his mother. His dad could only handle an hour or so every few days, more than that sent his blood pressure skyrocketing. At this point in his mother's illness, all conversations led to finding Jenna, no matter the topic.

While she wasn't necessarily a danger to others, aside from borrowing cell phones and racking up mega charges, she *was* a danger to herself and an easy target for charlatans who preyed upon her pain. She'd always been susceptible to shysters.

Part of him often thought she wouldn't be this delusional if she hadn't first been told by a psychic that Jenna was absolutely alive. After that, his mother had connected up with a swindler to help search for Jenna. Wearing the robes of a minister and claiming psychic powers from an omniscient spirit, the man had dragged his mother's tattered hopes from one end of the country to the other, following one "new vision" of Jenna after another. The only way Adam's father had been able to put an end to the charade, was to use the full force of the GBI to defrock, debunk, and imprison the man.

Adam could still hear the fight his parents' had when his mother found out. She accused Adam's father of caring more about his job than finding their lost daughter.

And it was all Adam's fault. With a heavy heart, and the world choking him by the throat, he entered his mother's room at the care facility. She sat innocently in a recliner, looking as normal as any middle-aged woman with graying hair and a wrinkling countenance. She had *Downton Abbey* playing on the television and a crochet needle working magic with a ball of yarn in her lap. He knew without asking that it would be something to keep Jenna warm. She filled a closet with stuff she made for Jenna every year. And every Christmas he'd convince her to donate it to the needy. She'd agree, but only because somehow, somewhere, something she made might find its way to Jenna.

Adam understood his mother's hope and determination to find her missing child. He'd learned every parent felt the same when a child disappeared. What he didn't understand however, and struggled to forgive, was how she'd disappeared along with Jenna.

"Mom," Adam said, his heart pounding as he crossed the room. He had to tell her she'd be moving next weekend. The time had come to put her in a more security-focused facility.

"Adam! I am so glad you're here." She stood, set her yarn and needle aside and hugged him. "You're just in time. Edith is going to claim Marigold and runaway. It's awful how her family and society has kept her daughter from her arms. I know how she feels. I could find Jenna if only I could go look for her." She glanced at the open door then whispered. "The nurses and your father won't let me go search for Jenna. Will you help me, Adam? Will you take me out of this prison so I can find my daughter?"

"Mom?" Adam's heart lodged in his throat. He planted his ass in a chair next to his mother's before his knees gave out. *Hell.* She'd asked for his help in searching for Jenna before, many times, but never with such direct clarity and never from an imprisoned perspective. It hit him head-on and laid him flat. Before he answered, he tried to put himself in the world he and his father had defined for her by placing her into a care facility.

Yes, life, fate, or perhaps Adam's action as a child, had led to Jenna's kidnapping. Dementia had stolen much more from his mother. But what had Adam and his father taken from his mother in their attempts to handle her disease? It had been years since he'd taken her out of the care facility, because she'd always look for Jenna and cry when she couldn't find her and he'd feel ripped apart—again.

Adam clasped his mother's hand and met her desperate blue gaze. This wasn't about him or his guilt. This was about her. So what if she spent the rest of her life this way? If he could give her a few hours, every now and then, to safely search for Jenna, then he owed it to her. "Yes, Mom. I'll take you to search for Jenna. But you have to promise me that you'll wait for me to do it and not call strangers to come get you. I'm moving you to a new home and then we'll begin our search, okay? I'll come as often as I can."

Tears spilled from his mother's eyes. "I promise." She turned to pick up the bundle of yarn. "I'm making this coat for Jenna. She always loved red. Do you think she'll like it?"

The sweater was for a small girl. Jenna had been six when she disappeared. He swallowed hard. "Yes. It's perfect, but like me, Jenna will be all grown up now. The sweater will be too little."

His mother paused. Her smile faltered. "It can't be. She can't be different. How will I find her if she's not the same, Adam?"

Adam pulled out his wallet and flipped to the last age-progressed picture he had a forensic artist do of Jenna. He'd had it done on a regular basis for years, but stopped a few years ago. He'd shown it to his mother many times before, but she'd always turn away, denying it was her little girl. "We can use this as a start."

His mother cradled the photo in her hands then sighed. "This isn't my Jenna, but maybe this woman will know where my Jenna is."

Adam exhaled. "We'll ask her if we find her. The nurses say you played the piano last week. You should do so more often. I remember how you used to play and—" he bit his tongue rather than share the vague memory of playing musical chairs with Jenna as their mother played the piano. Jenna always won.

His mother shook her head. "No. They're mistaken. I don't remember how to play anymore. The music died."

Adam nodded. "Maybe it was someone else then." He let the subject go, deciding that showing her the video of it, would only upset her.

"*Shh*, Edith's back on. See, she's claiming Marigold."

Adam leaned back in his chair, his gaze focused on the television, but in his mind he didn't see the screen, he saw a little black and white puppy on the edge of the woods.

He wanted to hold the puppy. He ran for it, calling, "Puppy! Puppy! Come pway."
He laughed and ran faster, stumbling in the pine needles. The puppy disappeared into
the trees. Sweat blurred his eyes and he wanted to cry. "Puppy!"

"Adam! Come back here, right now."

"Puppy. I want puppy!"

"Adam. Stop! Come here."

He ran faster. The tree branches stung his face as he hurried after the puppy,
determined.

"Adam! Adam!"

He didn't remember much more about chasing the puppy, but he remembered his
mother snatching him up. He remembered kicking and crying. "I want puppy to pway."

"A little boy who doesn't mind his mother, can't play with a puppy right now. Behave
and we will see about playing with the puppy later," his mother said firmly.

She carried him from the woods and her evolving panic would echo in his mind
forever. The swing, still in motion, was empty. At first his mother turned in a circle,
calling for Jenna. When no answer came. She ran around the park, yelling louder and
louder. "JENNA! OH, GOD! JENNA WHERE ARE YOU?"

Jenna had vanished. Their lives were never the same.

Downton Abbey ended and Adam hugged his mother goodbye, making her
promise again to wait for him before searching for Jenna. He left the care facility,
bracing for the battle he'd have with his father. After years of giving in to fruitless
searches for Jenna and dealing with Linda's grief and ridicule that he wasn't doing
enough, Vince Frasier drew a line in the sand, deciding the search for Jenna only
fed Linda's delusions.

Adam knew his father was right, but at this point, what did it matter? His
mother would never recover. Why not give her an outlet for her desperation? Maybe
he could stop her from attempting another escape. By "looking" for Jenna, he'd be
doing exactly what he usually did for the FBI in his chase for the Artist of Death.
He'd be hunting down someone impossible to find. Except the Artist of Death
regularly left evidence of his existence, if not clues to his identity. Nothing about
Jenna had ever surfaced.

It had been a little over six months since the Artist's last revelation, and as sick
as it was, Adam chomped at the bit for more evidence. As he expected, nothing

from the Golden Gate Bridge crime scene had given a hint to the Artist's identity. The upsides were, Teri McClutcheon's family got closure and Adam crossed off one more name on the long list of the missing.

His cell rang. "I'm on my way to your house, Pops. What's up?"

"Adam? Is that you? I can't hear you."

Adam frowned. The connection sounded clear. "Do you have your hearing-aid in?"

"What did you say?"

Adam clenched his jaw. "I'll be at your house soon." He was a little over five minutes away.

"Hold on. Let me get my hearing-aid." After a short silence, Vince returned. "Did you tell her about the move?"

"Yes. She's fine with it. Did you know she feels like she's in a prison?"

Vince sighed. "She's been asking why I keep her locked up for about six months now."

"You should have said something. Maybe if we'd taken her out of the facility for a few hours, she wouldn't have tried to escape." And he should have been more involved than just fly-by visits on a weekend every so often.

"Take her out to do, *what*?" his father's voice rose. "All she wants is to search for Jenna. She doesn't want to eat, shop, see a movie, or visit any museums or gardens. Nothing but to aimlessly wander around searching for Jenna. And God forgive me, I just can't do it anymore."

Adam's stomach sank at the edge of despair in his father's voice. "It's okay, Pops. We'll talk about this. We'll fix it."

"You can't fix it!" he cried.

The cry was followed by a tense silence as Adam searched for the right words. His father spoke first. "Adam, I'm sorry, I didn't mean to dump on you. But it can't be fixed. I've spent years trying and you're not going to waste your life, too."

"Hold that thought. I'll be there in a minute."

Adam disconnected the call with the surreal sense that the world around him, which had been on auto-pilot for a while, had suddenly plunged into a deadly spiral. His father was on thin ice, too. He turned up the radio, searching to chill for at least a few minutes, but what he heard didn't help. The clip on the WGGS radio of Grace DuMond talking about the St. Claires pissed him off. It seemed that even twenty years after the fact, the St. Claire's tragedy was still fodder for gossip.

"I met up with the elusive Eva St. Claire today after the charity auction for the National Victim's Assistance Program. Now that Hayden's Hell *has been released, I asked her which victim would be the subject for her next book. Since St. Claire attended Mason Smith's trial, perhaps Angel Banning? I also asked if she'd tell her poor mother's story. For those who don't remember, her father, the multi-millionaire businessman murdered her mother, then shot himself. But as usual, the St. Claires had nothing to say. You can go to GraceDuMondreports.com to see the news clips of that tragedy. Meanwhile, rap singer, High Five has been arrested for—"*

Adam snapped off the radio and rode in silence for the rest of the way. Already on edge, he walked into his father's house to find Vince on the computer with Eva St. Claire's name in the search box and lost his cool. Coke cans, beer cans, and pizza boxes, at least six of them ranging in age from a day to at least a week or two, by the looks of the greasy remains scattered the living room tables. The kitchen was worse. The dishes were all dirty, and had been for a while.

"Are you trying to kill yourself?" Adam demanded. "If the smell doesn't get you, there's enough sodium in the leftovers to send your blood pressure skyrocketing." His father had never been neat, but the house was in bad shape.

Vince shrugged. "Cleaning lady quit over a week ago and I haven't had a chance to hire a new one."

"If you live like this, it's no wonder she quit." Adam took a good look at his father, remembering the despair he'd heard over the phone. *But it can't be fixed. I've spent years trying and you're not going to waste your life, too.* All Adam's hot air dissipated. "You know what, Dad?"

"Yeah, I'm a slob. I'll clean it up. I wasn't expecting you this weekend. Then Linda pulled that stunt, I couldn't sleep, and I discovered the St. Claire's Hayden bomb. The mess doesn't seem to matter compared to that. Not much has these days, but this is really big."

"That isn't what I was going to say. *Haden's Hell* and finding the killer aside, you need to divorce Mom and get a life. You're right. You've spent too many years trying to fix what can't be fixed. Mom may have checked out when Jenna vanished, but you at least found time for a fishing trip every now and then. Living like this is going to kill you and quite frankly, I want my kids to at least have a grandfather to fish with when they are growing up."

Vince's jaw dropped open, his head already shaking no. Adam picked up pizza boxes and prepared for a fight, but was too ragged out to deal with the mess or trying to explain the promise he'd made to his mother. "Let's go eat and we'll clean up in the morning. My treat."

His father glanced back at the computer screen, clearly wanting to dig more into the St. Claires. "It's not football, Dad. You aren't going to miss a touchdown by getting a meal first."

Grumbling, Vince hefted himself from the chair. "Yeah. Yeah. You're sounding as if I'm a two-year-old who needs coaxing."

"If the mess fits…"

"Funny," his father muttered as he walked outside.

Adam shut the door, wishing he'd found something amusing. He needed a laugh.

DAY 2
SUNDAY, MAY 11TH

8:00 A.M.

You shouldn't have gone."

Eva looked up from the cup of morning coffee she was brooding over. The warm sun pouring through the ruffled lace curtains and gleaming across the polished wood of the table did little to ease the chill in her gut.

Iris stood in the doorway, her cheeks flushed and her hair windblown. She'd already been for a ride. It was just 7:00. "I haven't intruded into your thoughts, but I can feel your fear. It kept me up all night. You will tell me what happened or I'm barging in."

Eva closed her eyes. "Sorry. Grab some tea and I'll spill. I lost my cool with Smith, but it may lead to something important."

"Sounds complicated. I need caffeine and sugar, first. I don't know how we would survive without Lannie." Iris went to the buffet and poured a cup of Earl Grey. "Oooh, Devin nailed it. Chocolate covered Krispy Kremes." She grabbed the whole plate of donuts before coming to the table.

Eva stabbed her spoon into her oatmeal, grumbling for the millionth time how she envied Iris's metabolism. Eva gained pounds just smelling Krispy Kremes. Iris ignored the comment and bit into a chocolate iced-glazed donut with a moan.

"Just rub it in," Eva muttered. "I saw the news clip of the three of us leaving the Fox yesterday. You looked like a runway hit, Devin could nail *People Magazine's* next sexiest man alive, and I look like a Weight Watchers dropout."

Iris rolled her eyes. "You're gorgeous and you know it. You're just a little more of a Renaissance woman than Kelly Rippa could ever dream of being even with implants everywhere possible. Grace DuMond almost got her microphone shoved into her big mouth yesterday. For a brief second when she asked about you writing about Mom, Devin saw red."

"I saw more than red," Devin said from the doorway. "But I'd have only snatched her mic away as well as her assistant's camera. I've had it with shit in our faces." Devin muttered. He eyed the donuts on the table. "And losing out to an early bird sister." He rushed and grabbed the last chocolate iced donut from the plate just as Iris reached for it. Shirtless, he had clearly just tumbled out of bed. His hair stood out every which way, and his pajama pants sat cockeyed on his hips. "I had a nightmare. I'd miss out on this if I didn't wake up."

Inhaling the smell, he smiled. "You'll also be relieved to know that rather than rearrange DuMond and her camerawoman's faces, I'm calling in a favor and having them sued for something." He narrowed his gaze at Eva. "You should have mentioned how obnoxious she's become."

Eva shrugged and sighed, seemingly dismissing DuMond from her thoughts. "I ignore all the pesky reporters. There are more important problems to face."

"DuMond's behavior was more than pesky, it bordered on emotional harassment." Rather than sit down, Devin leaned against the buffet, eating his donut in three bites. "But then why should I worry about DuMond when you insist on beating yourself up. You're going back to the cabin today, aren't you?"

"I have to." Eva focused on the coffee in her cup.

"No," Iris whispered. "Why?"

"I was about to tell you. Yesterday, I goaded Smith into losing control. He said, '*We* are coming for you.' Not *I* am coming for you. He has someone on the outside working with him. I called Zeb last night and put the security team on alert. I have to go back to the cabin and make sure I am not missing something important. Like, how long has Smith had someone helping him? Was someone helping him torture and kill Kaylee?"

"Great news," Devin muttered. "A deranged killer and UNSUB are after my sister."

"Thank, *God* Smith is locked up for life," Iris said. "What are we going to do?"

"We hope. You still have his card?" Devin asked.

Eva met her brother's gaze. "Why? And what does 'we hope' mean?"

"Whose card?" Iris asked.

"You know, I never know why. I'm going back to bed. I'll tell Lannie to get only chocolate iced donuts tomorrow and to ready a room for Aunt Zena." He grabbed a handful of bacon and the two-pint carton of milk before exiting the room.

"The cheat. He didn't have a vision of donuts after all. When's Aunt Zena coming and whose card is he talking about?"

"He drives me crazy." Eva frowned at Iris. "Aunt Zena is supposed to be here in two weeks. Devin says it'll be sooner. Not good. And he's talking about Adam Frasier's card. The man from the auction yesterday. He's FBI."

Iris sighed. "I now know what inspired Michelangelo to sculpt David. That man defines perfection, don't you think?"

Iris looked expectantly at Eva. Eva stirred her clumpy oatmeal and shrugged. "I really didn't notice."

"Liar. Any woman with a pulse would notice. He's coming to the gallery today. Wants to buy one of my paintings. Something about my swing sets gets to him."

Eva shook her head. "Seems just a bit too…insinuating don't you think? First my books, now your paintings." Eva was aware her conclusion at the end of *Hayden's Hell* would ruffle GBI feathers, but she literally called it like she saw it. Those murders did not fit John Carlan's MO. "Makes me wonder what he really wants."

"Justice…forgiveness. I think he's like us."

"Psychic? You read his mind?"

"Not yet." Iris dolloped honey into her cup. "He's not psychic that I can tell. Haunted and driven is how I'd describe his vibe. Much like you," she said pointedly.

Eva refused to comment, discovering how Devin felt under Iris's needling over Dr. Caro.

"Damn Devin," Iris muttered. "I wanted milk for my tea. You can't go to the cabin alone, Eva. Promise you'll take Paddy with you."

"I already asked him." A grim smile tugged her lips. "*He* threatened to lock me in my room to keep me from going."

"Ha. A dose of your own medicine." Iris squeezed Eva's hand. "How will you find out who is helping Smith?"

"I've already sent an email this morning requesting a list of Smith's visitors. Hopefully, they'll give it to me. After I see if I missed anything at the cabin, I'll dig deeper into Smith's life."

"Be careful."

"Paddy and I will go armed and take Blue, too." Being a cat person, Eva had really *big* reservations three years ago when Paddy brought the steel-gray wolfhound home from the animal rescue shelter. At a hundred and fifty pounds and nearly table high, Blue looked formidable, was ferocious when need be, but mostly considered himself to be a lap dog and didn't understand that only his head qualified—just barely. It took about a year, but he'd won Eva over.

"I wish you wouldn't put yourself through Kaylee's torture again. You look exhausted and the day is just starting."

"I didn't sleep well last night, but you already know that."

"Yeah, I do. I also know you can't keep up this pace. I, at least, escape through my art. And when I'm out riding, the world melts away. You don't ever leave it. Even when you're working a puzzle, your mind is still worrying over a case."

"Did Lannie bend your ear with her 'live, laugh, and love' line?"

"A little. But I'd already felt that way about these last two books and spoke to Aunt Zena."

"What? You're at the root of this conspiracy?" Eva cried.

Iris's frown turned into a sly smile, letting Eva know she wasn't going to like what came next.

"Tell you what." Iris said. "I'll delay searching for my mystery killer for…three months if you promise me that once you nail this partner of Smith's, you'll take a three month break from writing and anything to do with crime."

Eva frowned. "I escape it."

"When? Name one thing you do that isn't associated with murder?"

"Well, I…"

"Told you so." Iris popped from her chair, taking her tea cup. "It's a deal set in stone. I'll tell Lannie and Aunt Zena. They'll be pleased."

"But I didn't—"

"Tough. It's the price for lying to me. You noticed every detail of Adam Frasier from head to toe."

Eva frowned.

Iris left the room. Eva stabbed her now cold oatmeal and pushed it aside, wondering what in the hell she would do for three months even as she worried how many killers would claim more victims, if she didn't keep her nose to the grindstone. And she absolutely refused to think of Frasier as anything but a threat to be avoided.

11:00 A.M.

E VA WINCED AS SHE explained to Paddy why she'd returned last night with clumps of mud and grass stuck to her car. "Everything ended up being fine."

"No, it's not fine. It's dangerous. If you can't swear you were in your own lane last night then you don't need to be driving until this is all over." Paddy shoved the sedan into park and Blue whined from the backseat, reacting to Paddy's upset and already recognizing the rural cabin as a "bad" place for them. Located between the small towns of Hiawassee and Dillard, Georgia, most people would never know that a monster stayed here or of the tragic death that took place in the simple cabin with homespun quilts and a bedside Bible. All they would see was a picturesque view of rolling mountains. All they would hear would be birds and a creek bubbling across the pasture. Sunshine bathed the sloping glen with bright warmth, making the yellow and white flowers sparkle.

She could *almost* hear the laughter of children playing in the field, but not quite. The happy fingerprints of life always escaped her. She knew only the violence. She'd never be able to run free without worrying about the snakes in the grass just waiting to strike and kill. She rubbed her temple. "You might be right about the driving."

"Might be?" he exclaimed, incredulous. "I'll not be losing you, lass. Not in a car accident and not to the evil inside that cabin there. You promise this is the last time?" Paddy's voice was thick with emotion.

"I wish I could," Eva whispered, her heart pounding. She gave the car door a sweaty-palmed shove and forced herself out of the car. Paddy exited and freed an anxious Blue from the back. The dog immediately searched the area, his powerful muscles tense, ready to attack.

Eva moved to the porch, hearing the old wood creak and feeling the heat of the sun streaming through the pines. The moment she opened the door, cold air hit her hard and grew colder with every step she made. She shivered as her vision blurred and the sweet scent of baby powder choked her. Jarring music pounded at her and pain throbbed from every part of her body. She latched onto the vision, falling into Kaylee's sobs and her ensuing hell.

"I am the god...I am the god...time for cake," the grating voice yelled to the discordant noise playing at an ear-splitting volume. Kaylee screamed as cruel hands grabbed at her.

More potent than before, the fingerprints of violence from the past pulled her into the horror faster than ever. Surrendering her mind completely, she slipped into the dark evil, too brutal to bear. Somewhere in the cold blackness, Eva lost herself.

LET GO, EVA. LET it go.

The vision began to fade. "No!" Eva cried, doubling over with pain, wanting to cling to Kaylee and comfort the girl. "That's not true, Kaylee. Don't believe him." She fisted her hands, wanting to obliterate Smith, wanting to pull Kaylee into her arms and make the evil and the pain disappear. Her impotency twisted around her, choking her as sobs welled in her throat.

"I am so sorry, so, so, sorry," she cried, devastated that she could do nothing to help Kaylee.

Let go, Eva. Let it go.

Disoriented, Eva reeled.

That's enough.

"No." Fighting the voice, she mentally searched for Kaylee.

No more, lass!

The forceful shout ripped at Eva, leaving her gasping and shaking with a chill no warmth could ever reach. She hovered in a smoky gray world where every sound and image wobbled drunkenly in a distorted haze, until reality and light stabbed through her consciousness. She came back to the present, bereft and in pain.

Eva opened her eyes to find her knees aching from the hard wood floor. Paddy and Blue, her odd guardian angels, stood over her.

Blue whined, nudged his wet nose into the crook of her neck and swiped a slobbery kiss there. She patted his head. "I'm okay, boy."

Taking Paddy's outstretched hand, she stood on shaky legs.

From the tension creasing the elderly man's brow and the fire in his eyes, she could tell he wanted to curse a blistering streak to hell and back. "That's enough of it, lass. Lannie is right. You need a break from this," he said, determination hardening his voice even as he shuddered. "It's as if you were a prisoner to the evil. I kept calling, but you couldn't hear me. It's been almost an hour."

Eva shook her head, searching for clarity, but only felt dizzier and more disoriented. "Lannie talks too much." She shook her head again. "It's been an hour? *Really?*" For her, it seemed as if only minutes had passed. She swung a 360 around the interior of the cabin and moaned with disbelief as a heavy wave of guilt slammed her. The confused pieces of Kaylee's horror flooded together and coalesced into a chilling certainty.

"How did I miss it all before?" She cried to Paddy. "I just assumed Smith was ambidextrous…Smith used his left hand to hurt Kaylee in one vision. Then he used his right hand to hurt her. Then in some visions, two shiny, hairless Smiths are hurting Kaylee, one right-handed, one left-handed. Both doing different things…I need air!" She hurried to the porch and drew in several deep breaths of the mountain air. Blue stayed by her side, leaning against her to offer comfort.

Paddy joined her outside and cleared his throat. "Don't be so hard on yourself, lass."

Eva swung around. "I missed all the clues, even to them wearing different colored shirts at the same time. Since they were both hairless and bulky, I assumed Kaylee was delirious with pain and the visions were of different times and days all rambling together. I was wrong."

"How could you know? The bastard must look very similar to Smith and can't be far from the fringes of Smith's life. Do you remember seeing anyone similar in looks at the trial?"

She tried to remember, but her head hurt too much at the moment to think.

Would it be as simple as that? Finding a balding man associated with Smith? Someone in a position to aid and abet Smith's evil?

Officer Hatchett came to mind, but she dismissed the thought of singling him out. He wasn't the only balding prison guard around.

Paddy set his hand on her shoulder. "You'll find the bastard. I know you will, but you'll not be doing this here again. If you won't draw the line, then I will. God didn't bless the St. Claires with gifts for you to kill yourself using them."

Bless? More like cursed, but she didn't argue with Paddy. They'd been down that road too many times already. She slipped on her dark sunglasses, hoping to ease the sunlight's painful edge. Lannie's warning from yesterday rang in her mind. The post vision migraines were getting worse. "Let's go."

Walking to the car, the sense that she'd failed Kaylee sat heavily on her shoulders. She had to expose the truth. She couldn't bring comfort to the little girl, but come hell or high water, she'd get Kaylee justice.

On a steep mountain curve, an explosive pop and Paddy's curse snapped Eva from her thoughts. Her heart slammed into her throat. They were on the hairpin turn of a steep mountain decline. The car wrenched sideways, heading straight for the guardrail and a drop off there'd be no surviving. Eva gripped the car door and wrapped her arm around Blue, bracing for death. Her life flashed in a blur with a punch of regret that hit her gut like a wrecking ball. She hadn't really lived yet.

Suddenly the car jerked hard and the back-end fishtailed, then whipped around. Instead of plunging through the guardrail, the car went backwards down the road. Eva wasn't sure exactly how, but in a head-spinning turn the car flipped around and slowed to a stop. They landed on the shoulder of the opposite side of the road, barely missing an oncoming pickup truck. All one-hundred and fifty pounds of Blue was in her lap and Paddy's expletives had doubled in volume.

Easing Blue's snout from her face, Eva gasped. "What happened?"

"Flat tire…I think," Paddy said between curses. "The sons-of-bitches are brand new, too."

A thump on the window startled them both and Blue erupted into action. He sprang from Eva's lamp to lunge himself at the man standing at Paddy's window. The man leapt back. Wearing work-stained jeans and a plaid shirt; he looked twenty-something and worried.

"Easy boy." Eva grabbed Blue's collar as she fished her purse from the floorboard, ensuring her Glock was in reach.

Paddy cracked the window. "Hey man, y'all okay? You need help with that flat?"

"I'll be right out," Paddy said and rolled the window back up.

Eva bit her lip. "We have roadside, just call."

"It'd likely be an hour or more wait. He looks harmless enough. Not every stranger is a killer. You are armed though, right?"

Eva patted her purse.

"Good. Stay in the car with Blue. This won't take long. It goes without saying, shoot first, if it becomes necessary, and ask questions later."

Eva glanced at the window. "Be careful. Also, find out how we can contact him. Every good Samaritan deserves a thank you."

Within twenty minutes the men had the tire changed and she and Paddy were on their way back to Atlanta.

"Let's not say anything to Iris or Devin," Eva finally spoke into the heavy silence. She could see Paddy still looked too upset to talk about it. "There's a lot going on. I don't want Devin to feel as if he should have seen this, okay?"

"I hear you, lass. Devin may be a man now, but inside he's still that boy who feels he should have stopped what happened to your parents. You tell him about this and he'll dive right back into guilt and depression."

"You know us all too well, Paddy."

"Not well enough. I never in a million years saw your parents' tragedy coming."

No one had. There'd never been a hint of it in her parents' relationship or actions. As her post-vision headache worsened, she closed her eyes and covered her face with her jacket. She tried to shut the world out for even just a few minutes, but failed as usual.

1:00 P.M.

AFTER DINNER LAST NIGHT, Adam spent a couple of hours delving into every article he could find about Eva St. Claire, her siblings, and the murder/suicide of her parents. He even bit the bullet and checked out Grace DuMond's videos on her website. He had to give the grating reporter points for being thorough.

He learned more from her than he had from the other sources. The facts of the crime itself were cut and dry, but the events leading up to the tragedy, cast a mysterious shadow over it all. Eva's parents seemed to have prepared for their deaths. A month prior, their mother had had a family mausoleum built in a rural cemetery in the mountains and their father had placed people to keep his enterprises running smoothly in the event of his death. In the video clip, Grace DuMond stood in front of the scrolled iron and polished granite mausoleum. The phrase, *Love became a bridge too far,* engraved the top of the impressive stone structure. The reporter asked the shocking questions, "Was this a murder/suicide? Or a suicide pact? We'll never know."

Damn, what a hell Eva and her siblings had faced.

Love became a bridge too far was an odd epitaph. He'd only heard the "bridge too far" phrase referencing military action too extreme in its objective to realistically succeed. It stemmed from World War II's Operation Market Garden where Allied

Troops failed to break Germany's hold on bridges to Holland in September of 1944. Had they succeeded, the war could have been won in mere months. Instead, it raged on for another year of death and destruction.

Adam had gone to sleep and woke up with that thought rambling around in his mind along with own his parents' situation. His father couldn't keep living this way. He'd spent the morning helping his father return from the dregs of bachelordom before bringing up the subject of divorce again. They'd even mowed the yard and trimmed the hedges. After to die for BLT sandwiches made with ripe tomatoes from the local farmer's market and extra crispy thick bacon, they sat drinking an icy beer.

"I meant what I said last night, Pops."

"We aren't even going to discuss it."

"Why not?"

"I don't shirk my responsibilities."

"I'm not suggesting you do. I'm asking you to stop, in your own words, wasting your life. Find someone to share a meal with, go to the movies, or take a vacation. This is your retirement. Besides restoring your muscle car, all you've done is visit Mom. You don't even fish anymore. Find a senior center, make some friends, do something fun."

"A senior center?" Vince rolled his eyes. "Did you smoke, rather than cut, those weeds out back? You know I'm not the bingo/ice cream social type."

Adam sat forward and met his father's gaze head on. "Fine. But do something with your life. Go fish. Play golf. Whatever you have to do so you can look in the mirror and not think you've wasted your life taking care of Mom."

His father winced. "Hell, I didn't mean it the way it sounded. I loved your mother. And I should have—"

"What, Pops?"

"I don't know. I should have done something different or better. Maybe I should have—"

"No. No you shouldn't. And no you couldn't. Tragedy and disease struck and you couldn't have stopped either of them from happening. Neither can you fix either of them no matter how hard you try or what you do."

Vince shook his head and Adam gritted his teeth. It was time he and his father had a frank conversation about Jenna and Adam's mother. Always before, they'd have a word or two, but the subject had been too painful to fully face.

Adam took a long sip of his beer. "Okay, Dad. You want to play the guilt card. Then I'll ante into the game. It's all my fault. If I hadn't run into the woods after the puppy. If I had listened to Mom yelling for me to stop, Jenna would have never been left on the swing."

"Don't you dare go there," his father cried, glaring. "You were four years old for God's sake."

"You can say that until you're blue in the face. I can intellectually understand how insane my guilt is, but that doesn't make it go away. While we are at it though, let's deal Mom into this hand as well. Why didn't she snatch Jenna off the swing and bring her along after me?"

"Because she didn't think it through. It was a split second reaction to run after you. You know, she cried every night because she left Jenna and there was nothing I could do to console her. She couldn't forgive herself."

"Which sent her spiraling to where she is now. A woman lost from any sort of reality and incapable of living life, much less relating to others. So why are you following in her footsteps?"

"What do you mean? I'm not anything like—"

"Heading down the road you're on, where will you be in ten or fifteen years if your arteries and heart survive your lifestyle?"

Vince set his beer down and stood. "I don't know. I'll be here. What in the hell do you want from me?"

Adam rose and put his hand on his father's shoulder. "I want you to be happy."

Vince narrowed his gaze. "So stop just existing and start living? Enjoy life and have fun?"

"Exactly." Adam smiled.

"Well then, I'll follow your lead. Like son, like father."

Adam's eye twitched. "This isn't about me."

"Yeah. It is. You're so driven to find this death artist that you make my life look like a Disney vacation. You going to take her out?"

"Who?" Adam had yet to tell his father about his promise to his mother, so how would he know?

"Iris St. Claire. If I'm not mistaken, she gave you a look yesterday."

"You're mistaken. My guess is she's barely old enough to drink."

"Twenty-four."

"Hell. I was thinking twenty-five. What do you take me for?"

"A blonde wearing zebra heels is kind of dazzling. I was just making sure you didn't get hung up on the wrong sister. It's Eva we need information from."

"They could both be wearing tiger print bikinis. I'm not asking either of them out. It would be beyond unethical."

"Then how are you going to find out who Eva interviewed? Me, you, this 'make myself happy' shit, all of it is nothing compared to finding out who murdered Tony and his family."

"It will happen. I promise." After their epic fail at the auction and a restless night, Adam had pretty much decided the best way to approach Eva St. Claire was to tell her point blank that someone she interviewed murdered the Haydens. But he could only do that at the right moment, and he didn't know when that would be. "Were you serious about writing a book?"

"Maybe. Some of it was just off the cuff, but I've been toying with the general idea for a while. You think she was just blowing smoke?"

"About finding your Andy Griffith-like bounty hunter interesting?"

Vince nodded, frowning. "Yeah."

"I don't think blowing smoke is even in Eva St. Claire's universe. I think she meant it."

"When you ask her out, take her to the Capital Grille. It's fancy enough for their pocket, but won't completely empty your wallet."

"Pops!"

"Lunch never hurt anybody."

"Then take your own advice."

"Deal."

"Who?"

"Remember Helen?"

"From the GBI? She's still there, right?" An ill feeling crept along Adam's neck. "You're not to go fishing around on anything to do with Tony."

"Who's fishing? I'm just catching up with an old friend and getting the scoop on what other destruction Geena Winters has caused. You know she's SAC of

Region 10 now."

Adam shook his head, having a hard time dealing with Geena being Special Agent in Charge of *anything*. "That's bad news for everybody. Thank God you're here and not there. Working with her was bad enough. Working *under* her would be worse than torture," Adam said, hoping his father would see the upside of being forced into an early retirement by the woman.

"There is that," Vince muttered. "You'd better get going. You're already late to Iris's art gallery."

Adam left in a rush, feeling like he'd been blindsided by Columbo. Like son, like father, like hell. His father had twisted everything around and danced away on a zinger. This conversation wasn't over yet.

2:00 P.M.

ADAM ENTERED DIMENSIONS ART Gallery off Slaton Drive and West Paces Ferry Road in Buckhead, and found himself in another world, or multiple worlds to be exact. Scented a pleasant ginger-cinnamon, the art gallery was unlike any he'd ever seen. Iris was busy with another customer, so Adam explored. The walls and ceiling of the studio's center appeared to be a galaxy from space and the art hanging along the walls were of fiery planets and alien species. Rooms led off to both the right and the left of the center display.

The first room immersed him in an undersea odyssey with paintings so vibrantly real he wanted to touch them just to make sure they weren't. Even the way the ceiling was painted, gave the effect of being underwater and looking up to see the sunlight distorted by the waves. Another room sent him into a jungle full of wild animals. Had Iris painted all of these vastly different pictures? He started checking the signatures and found many different artists were on display.

"Thank you for waiting, Mr. Frasier. Find anything interesting?" Iris joined him, pretty in pink. Her shoes, jacket and shirt reminded him of cotton candy. Even her jeans had pink crystals on the pockets.

Adam held out his hand. "Adam, please. This isn't what I expected. The gallery itself is…a work of art."

"You get it then. Creating the right world only enhances the art. Some would say anything but a plain wall detracts from the painting."

"And they would be blind. I see many different artists on display, but where are your paintings?"

"The back room. Mine require lots of light to really come alive. Let me lock the front door and we'll head back."

He followed, wondering how she navigated so gracefully in six inch stilettos. When they entered the back "room" he had to blink twice. Not only was it bright, but the marvel of glass, iron, and stone craftsmanship took his breath. "This is like a Victorian era observatory fit for a king."

Her brows lifted. "Close. It was actually dismantled from a summer palace in Bavaria built for a princess born on the wrong side of the blanket and reconstructed here."

"Impressive and so are your paintings." Iris's art filled every alcove, nook, and wall. In one corner, adjacent to a gurgling fountain, stood an easel and painting paraphernalia scattered over the surface of several nearby tables. "Is this where you work?"

"Yes. I have a studio at home, too. My swing set collection is over here." She led the way to the right. Inside a scrolled alcove were about a dozen paintings. All beautiful. And all of them had an empty swing somewhere amid the flowers and sunlight.

"Do you ever put people in your pictures?" he asked, wondering if the tragedy of her parents' death played a significant role in what she painted.

"No. Rather than filling the space, I think people want to imagine either themselves or someone they love into the scenes."

He snapped his gaze to hers. He'd gotten his answer. Yes her parents' death greatly affected her art. He also surprisingly realized why he'd been drawn to her paintings. He'd imagined Jenna swinging in that happy, peaceful place. Iris's blue gaze seemed way too knowing.

He focused back on the paintings. After studying the composition of each, he chose one.

"You're in luck. I do have enhanced prints of this painting. So you can either buy the original or—Dear God, he's coming!"

Adam spun around at the sheer terror in Iris's cry and reached for his Taurus PT111, but left the compact 9mm secured at the small of his back when no threat appeared.

They were alone in the gallery. Iris's eyes were huge. She'd turned white as a ghost and wavered dangerously on her heels. He caught her arm, suddenly feeling odd, as if an image of Jenna and her golden blonde hair glinting in the sun merged with Iris's. He shook his head and focused on Iris.

"I need my phone. Must call Eva. Danger." She stumbled forward.

He slid a steadying hand to her back. "Who's coming? Where's your phone?"

"Desk. Back there."

Adam eased her into a strange sofa with a half a back. "Sit here. I'll bring it to you. But first tell me, what danger? Who's coming?"

Iris shook her head. "Eva. Must call Eva."

He ran for the phone and had a heart-stopping moment when he returned to find Iris shivering uncontrollably and unresponsive to his questions. Her pulse and respirations raced. He called 911 from his cell phone. Then found Eva in Iris's contacts and connected the call.

She answered immediately. "Iris, I think—"

"It's Adam. Something's wrong with your sister. Does she have a history of seizures?"

"Not exactly. Where are you? What happened?"

"Dimensions." Adam explained what happened. "I've called 911."

"Paddy and I are minutes away. We'll be right there. Just stay with her and tell her everything is fine. Tell her I'm safe."

Adam wanted to know what 'not exactly' meant, but decided Iris needed reassuring more than he needed to interrogate Eva. He did as Eva suggested, speaking clearly and firmly to Iris. Iris's shivering seemed to ease, but her eyes remained shut and she continued to shake her head as if in the grip of a terrifying nightmare.

Eva hadn't lied. Within minutes, she ran into the gallery like an avenging warrior followed by an older gentleman who had a monster on a leash. No stranger to big dogs, Adam had to pick his jaw up off the floor at the size of this one. Eva cried out for Iris and the dog barked, lunging toward where Adam held Iris.

"Easy boy," Adam whispered. "I'm not hurting her."

"Friend. Blue. Friend," Eva told the dog firmly. Blue sat, but didn't look convinced. The older man patted the giant on the head and repeated Eva's command.

"Sorry," she said as she joined him, bringing with her the scent of Ivory soap that brought a flood of childhood memories. He shoved them aside, but still sucked in another deep breath of her scent. He nodded toward the monster. "With that beast around, it makes me wonder why Iris was so worried about you. What's going on?"

"I don't know. She was fine this morning." Eva pressed her hand to Iris's cheek. "Iris, I'm here. Everything is okay. Let it go. Please. Just let it go."

The paramedics rushed into the room. Relieved, Adam motioned for them. But the dog leapt to his feet and barked. They retreated a few feet. The older gentleman pulled the dog back to a sit, soothing him with several commands.

Iris sat up and cried out again, knocking Eva back. Adam steadied Eva with a hand to her hip, noticing that her jeans and a form-fitting top revealed an intriguing figure the suit she had worn yesterday had hidden. She pulled away from his touch quickly and put her hand on Iris's shoulder.

"Eva, he's coming for you," Iris cried.

Eva bent down. "Look at me, Iris. Look at me. I'm here. I'm safe."

Iris shuddered hard. "No, you're not safe."

"It's okay, love." Eva glanced toward the paramedics. "You can check her out, but I'm sure she is all right. She has these nightmares that it's hard for her to wake up from."

What just happened was no nightmare. Adam was about to set the record straight when Eva turned to him, her gaze imploring. She mouthed two words that completely floored him. Trust me.

Anything he had to say evaporated as he noticed her appearance. As pale as her sister, Eva's features looked drawn with stress, and deep shadows darkened her bloodshot eyes. In comparison to yesterday's cool confidence, it seemed the sisters had suffered a serious shock.

Iris glanced around, frowning with confusion. When she saw the paramedics, she cursed. "Hell. I'm sorry. I'm fine, really."

"We'd still like to make sure, ma'am," one paramedic said.

"Let them check you out," Eva said. "Dr. Caro will want to know."

"Fine." Iris held out her arm and smiled at the paramedics. "I'm all yours." As they approached Iris, both of the men kept a wary eye on the monster who sat watching their every move.

IT WAS BECOMING ONE HELL of a day. Eva bit back the hundreds of questions gnawing at her. Until she and Iris were alone, all she could do was guess at what happened and who might be coming after her. Maybe in some weird connection, Iris had sensed the brush with death Eva and Paddy had with the flat tire. The timing for that was completely off. It'd been about two hours ago. What if Iris had psychically reconnected with the killer who'd nearly destroyed her mind a few months ago?

She'd known it was too soon for Iris to subject herself to the world again. She didn't think a worse scenario could have played out. The nightmare excuse clearly did not hold water with Adam Frasier, which meant Eva had to come up with a satisfactory explanation for it all. But after everything today, her brain and body were a pile of mush. That's why her knees felt weak and her pulse raced.

It had nothing to do with Adam's proximity or larger-than-life presence. He absolutely had not intruded into her dreams last night. She had no room in her mind for anything about him, even his scent reached her in ways she didn't want to think about. Being hypersensitive to perfumes, she rarely wore any and found most cologne overbearing, but she actually liked his light and refreshing scent.

Her cell vibrated, and she thankfully escaped Adam's side to answer Devin's call.

"Have you seen or heard the news?"

"No. I'm at Dimensions with Iris, Paddy, Mr. Frasier, and a couple of para-medics. Iris had a "nightmare.""

"I'm not surprised. Smith is on the loose."

Eva gripped the phone, her heart stopping for a full beat before pounding painfully hard. "How? When? What happened?"

"I don't know the details yet. Just saw his picture being flashed on the tube and something about a transport crash this morning. They've just now figured out Smith is missing. You need to tell him."

"Tell who? What?" She whispered, glancing past the paramedics tending Iris to Adam. He had his gaze focused on her and Eva turned away.

"You know who," Devin said. "Tell Frasier about Smith's accomplice."

"I don't think so." It was bad enough the FBI agent had witnessed Iris's psychic trance. She couldn't just declare Smith hadn't worked alone.

"*No* isn't an option this time."

"Why? What are you seeing?"

"Enough to know Frasier is essential."

"We'll discuss it later. Meanwhile, Paddy will drive Iris home and I'll be along later. I need to check something out."

"If it's about Smith, take Frasier."

Damn Devin. She bit back her adamant 'no' and changed the subject. "When Iris gets home, find out if the nightmare is the same as the last time she connected to the killer. She's worried that I'm in danger, which is different than before."

Devin cursed. "Why aren't you coming straight home then? Show some intelligence and—"

"I'm only going to the library before they close, okay?"

Devin sighed. "Nowhere is safe, you know that. Just be careful."

"Always."

Rejoining the paramedics, Eva learned Iris's pulse was up to 130, blood pressure was normal, and after numerous questions about the date, year, president, and a few math problems, they declared Iris fine. They did recommend, she see her doctor tomorrow, and for Eva to call 911 or bring Iris to the emergency room if she lost consciousness again, had a seizure, or became disoriented.

As the paramedics packed up their equipment, their radio squawked. All Eva heard was garble, but one paramedic told the other there was a four alarm fire at a mansion not far from the governor's estate, just blocks from the art gallery. They hurried off.

Eva focused on Iris for a brief moment then it hit her. Angel Banning had lived near the governor's. That wasn't far from the art gallery. Smith was on the loose and could have easily passed close enough for Iris to make a psychic connection with him. Eva had to find out which house was on fire.

"Paddy, take Iris and Blue home. I've got to do something first so I'll drive Iris's car and—"

"*No,*" Iris and Paddy practically shouted in unison.

Eva pressed her fingers to her pounding temple. "Not so loud."

"After the morning you've had, you aren't driving anywhere. You can't even be in the sunlight unless you close your eyes. I'm driving you both home now and that's final."

"I'm better," Eva said. "Honestly."

"I can help," Adam said.

"She can't go anywhere," Iris whispered. "She needs to come home where it's safe."

"Home might not be the safest place to go. That was Devin on the phone. Smith escaped during transport today and is on the loose." The verbal bomb, hit everyone. Paddy cursed causing Blue to bark. Iris abruptly stood; her heels clicked on the marble floor as she paced, muttering, "*What the hell!* Can't good win for five freaking minutes?"

Adam pulled out his phone and walked away engaging in an intense, but whispered conversation.

"You're coming home. Lannie will kill me if ya don't," Paddy said emphatically.

Eva shook her head. "Don't you see? Now more than ever, we can't lose a minute in hunting down the truth."

Adam returned, his expression grim. "Apparently, a stolen dump truck ambushed the transport van by knocking it into a ravine. Officers lucky enough to survive the collision received a bullet to the head. After untangling the wreckage, the authorities have determined Smith and two other prisoners are missing, the rest died in the accident."

"You need to tell him right now. Or I will," Iris said.

Eva clenched her jaw and glared at her sister. They never aired their psychic laundry. *Ever.* It was going to be hard enough to explain Iris's telepathic incident.

"Tell me what?" Adam demanded.

"Nothing unusual," Eva muttered.

"Smith threatened her life yesterday."

"Killers do that," Eva replied.

"It was more than hot air. Smith pretty much told Eva that he and his partner were coming after her."

"His partner?" Adam's sharp gaze cut into Eva. "And you didn't tell anyone? Today might not have—"

"No!" Eva cut him off. "I shoulder a lot, but not this. I goaded him into losing his cool and he yelled, 'We're coming for you.' Based on that and my, uh, gut instinct, I'm digging back through everything I can find on Smith, looking for a *we.*"

"Well, that *we* happened today. But even if you'd said anything. I doubt that one statement would have altered his transport arrangements. What is a sure bet is he will follow through on that threat, which means you shouldn't go anywhere without a bodyguard. Not even to the library."

Eva frowned. Adam had great hearing. She'd been whispering to Devin. "Thank you, but—"

"Is she always this contrary?" Adam looked to Iris and Paddy and Eva gritted her teeth.

"Yes," Iris and Paddy said in unison.

Iris smiled. "You can drive me home, Paddy, and we'll come get my Miata tomorrow. I think Eva just got herself a bodyguard for the day."

"I didn't—" Adam said.

"He's not—" Eva interjected.

Iris waved her hand as if shooing pesky flies. "Yes, you both are. Besides, if I don't miss my guess, Adam has something important to talk with you about, Eva."

Adam's jaw dropped and Eva cursed. It seemed Iris was determined to wave her psychic ability in front of Adam like a red cape before a bull.

"Come on, Paddy," Iris took Blue's leash and led the away. "Don't forget to set the alarm when you lock up, Eva."

Paddy moved a few steps, his gaze bouncing between Iris and Eva. "You sure about this?"

"Positive," Iris said with an impish smile.

Paddy looked torn, clearly wanting Eva's okay.

Adam spoke up, setting his gaze on her. "My flight to D.C. isn't until ten thirty. I have some spare time, especially to search for a lead on who sprung Smith and murdered four officers. Are you game?"

Eva sighed and frowned at the challenge in Adam's gaze. Should she kill two birds with one stone? Dig safely into Smith's life for a few hours and nip in the bud Adam's reasons for coming around yesterday and today? Or, should she call a cab and lone-wolf it as usual? Whatever she decided, she needed Iris and Paddy safely home. "Don't worry, Paddy. Take Iris and Blue home. Tell Lannie, I won't be long."

Paddy nodded and followed Iris. Eva waited until the coast was clear and gave

Adam a grim smile. "Sorry to put you through that. I'll call a taxi and you can be on your way."

He shook his head. "No can do. Your family thinks you're in safe hands and that's exactly where you'll stay, or I call Iris and tell her you bailed. Who is Lannie?"

"Our housekeeper whom I may have to send on a long vacation with my soon-to-arrive aunt to stay sane. Listen, I appreciate your offer, but I can take care of myself," she patted her purse, feeling the reassuring bulk of her Glock.

"Good. Two capable people are better than one."

Eva glared at Adam. *Now* what?

3:00 P.M.

EVA DIDN'T HAVE ANY more time to waste. The sooner she tackled her agenda, the sooner she could ditch Adam. She gave an exasperated huff and started for the office. "Fine. We need to hurry."

Adam followed. "Your wish is my command. What can I do to help?"

"Crawl back into your bottle and disappear," she muttered, turning off the lights.

He chuckled and followed her as she closed the gallery, set the alarm, and locked the door. Once outside, she slipped her dark sun glasses on and still winced at the bright sunlight.

Adam fell into step beside her, too close for comfort. The combination of his handsomeness, size, and charisma left very little to ignore and she fought for distance. "We've a fire to catch, Frasier."

He arched a brow. "Frasier, is it, Eva?"

She ignored the smooth warmth of his tone and nodded. "St. Claire will do."

"We'll see," he said. "What's this about a fire?"

"The one near the governor's mansion. Angel Banning lived in the area."

Adam caught Eva's arm and swung her to face him. "The rescued girl whose testimony sent Smith to prison? Son-of-a-bitch." His face flushed. "If he got to her—"

Eva shook her head and set her hand on his then quickly pulled back at the heat she'd felt. "No. The family moved to an undisclosed location before the trial.

As of last month, their mansion was still up for sale. I pray no one has bought and moved in since. We won't know till we get there."

"Let's go, then." He led the way to a souped-up Batmobile-Mustang, obviously not a rental.

This time Eva lowered her glasses and arched a brow at him. Did the man have super hero aspirations?

Adam shrugged. "My father's revisiting his teens. Even had to have the 'responsible driver' talk with him last month after he got a ticket for Exhibition of Acceleration because he smoked his tires at a red light. He's had so many violations that he'll likely have his license suspended if he gets one more."

A reluctant grin tugged at her lips. "Are we talking about the same sedate, bookish gentleman I met yesterday?" Vince Frasier's bifocal, absentminded professor-like image in no way matched the muscle car.

"Sedate?" Chuckling hard, Adam got into the car.

Eva sank into the seat, immediately set even more off-kilter by the deep rumble of Adam's laughter, the twinkle in his green eyes, and his intriguing cologne.

A little over six feet, and judging from the fit of his jeans and pullover, well-honed, Adam cut an impressive figure that filled space—*fast*.

He maneuvered into the flow of traffic, adeptly shifting gears. His knuckles brushed her knee and her pulse sped at the tingling sensations that, surprisingly, diminished her headache. Only being able to lounge in the angled bucket seat, and not sit anywhere near normal, left Eva feeling more vulnerable and oddly more feminine than she had in a long time.

She clenched her jaw and shifted her knees toward the door, already blasting Iris for disrupting her status quo.

"I take a left at the next light, right?" He kept his gaze on the road, as if completely unaware of the havoc he created.

Blinking, Eva refocused her mind. "Yes."

They reached the light, but traffic to the left onto West Paces Ferry Road sat at a standstill. "Take a right and we'll circle around to come up Habersham. The Banning's estate is a few houses from where Habersham intersects with West Paces Ferry. Smith kidnapped Angel off of Habersham. She wasn't supposed to leave the driveway of her home with her scooter, but decided to visit her friend around the corner."

"I've yet to understand how evil so often finds that vulnerable, split-second moment of human error to strike in."

"It's because evil is always there, lurking and looking to harm no matter what the surroundings are. People don't realize the monsters are there until they fall victim to them. Even in neighborhoods like this, they're there. A young woman named Julie Love ran out of gas not too far from the governor's mansion and disappeared. What happened to her didn't come to light until over a year later. The girlfriend of one of the men who'd raped then killed Julie, went to the police. They'd kidnapped Julie from the side of the road as she walked to get help from a nearby mansion. Making people aware of what's hiding beneath the surface of life is why I write true crime. If one book can save a life then it's worth it all. No woman should let her gas go below a quarter of a tank. Ever."

"I owe you an apology," Adam said softly. "From my perspective with the FBI, sensationalizing a killer's crimes—such as writing a book about their depravity—only feeds the sickness and encourages others to act. I didn't consider true crime stories to be warning manuals."

"I suppose that would depend on the writer and the perspective in which the story is written. You don't view John Douglas's books as sensationalizing a killer's acts, do you?" The legendary FBI profiler had written several chilling books, delving into the minds of the most notorious serial killers known.

"No. His non-fiction books are gold when it comes to profiling. Every agent dreams of being as good."

"You haven't read one of my books yet, have you?"

"Guilty. But I will."

"I'm not much different. I tell the story as best as I can, so readers will understand what happened. Then maybe, when faced with a situation or a crime in progress, they'll stop it from happening." Eva frowned, wondering why she wanted Adam to understand her work.

"Makes sense."

"Good. Then make sense of why you spent five thousand on books by an author you've never read. While I believe your father will enjoy them and it was for a worthy cause, it's clear there's another reason."

"Nothing like striping a man bare. You're right, but I'm not sure what to say just yet. You know my father and Tony Hayden were pals and he's long believed Carlan didn't murder the Haydens. According to my father, you also question Carlan's guilt."

She'd known in her gut this was related to *Hayden's Hell.* "I do. I don't recall, your father's name coming up in any of the records surrounding Tony's life, and no one mentioned their relationship in my investigation."

"My father and Tony worked in different departments at the GBI, and it has been fifteen years. But it's curious why no one mentioned my father. Who did you interview for the book?"

Eva frowned. A strong sense that there was still more Adam Frasier wasn't saying weighed heavily on her. Just then, a fire truck came blaring through a red light and swerved onto the road. Adam slammed on his brakes and his arm swung over as she flew forward. The back of his hand pressed against her breasts just as the seatbelt locked down. Her sunglasses went flying into her lap. She gasped, stunned. Their gazes met and heat zinged.

Before she could speak or move, his hand settled back on the gear shift, his gaze focused on the road, and he flew in the fire truck's wake.

Eva did the only thing possible; she ignored anything remotely personal and held on for dear life. Snapping her dark glasses back on, she focused on the unfolding drama ahead. They got as close as they could to the intersection of West Paces Ferry and parked the car, walking the last block with quite a few spectators. News vans were everywhere. Eva thankfully noted Grace DuMond's network had yet to arrive.

Despite ten fire trucks and dozens of firefighters, not much could be done to save the Banning's mansion. Flames and smoke billowed not only from the house but the woods surrounding the estate. The place stank as if it had been doused in gas before being ignited. The FOR SALE sign by the road lay trampled into the dirt.

"Smith and his partner-in-crime were here," Eva whispered. Looking at the damage, she had little doubt.

The scorched earth before Eva sent chills down her spine as Smith's 'were coming for you' rang over and over in her mind. This fire had a well-planned feel about it. Adam dug out his phone.

"Who are you calling?"

"Same person I spoke to earlier. Major Brad Warren, he's commanding officer over field operations for the Georgia State Patrol. We grew up together. Don't know if the police have had the time to connect Smith with the fire, but it can't hurt to alert everyone he's been in the area."

"Good. I'll call the real estate agent. Her name is on that sign in the dirt. Smith may go after her to find Angel Banning's family."

"*Hell*, quick thinking."

"It may already be too late." Cursing herself for not calling the moment she heard of the fire near the governor's mansion, Eva turned away and called Jillian Miles. She'd spoken to the woman twice before. It was how Eva had been able to contact Angel Banning's parents for input into Kaylee's book.

Jillian answered immediately.

"You're safe?" Eva asked. "Smith escaped today and the Banning's mansion is now on fire. He might come after you to get to them."

"*Dear God.* I'm heading to the office right now. Sally, the agent on duty this afternoon isn't answering my calls."

"Call the police. Do *not* go to your office. Where can I meet you close by?"

"There's a Starbucks one block down from my office. But what about Sally?"

"Let the police go in first. If all is well, no harm. If not, I'm afraid there won't be anything you can do. Do you keep information on where the Banning's are now in your office?"

"No. Not there. I didn't want any chance their location could accidentally be made known."

"Good. You may have just saved them more trauma."

"Smith on the loose will hit them hard."

"See you in about twenty minutes." Eva disconnected the call and met Adam's grim gaze. "You heard?"

"Enough. Let's hurry. Brad has troopers on their way to the area. He's contacting the other authorities and the GBI taskforce assigned to recapture Smith. They'll set up road blocks and start canvassing surveillance footage of the area."

She and Adam fell into step, quickly returning to the car just as Grace DuMond's news van arrived. The reporter and her camera crew were late. Eva saw the moment Grace spied her with Adam. She pointed toward Eva, yelling at her camerawoman to move her ass. DuMond made an impossible high-heeled dash with her camerawoman in tow, dreadlock's bouncing. Eva had always thought anyone who insisted on wearing the same color all the time was strange. With DuMond consistently in red, and the camerawoman in black, the two made an odd couple.

"If she isn't wearing Prada, then she should be," Adam said dryly. "I heard her on the radio last night. She's worse than obnoxious." He unlocked the car with the remote.

Surprisingly, Eva found herself laughing at his movie joke, thinking the Devil DuMond likely *did* wear Prada. Red Prada everything.

She opened the car door, sent DuMond a queenly wave, and ducked into the Batmobile. Adam made a turn worthy of a stuntman and left with dirt and dust flying at DuMond.

"I should send her red shoes with pitchfork heels."

"Do they really make those?" he asked.

"I'm sure. There's a shoe for everything these days."

Adam floored the gas once they cleared the rescue traffic and they made their way to Jillian's office. Eva patted the dash. "I for one am thankful for your father's Batmobile. DuMond ate our exhaust today."

"Me, too." Adam laughed. With Batman worthy speed, he adeptly maneuvered through the traffic as he drove back into the heart of Buckhead on Peachtree Street.

3:30 P.M.

ADAM PULLED INTO THE Starbucks and Eva saw a police car down the street. Its blue lights flashed as it stopped in front of Jillian's office. Two police officers, weapons in hand, quickly, but cautiously entered the building. Jillian, inside Starbucks, stood at the glass door watching anxiously. Eva prayed she was wrong. That Jillian's employee would be fine.

Eva and Adam approached Jillian, who joined them outside where they could see the office. Jillian's phone rang. She answered then cried out, turning ghost white, and ran for her office. "Sally! Oh, no. Sally."

Grimly, Eva fell into step and caught Jillian's arm to steady the agent.

Adam did the same on the other side. "Was that the police? What did they say?"

Tears spilled from Jillian's eyes. "I don't know exactly. This is my fault. I was supposed to work this afternoon, but went to a fundraiser at the Botanical Gardens. Sally filled in for me."

Eva had to bite her tongue to keep from saying it would have been worse if Jillian had been there. She had no doubt Smith would have gone to any length to get to the Banning family. Less than a minute later, they reached Jillian's office. The blinds covering the plate glass window were open, allowing Eva to make out the shadows of the antique décor between the slats.

Adam pulled Jillian back from barging through the open door. "Wait a second," he told Jillian then called out. "Officers, the realtor, Jillian Miles, is here."

An officer appeared at the door. "You three can step inside. Don't touch anything though."

Eva knew the second she walked into the office that Sally was dead. A chilling cold rushed down her spine and she heard the reverberating echoes of the woman's cries.

"I told you I don't know. Please!" Then an image slowly appeared. A woman, middle-aged but hip, with spiked, salt and pepper hair sat tied to an office chair, sobbing. Slashing cuts tattered her white blouse, turning it red.

"Around and around she goes. Will she tell us and live? Nobody knows."

"No, no! Please. I don't know," the woman screamed.

A black leather gloved hand, large like a man's, holding a black KA-BAR knife appeared. The hand shoved the chair into a spin and placed the knife close enough to slice into the woman as she spun. Laughter followed. The woman screamed and suddenly convulsed into spasms. When she came to a stop, she sat slumped in the chair, her eyes open and sightless.

"Shit. You killed her, Mason."

The knife blade slid to the woman's chin, lifting her face up for a second then fell away. "I should have fucked her first. Now we have to wait for the other, bitch."

"Not here."

A blur of the room passed until a black and white painted face came into view. He had the same shape and build as Mason. His eyes were made into black upside down crucifixes with red contacts at the centers of the crosses. His mouth gleamed like a black serpent as did his black hair which had been caught up into a Gene Simmons KISS-like ponytail.

"Why not?"

The black-mouthed smile widened. "Because we're smarter than that. If she doesn't show up by the time I get back then we'll go after St. Claire. Are you sure you didn't tell anyone what I did to Kaylee?"

"Positive. We need to kill that scary bitch."

"Not until I find out how St. Claire knows."

"What does it matter?"

Eva shuddered hard, gasping for air. She blinked and the room came into focus. Adam was staring at her. Jillian stood crying and talking to the two officers who were refusing to let her go to the back room.

"I need air," Eva whispered and wrenched around, stumbling back out front. This was the first time she'd ever been caught up in a murder just moments after and it had left her shaken. She leaned hard on the glass window and braced her hands on her knees as she fought dizzying nausea and pain. She'd been in Mason's point of view and could still feel his excitement and bloodlust reverberating in the room. She had no idea if it'd been five minutes or two hours since Smith had been here. The fire at the Banning's had been burning for a while.

She'd seen the masked face of Smith's partner—a sick anti-clown who preyed on children? But the man hadn't been bald.

"Are you okay?" Adam followed her outside. He gripped her shoulder, and leaned close, deep concern creasing his brow.

Eva looked up, drawing in a deep breath of air. That's when she saw Mason Smith. He stepped from the shadowed recess of a building across the street. His bald head gleamed in the sun as he pointed the wide barrel of an unusual pistol right at her.

4:00 P.M.

Gun. Get down," Eva screamed. Launching from the wall, she plowed hard into Adam, knocking him backward and landing on top of him. The plate glass window shattered. An explosion of glass cubes rained down on them. Adam rolled with her across the rough sidewalk until he hit the protective cover of a car parked against the curb. Bits of glass pressed sharply against her jeans and shirt.

"Shooter. Six o'clock, on the run," Adam yelled as the officers called out from inside the office.

The policemen, pistols at the ready, eased from the doorway, one high, one low.

"It's Smith," Eva gasped. She lay stunned beneath Adam with her nose buried against the scruff of his firm jaw. Inadvertently, she drew a deep breath of his cool scent. The distant sound of sirens wailed above the roar of blood in her ears. Hard male muscle pressed her back against hot cement and his lean legs were tangled up with hers.

"Which way?" One policeman asked.

"Left. Behind the red brick building across the street," Adam said.

"Keep down, backup is on the way," the other policeman said before they took off after Smith.

Blinking at the bright sun, Eva blindly dug for her Glock in her purse wrapped around her wrist. "How do you know which way Smith went?"

Adam nodded to the left. "Mirrored glass, next door. I've had a view since you shouted 'gun.'"

Craning her neck and squinting hard, she could see the opposite side of the street and the advancing policemen in the mirrored storefront. She had to do something to help. Smith could not escape to kill again. She could now ID the partner, provided the man still had his makeup on and rock star hair. How could she reveal that to anyone? She had to go hunt for him herself. "Move off. I have my Glock."

"For what? You plan to run after Smith, too?"

So mad she could spit, Eva squirmed against his weight. "Maybe. Some FBI agent you are, Frasier. He's escaping."

Adam eased to her side and glared at her, blowing all the hot air out of her bravado with a single look that only a more than capable, calm man could give. "Well, Ms. Saint, only a greenhorn civilian would be naïve enough to brandish a weapon with armed cops on the hunt. This isn't the movies. Hide the Glock. You're going back into that office with your friend, Jillian. Period."

Eva shuddered hard at the thought of facing Sally's death again, but knew Adam was somewhat right about her knee-jerk reaction. Running around right now with gun in hand could get her killed. Her hot air deflated beneath his common sense. She'd never been in the heat of an investigation before. She'd always lone-wolfed cold cases.

Going to Jillian and leaving the killer chasing to the police was the levelheaded thing to do—and the hardest for her to face at this raw moment. Telling herself that Sally had died from a stroke or heart attack instead of hours more of torture was little consolation. Smith and his clown partner had tortured Sally and she'd died.

Adam narrowed his gaze at Eva. "You want to tell me what happened when you entered Jillian's office a few minutes ago?"

She sat up, pushing Adam further away from her. Her sunglasses lay mangled on the sidewalk. *Damn.* "Nothing. I just needed some air. I get migraines." She tucked the Glock into her waistband, under her shirt. Just in time, too. Dozens of police cars sped from both directions down Peachtree Street right at them.

Adam stood and helped Eva to her feet. Ghost white and crying, Jillian stumbled out of the office, her heels crunching on broken glass. "She's dead. He tied her to a chair and cut her. Everywhere. This is my fault."

Eva moved to Jillian and hugged her. "Shh, it's not your fault."

The squad cars squealed to a stop at different points, and an army of Atlanta's finest established a perimeter around the area. Two more cars, unmarked and flashing blue lights, pulled to a stop at the realtor's office. Four men ejected from the cars, weapons drawn.

Eva hated that the situation had proved Adam right.

Adam held up his hands. "Special Agent, Adam Frasier. Author, Eva St. Claire and realtor, Jillian Miles, this is her office."

Two detectives entered the office, two approached, one shiny bald like Smith, the other shaggy blonde. Shaggy blonde lowered his weapon while shiny bald kept his gun aimed, more at Adam than her or Jillian.

"Ms. St. Claire, I'm Detective Rollins," said the shaggy blonde. "I've heard a lot about you from Sheriff Doug Grant. I, too, am a fan of your work." Rollins and his Southern drawl reminded her of Alan Jackson—mustached, wearing worn jeans with a western-style blue plaid shirt that brightened his eyes. "You ladies need to move inside where it's safe."

Jillian shook her head and stared fearfully at her office doorway. She was pale, red-eyed, and shaking with shock.

Eva forced a grim smile. "We were about to do that, but considering the situation, it might be better for Jillian to either go to the station or let us take her home and you can contact her there."

"We'll see what we can do, but with the manhunt for Smith in progress I have to ask you to step inside for now." He frowned at Adam. "Special Agent Frasier, is it? Let me see your badge. You're news to me on this. You just get here?"

"Do it slowly," the shiny bald detective said. Eva shivered at the man's menacing tone. She realized she'd never noted so many bald men before. Maybe it was because she'd never been looking for one. How did the shiny bald twin of Smith from Kaylee's vision match up to the sick clown she'd seen. Did Smith have two partners? Or had there been a shiny bald, Smith-look-alike beneath the masking makeup and a Gene Simmons's wig?

Adam carefully pulled out his wallet. "Not officially on the case. I'm with Ms. Saint…Claire. Following her uncanny, gut instincts is what led us here." Adam arched a questioning brow at Eva.

Wishing for her dark glasses, Eva shrugged. "Just logical deductions, Frasier." Taking Jillian's hand, she drew a deep breath and braced herself to reenter Jillian's office. "Come on, we'll go to just inside the door. It's only until they can find out everything they need to help Sally get justice, okay?"

Jillian nodded and burst into tears again. Eva felt like doing the same thing the second she heard Sally's cries again. Forcing her way to a sofa and dragging Jillian with her, Eva sat. With her head pounding again and fearing she'd vomit from the pain, she prayed the detectives would hurry. Realizing she'd seen the unusually wide barrel of Smith's pistol before didn't help. She'd had an up-close view of it, from Kaylee's eyes, when he'd violated her with it.

Adam pacing the room only added to her tension. The bald detective, whom everyone called Curly, remained as uneasy as ever. He kept his hand on his gun and his eyes on Adam as the other men checked over the crime scene.

After fifteen minutes, Eva had to do something or go insane. She chewed two of her migraine tablets, slipped her Glock from her pocket back into her purse, and pulled out her phone. Turning up the volume, she streamed a live news video of the manhunt for Smith. She was even desperate enough to listen to Grace DuMond's rambling as she and another reporter stood camped out in front of Smith's parent's house in Conyers, Georgia. They'd have a long wait for Smith's parents to return.

It was church night. With Mason Smith's escape, the Reverend Smith and his Holiness Congregation would likely spend more hours than usual praying and handling snakes, to prove their righteousness and eradicate any possibility they contributed to raising a monster.

The distraction helped her survive the wait before the police let them go even though Smith had yet to be captured. The Fulton County Medical Examiner's Office had whisked Sally away. Jillian and her family, under police protection, planned to check into an upscale hotel with additional 24/7 security. When Detective Rollins cleared Eva and Adam to go, he handed her his card with an interested smile. "I'd like to discuss a book idea with you sometime."

Eva smiled. "We'll see. Thank you for your assistance today." She grabbed Adam's arm and hurried out the door. When she turned back for a final glance, she saw Curly standing at the shattered window, staring at them. What would he look like in sick clown makeup and a wig? His pudgy shape wasn't too far from Smith's.

"Curly needs to have his name changed to Stony or binge watch the *Three Stooges* and find a better disposition," Adam said.

"Do you have eyes in the back of your head?"

"Nope. I can just feel his scrutiny. He wouldn't be the first detective to take issue with FBI intrusion."

"But you aren't officially here." Eva picked up her pace.

"Doesn't matter. He seems a little more hostile than usual, though."

Eva felt as if Mason and the sick clown lurked in every shadow. She'd never been this spooked on a case before. They moved swiftly to the car still parked down the block at the Starbucks. Police were everywhere around them, but it did little to ease her apprehension—take away the makeup and Mason's partner could be almost any similarly shaped man—even a cop.

"Does every Tom, Dick, and Harry use the 'I'm writing a book' line on you?" Adam asked as he started the car.

Eva welcomed the distraction from her racing thoughts. "Pretty much."

He shook his head and pulled into the Buckhead traffic that had become a nightmare after having the main thoroughfare blocked off. "Which way to your house? Or do you want to catch dinner first. I'm starving."

She glanced at her watch. "I'm not going home yet and no time to eat. You can drop me off at the Ritz Carlton just up the street and I'll catch a cab."

"I already told you that isn't happening. It's after 6:00. The library is closed. Where are you going?"

"To church."

Adam blinked. "Okay. I'm game. It's been a while. But I'm going to need sustenance." He whipped the car into McDonald's and zoomed into the drive-thru lane. "What do you want?"

"You eat this—" She flapped her hand, searching for the right disgusted words. "Artery clogging, cardboard junk?"

He grinned. "With relish at times, just don't tell my father. He thinks I'm a health food Nazi, but somebody has to preach to him about his diet. Have you ever tried it?"

"Never, Frasier."

"You sound like the grump from *Green Eggs and Ham*." He pulled up to the window. "I'll take two double quarter pounders with extra cheese and onions meals. Supersize the fries. Add two apple pies and two large sweet teas with lemon. I need lots of catsup, too." He looked at Eva. "What do you want, Ms. Saint?"

She snapped her dropped jaw closed and shook her head. "I'll be the designated driver, Sam I Am. Somebody will need to rush you to the hospital."

He chuckled. Moments later he paid for the food and handed her the bags.

"What do I do with this?"

"Since I'm driving, you're the designated server. Dump catsup on mine and add a handful of fries then hand me the sandwich in the box, my fries, and a couple of napkins. Which way to church?"

Eighty-five South to I-20. It's in Conyers."

"Geez, I could have had a chili dog and onion rings from the Varsity. It's been ages."

"The Varsity is—"

"The best greasy spoon in the South," he inserted.

"—worse than McDonalds," she finished. "And yes, I tried it. Once."

"We'll fix that. You live out toward Conyers?"

"I don't need fixing. And no, I don't. I live up in Alpharetta. Reverend Smith and his wife live in Conyers. If I don't miss my guess, Mason's father will be busy handling rattlesnakes and Mason's mother will be all by herself in the Sunday School room praying. It's the only time she'll talk. She never speaks a word when her husband is present and that's most of the time."

"You can't be serious."

"It's true."

"I believe you about her. I've read up on the Reverend and his cult. You can't be serious about going there."

"You didn't listen. Right now is the only time she'll be free of him until God knows when. There are reporters camped out in front of their house. I didn't see any at the church yet, but who knows. Reverend Smith will go on lockdown as soon as the media hits them. I need to ask her some more questions about Mason's childhood. Friends he had. Anything that might give a clue to who his partner is."

"And what if Smith decides to pay a visit to his not-so-beloved parents?"

"Won't happen at the church during a Sunday night service. He's deathly afraid of snakes and exorcisms, which is exactly what they do at night. You know that's why the Reverend Smith adopted him. Mason was the most out of control, vicious child in foster care. Reverend Smith's great plan was to cast out the boy's demons and prove to the world how great his spiritual powers were."

"Does he think he's God? Who did you learn that from?"

I am the god…I am the god… The chant from Kaylee's vision flashed through Eva's memory. Psychiatrists had diagnosed Mason with delusions of grandeur. Something he'd learned from his adopted father maybe?

"From Mason's mother. As I said, she talks when her husband isn't there and she's sure he won't get wind of what she's saying. She trusts me."

"Why is she the only one praying in the Sunday School room? Why aren't the other women with her?"

Eva laughed. "Supposedly, because the other women have to watch how manly their husbands are, so they can be awed by their mastery over evil serpents. Mrs. Smith stopped a snake from biting her husband's neck one time, handling it so well that the men were extremely impressed by her ability. She was then banned from the snake handling services to dutifully pray for humility."

"It's hard to believe suppressive cults are prevalent in this day and age. I don't understand why or how it's possible."

"Fear, community, the need to be told everything rather than make a decision, I could go on and on. It's sad."

"It's sick. Speaking of which, is my hamburger ready yet?"

Eva looked down at the bags. She had to admit that her mouth watered at the smell of fries and onions. Her oatmeal breakfast had disappeared ages ago. "You're really going to eat all of this?"

"No. Half of it is yours."

"*What?* Absolutely not, Frasier." She'd exit the car twenty pounds heavier in all of the wrong places.

"Have you never eaten a hamburger before, Ms. Saint?"

"Of course, I occasionally have a Wagyu burger. It's a healthier—"

"I know all about the praises of Wagyu. One McDonald patty and a few fries aren't going to kill you and will likely help your headache, too. When was the last time you ate?"

"I ate," she muttered, knowing he was right. She quickly fixed him his catsup-drenched, fry-stacked burger so he'd shut up and focus on something besides her. "Here," she handed him the box, his fries, and some napkins. He placed his fries between his legs, balanced the hamburger box on his thigh, and proceeded to devour the meal.

She got hungry looking at him. For food that was. Nothing else. "What if I said I was a vegetarian, Sam I Am?" She found herself muttering.

"Then you'll have sweet tea, fries and an apple pie. Now eat."

Eva grumbled, but bit into a fry. Five fries later, she opened the box and glared at the gigantic hamburger. The smell of onions did her in. She settled on eating one of the patties covered in cheese and onions and skipped the bun. It wasn't the best she'd ever had, but it wasn't the worst either. And she had to admit, she felt a lot better afterward.

"Never say never, Ms. Saint. You liked it didn't you?"

"It was edible. Thank you."

He shook his head and laughed. "You're welcome. It's a good thing you write true crime."

She frowned. "Why is that?"

"Because if you'd been Dr. Seuss, poor Sam I Am would still be running around with a plate of green eggs and ham. Seriously though, as thoroughly as you've dug into Mason Smith's life, you're likely the best profiler available for finding him. You're on par with the BAU analysts and The Profiler program. Do you go this in-depth with every case you write about?"

"Yes." Eva had done as much research about the BAU and their methods as she could, in order to write better books. Most people thought the BAU operated like the *Criminal Minds* television show, but that wasn't how the unit worked at all. They were researchers and analysts who provided support. Not super agents who drive bomb laden ambulances into central park to keep from blowing up a hospital. She looked Adam's way. He appeared more than capable of doing that, though.

He wiped his chin with a napkin. "Did I get catsup on myself?"

She blinked, realizing she'd been staring. "A little, Frasier, but you got it. How long have you been with the FBI?"

"Nine years."

"Why?"

He sucked in air, and his grip on the steering wheel tightened. "If I tell you the truth, will you start telling me the truth?" he whispered.

"I have."

He shook his head. "No, you haven't." He sighed. "When I was four, I ran into the woods after a puppy. My mother left my six-year-old sister on the swing to chase after me. When we returned, my sister had vanished and was never heard from or seen again. It destroyed my mother, and our family. For me, every case I help solve, every killer I help stop, I come one step closer to redemption."

Eva curled her hand into a fist to keep from reaching for Adam. The conversation had gone from Dr. Seuss funny to a heart-wrenching burden that no child or man should ever have to bear. The switch smacked her hard. She hurt for him.

"I'm sorry," she said. She didn't try to tell him it wasn't his fault. She knew all too well the guilt a child carried when tragedy struck. She would forever wonder if she could have done something, anything, that would have stopped her father from killing her mother.

"Me too. But as you so adeptly put it, evil constantly lurks and it seems in Mason's case was nurtured. I remember reading that he'd received frequent and heavy-handed punishments from his uber-religious father."

"From the age of seven until he left at seventeen. Before that we don't know. His adoption records are sealed. What I'd planned to do at the library today was look for that needle in the hay stack. Since he was adopted in Rockdale County, I wanted to do a search for articles where a boy in his age range was abandoned, orphaned, or taken from an abusive parent, or something, anything." She left off that she was looking for identical twins. It would so easily explain her visions at the cabin.

"I can make that happen," Adam said. "When I go in tomorrow, I'll set the wheels in motion."

Eva sucked in air. She didn't want to be beholden to the FBI for anything. She didn't want to be involved with the agency on any level, even on the distant fringes of a case. When she returned home, she would hog-tie Devin until he told her what his vision of Adam was. Right now, hunting down Smith was more important than anything else.

6:30 P.M.

ADAM KNEW THE ATLANTA suburbs could go from city outskirts to backwoods rural in a heartbeat, but the country road they'd taken off Interstate 20 still surprised him. They'd wound past ramshackle farms and acres of corn and hay fields, before reaching the Holiness Church of God. Situated on a knoll with ancient live oaks and a miniscule graveyard, the one-room schoolhouse looking structure needed paint and more than a few prayers. There were less than ten cars parked in front. The theme song from Deliverance played in the back of his mind.

"No reporters yet. A good sign for us. Take the dirt road on the left, just before the graveyard. There's a picnic area in a copse of trees where we can park unnoticed. It won't be dark for a couple of hours yet. I'd rather not encounter the Reverend Smith, or his congregation and their company of serpents again."

"Again? I think you'd better explain that." He slowed the car to a crawl and eyed Eva. In their short time together, he'd gained a healthy respect for her investigative research skills, but also realized she said a whole hell of a lot less than she knew. He wanted inside her head as much as he wanted to cross the line she'd drawn between them. He'd never lacked for feminine company when he'd wanted it, nor did he have to pursue it. Women were never far away and a certain look always brought them closer.

Eva winced. Not a good sign for him, Adam thought. "When I interviewed Mrs. Smith the first time, it was sort of by accident. I'd come here to observe a snake handling service and she intercepted me beforehand. We talked and made plans to speak again in two weeks. I returned as scheduled, and parked with the rest of the cars up by the church as I had before. Someone from inside the service saw me though, because everyone exited the church, snakes and all, to give me a very unwelcoming greeting. Smith thought I was a reporter and pretty much said he'd throw me into their rattlesnake pit if I came back."

"You didn't think it important to mention this earlier?"

"Would you have come here or insisted on taking me home?"

Adam cursed. "I ought to turn around now. Given my experiences with you today, it's a wonder that you're alive after one book much less eight, isn't it?"

"Yes, eight. It's been an unusual day and the Reverend Smith's threat was an isolated incident. Besides it was more hot air to impress his congregation than real intent. He'd never jeopardize his standing and ministry just to deter a pesky journalist."

"Take a page out of your own playbook, evil lurks. You might not think the Reverend himself would act, but what about one of his followers? Anyone of them might risk anything to protect or impress their leader."

"Point taken. Usually I take Paddy and Blue with me on isolated excursions."

"Where did you go this morning then?"

Her gaze settled on him, and the misty gray of her eyes stirred with dark emotions. "If you must know, I went to the cabin where Smith killed and buried Kaylee to remind myself how much she deserves justice and he the death penalty."

Adam's irritation with her evaporated. Was he being an ass? Had he been one all day? Standing in judgment over her, slightly condescending? Would he have viewed another agent, even one without his training, the same way? He parked in the shade next to the picnic bench, cracked the windows for ventilation, and killed the engine. "Let's do this then. Where is the Sunday School room?"

"In the basement. There's a door in the back."

"Lead the way," he said, beating down the urge to take charge. Under the post 9/11 Law Enforcement Officer's Safety Act, it was his duty to be armed even when he wasn't on the job. He always had a compact 9mm in a concealing band at the small of his back, but he still felt practically naked walking into a possible hostile environment without the Glock he'd left in D.C.

He stepped out of the car and his empty fry box landed on the ground. He picked it up. Hearing a growl to his left, he drew his weapon as he turned to face a mid-sized pit bull with fangs bared.

"Easy boy, stay," Adam said firmly. The dog growled louder, deeper. Not good.

"Here boy. Hungry?" Eva said brightly. The dog leapt into the car at her command. Adam cut his gaze to see Eva had dumped her remaining fries, hamburger patty, and buns into the car seat. The pit bull was on it in a slobbering second. Eva shut her car door and Adam shut his, cringing at what was happening to his father's prized leather seats.

"We need to hurry. Best to cut through the woods to the back of the church," Eva moved to the left.

He matched her stride. "My father's going to kill me."

"Better you than the dog, Frasier."

"What? Nice to hear where your priorities lie."

"Well, were you going to shoot the poor thing?"

"Poor thing?" He frowned. "I'd shoot the ground first, but his teeth and my ass were not going to meet under any circumstances. Let's hope he's alone." Adam kept a sharp eye out as they moved at a swift pace.

"He's new. Looks like he had on a wireless collar."

"Definitely not a stray. The Reverend Smith's welcome committee for newcomers, maybe? Were you actually going to attend a snake handling service when you first came here?"

"I needed more insight into Smith's life. Since he'd spent ten years subjected to the church's loving hands, I'd thought about it. But my second thoughts had me peeking in the windows first. That's when Mrs. Smith spotted me."

"Amend my earlier statement from a wonder that you're alive to a miracle."

"Somethings are worth the price you pay. But you already know that or you wouldn't be with the FBI."

Adam snapped his mouth closed, knowing she was right. He didn't know what his problem was or why he kept playing scenarios in his head that ended with her in serious danger, or even dead. He'd just met her and it wasn't as if she was a destitute waif on gang-riddled streets. She had money to do anything she wanted. So why was she pounding the pavement after a killer rather than living it up at a luxury spa?

They were close enough now that he could hear Bluegrass music stuck on hyper-speed, accompanied by high-pitched singing and shouting. He'd seen videos of several snake handling services when studying religious groups. The FBI's Critical Incident Response Group had been founded to prevent another situation like what happened with the Branch Dividians outside of Waco. What he'd learned in CIRG was that any threat to a group's ideology can be deadly.

Adam really hoped they didn't butt heads with the Reverend Smith. Adam didn't want to have to explain to anyone, especially his boss, how he ended up conducting an unofficial manhunt for Smith with a crime writer as lead. That Eva St. Claire, with all her interesting curves, and secrets was an infuriating puzzle he couldn't seem to dismiss, was hardly an excuse.

Up close, the peeling paint, uncut shrubbery, and sparse grass suggested the congregation of this Holiness Church of God would be better served if they'd put down their snakes and picked up a garden hose or paintbrush. The rhythmic stomping from inside the church added a chaotic beat to the over-the-top din of music. Instead of descending the stairs and entering the basement door, Eva went and tapped on a window to the right. A gray-haired, stern looking woman popped her face at the window so fast, Adam nearly jumped. Eva waved then pointed at the door. The woman smiled and nodded.

Moments later the basement door opened. Not more than five feet tall and hump-backed, the full-figured woman of about seventy wore a serviceable gray and brown dress that covered her from wrinkled neckline to black lace-up shoes. Her smile brightened the dullness of her blue eyes as she raised her voice to be heard. "How did you get past Goliath?"

"Gave him a Happy Meal on steroids. I'm sorry I didn't make it before."

"The Reverend is a difficult man. When I heard Mason escaped today, I knew you'd come again." She looked at Adam, her expression guarded. He settled a deliberately loving look on Eva as he pressed a firm hand to her back. They didn't have time for Mrs. Smith's suspicions or questions about him or his FBI status.

Mrs. Smith smiled again. "You found yourself a man, didn't you? I'm glad.

You need one. Both of you come on in."

Eva gasped. "I don't. He's not—"

Adam caught Eva's hand. "I keep trying to tell her she does, but she's a little stubborn," he said with a smile.

Eva glared at him.

Adam mouthed the words 'trust me' back at Eva and knew from the consternated furrow across her brow, he'd pushed the right wrong button. He added fuel to the fire by sliding his hand up her back. "You need to hurry, luv."

She startled and he bit his cheek to keep from smiling and glanced out the door to assure their escape route remained clear. Made of concrete cinder block and painted hospital green, the basement was a trap waiting to happen. Covering one whole wall was a large poster of a bald-headed man holding a snake in one hand and a Bible in the other. A bright, anointing light in the shape of a cross above shone down on the man. A crowd of children and several men bowed at his feet. Below that, Luke 13:5 The Time is at Hand, was printed in bold.

Adam moved closer to the door as Eva followed Mrs. Smith several feet into the room. Inside, the beat of the stomping continued but the din of the music diminished. While Eva spoke to Mason's mother, Adam kept one ear on the conversation and pulled out his phone. He downloaded the Dog Repeller App, something he'd been meaning to do for ages. The high-pitched signal would hopefully send Goliath running when they returned to the car—provided there was a car left.

Then he looked up Luke 13:5. The Reverend Smith clearly saw himself as being anointed by God, a leader of children, and above his fellow man—all dangerously unstable self-perceptions, especially when challenged. Men like that became the Jim Jones's or the David Koresh's of the world. Adam had a sudden image of himself and Eva landing in a snake pit with no way out.

How had he ended up here? More importantly, why had he ended up here? He set his gaze on Eva. She was the most complex woman he'd ever met. Even now, her gray eyes held genuine interest and concern for Mrs. Smith, the mother of the serial killer who'd as soon annihilate Eva as look at her.

Eva set her hand briefly on Mrs. Smith's humped shoulders. "I'm sorry. We do need to hurry, but first tell me how you are?"

"Best as can be, considering all. But you don't need to worry none 'bout me.

The Lord giveth and taketh as He wills. Guess you're wanting to know if I've heard from Mason. No, and I don't expect to, either. As I told you before, he left at seventeen and hasn't been back since. The Reverend done beat the fear of God and snakes into the boy. Mason knows that after what he's done, the Reverend would kill him if he showed up."

"Did Mason have any close friends while growing up? Anyone he made a connection with whom he might have stayed in touch with over the years?"

"Wasn't allowed to see folks often. He stayed in too much trouble for that privilege. He had a friend of sorts here at church. They hung out some after the services. A boy named Randy Bell. Last I heard he went up to Kentucky. But that's been near twenty years ago."

"What about people in his life before his adoption? Did he ever speak of anyone?"

She shook her head. "Not really. He didn't talk when he first came to us. He was seven and they said he and his siblings had suffered a bad trauma. Didn't say what that was. But we knew he could speak 'cause of his nightmares. Never did understand what he cried out, though. The Reverend believed it was demons talking."

"Do you know more about his siblings?"

"Sisters they were. Two of them, maybe more. Can't remember exactly."

"Did Mason have anyone who he looked up to outside of the home? A mentor, a teacher, anyone who he admired?"

Mrs. Smith frowned. "For a while he played the fiddle with the Rockdale Sunshine Band, took lessons from a teacher, a Miss Carroll. The Reverend considered that an acceptable use of time. Lasted about two years then Mason came home one day, smashed his fiddle against a tree and never played again. It was just after he and the Reverend fought. The Reverend wanted Mason to play for the church's services with the others and Mason refused."

"What kind of music did Mason listen to?"

"Gospel."

"Any Heavy Metal?"

Mrs. Smith frowned. "Heavy what?"

"Any other music besides gospel?"

Her eyes widened and she spoke with more passion than ever before. "No. Only gospel was allowed. Still is. Everything else is from the devil and will lead you to Hell. You remember that, child."

The woman fervently believed in her decree. Not that Adam held any sympathy for a man who'd tortured and killed young girls, but he did wonder if Mason had ever had a prayer in hell of ending up normal. Didn't sound like it. Adam had faced this issue before and had concluded as inhumane as it sounded, just as rabid animals had to be put down, serial killers had to be stopped and ended—no matter what their reasons for killing.

When Smith shot at Eva earlier, it had taken every particle of Adam's being to stay with her and not go after the bastard as the on-scene policemen had. Adam kept wondering why Smith had missed the shot. Two reasons came to mind. Smith wanted the cops chasing him so Eva and Jillian would be left vulnerable for his invisible partner to grab. Or a more chilling reason—Smith wanted something from Eva before he killed her.

As they left the basement, Mrs. Smith handed Eva a pen. "I answer the Line to Salvation calls. I promise to let you know if Mason contacts us."

Feeling anxious, Adam caught Eva's elbow. "We should go." The music upstairs had increased in frenzy and volume. Above the din, a deep voice chanted. "I am the Alpha and the Omega. Repent of your sins or perish to an everlasting Hell. I am the Alpha and the Omega…"

Ducking quickly into the shadows of the unkempt bushes, they escaped the church and the Reverend Smith's oppressive shadow without incident. When they reached the car, Adam found Goliath sitting patiently in the driver's seat.

"Any ideas on how to get him out and us in," Eva asked. "He looks kind of friendly now."

Adam showed her the app on his phone. "Better safe than sorry." He was relieved to see the car upholstery, though glistening with slobber, grease, and apple pie goo, appeared intact. Adam amped up the dog repelling signal before he opened the car door. Goliath took off whimpering and shaking his head.

"Where was that app earlier?" Eva handed him a couple of wet wipes from a packet in her purse.

"On my to do list." He wiped the seat, the steering wheel, and the gear shift.

"Well, I'll add it to mine, along with finding Randy Bell, a music teacher named Miss Carroll from Rockdale's Sunshine Band, and Mason's unknown siblings. But

I'll start on that list tomorrow."

"I think we should add the Reverend Smith to that list too," Adam said.

"Why?"

"In my experiences, zealots with big egos and big mouths cast a large shadow where they hide all kinds of bad things. Are you sure Mason and his father are estranged?"

"Are you suggesting his father is helping Mason?"

"Maybe. That poster in the basement with an anointed Smith preaching to a crowd of bowing children speaks volumes." Adam explained what he'd learned about men like Jim Jones, David Koresh, and even Warren Jeffs. Oppressive control, especially of the children, is what allowed the monsters to rule. "What would the Reverend Smith do to a child who didn't repent? Would he assure they perished in Hell? Is Mason a killing machine for the Reverend?"

Eva frowned. "An interesting question. If the girls killed were prostitutes on the streets then I could entertain that theory. But they're not. Mason is destroying innocence. Mason's father may be why Mason is killing, but he's not assisting in the kills. Besides, the Reverend is too skinny and wrinkled to be—"

Adam shook his head at Eva's unfinished sentence, puzzled by it. "Since when did being skinny and wrinkled keep a man from being a killer?"

Eva huffed with exasperation. "Don't you have a plane to catch, Frasier?"

Adam noted the time. He had a little over two hours before his 9:30 check in. Depending on traffic, he doubted he'd make it on time. Surprising, he was more put off at the idea of making his flight and leaving Eva to her own devices than missing his flight. Between his mother's desperation, his father's revelation on the Hayden murders, and Eva's investigation into Smith, Adam's life had turned upside down and his guts were inside out. "Yeah, I do. And you're likely right about Mason and his father. I haven't even met the Reverend but everything I've learned about him is so gratingly wrong and obnoxious, that I'm looking for him to be guilty of something."

"I can relate to that. I hadn't seen the child aspect to the poster. His oppressive control over women is what jerked my chains. But you're right. We should put the Reverend on the list of people to interview. I already know he won't talk to me, but he'd be compelled to at least meet with the FBI, right?"

"Right." Eva had come a long way from telling him to crawl back into his bottle and disappear. He sent her a comically smug look, cocking his chin in the air. "I have my uses."

She rolled her eyes. "We'll see, Frasier. We'll see."

He grinned. His life might be racing toward a train wreck, but somehow he was enjoying the ride and it all seemed to be wrapped up in a pair of misty eyes with soft curves and a hard ass attitude.

8:00 P.M.

EVA DIRECTED ADAM TO the St. Claire estate with mixed emotions. Neither Iris nor Devin had called, which meant they were avoiding her and her displeasure at being foisted off on Adam. He'd either grown on her or she'd become inured to his presence, because her irritation had...dissipated?

Surely not. *Diminished* was better.

The afternoon and evening with him had gone smoother than she'd thought possible and in truth, she'd made more progress with him along than she would have alone. She'd been safer, too.

Surprisingly, she wasn't chomping at the bit to ditch him as she had been at first. Not because of his appeal, of course. It was because he'd proven himself useful. Her cold case investigation had taken a bad turn into the hot zone of an active investigation, which meant she needed to think twice before making a move or turning down help—even if it came from a FBI agent.

Logically, she knew she had to go home, regroup, and refuel before continuing her hunt for Smith and his mysterious partner. On an emotional level, she wondered how many Sally's or Kaylee's were going to fall prey to Smith and his partner's knife before they were stopped.

Depending on what she dug up on the internet tonight, using the leads Mrs. Smith provided, she'd leave early in the morning to continue the hunt for Smith.

She'd have Paddy or Zeb from her security team, escort her. Facing the wide barrel of Smith's pistol had shaken her as much as nearly going over the cliff this morning when the tire had blown. She wondered if the double-barreled weapon was unusual enough to be traced. "Did you catch sight of Smith's weapon before he ran?"

Adam changed lanes to head up Hwy 400. "No. Why?"

"Hopefully there will be surveillance video, but his pistol had a wider barrel than what I'd call normal. He decimated that window in one shot."

"Wider and bigger? Smith and Wesson makes a Magnum 500. Biggest pistol you're likely to ever see. Kicks like a rodeo bull, though."

Eva shook her head. She'd seen the monster weapon in action and it wasn't what Smith had. "Everything else appeared normal sized, but it had two barrels." *Was she saying too much? Would Adam question how she could see that detail in a split second from across the street? And she'd yet to figure out how to bring Mr. Sick Clown into the investigation.* "Maybe my eyesight was off. My migraine was in full force."

"There are double-barreled pistols. Bad ass. Shoots two bullets at a time. I'll touch base with Warren to see what he can discover from ballistics and surveillance. If you're thinking to ID Smith's accomplice through a weapon, even an unusual one, you're heading down a long road. It'd be easier to find a needle in a haystack."

"Maybe." Eva directed Adam to her driveway. He made the turn leading to the security gate and slowed the car to a crawl. While there was nothing much to say, other than goodbye, her stomach still tensed, like that moment at the end of a date when awkwardness and anxiety rear their ugly heads.

"This has been an interesting day," he said. "You know, you're damn good at facts and putting them together."

She studied him a moment, reluctantly connecting to his "wanting a few more minutes before saying goodbye" vibe. "Careful, Frasier. That sounded like a compliment. It's what I do. I delve deep into the details of a crime, the killer, and tell the victim's story."

"You do more than that, but I'll let it go for now." He reached the security gate and Hank, one of the security team, directed a bright light into the car. Blinking, Eva waved at him, holding up four fingers with her thumb across her palm. It was their predetermined signal that all was fine. A normal wave meant trouble. Hank opened the electronic iron-gate.

Adam drove through. "Good set up," he said. "The perimeter monitored, too?"

"Twenty-four seven."

"Still, no system is perfect. You really need to be extra careful, especially when you're out. Smith could have killed any one of us or all of us when we walked from Starbuck's to Jillian's office earlier. He had to have been watching. I think he missed the shot at you on purpose, so I and the cops would chase him down, leaving you and Jillian—"

"Ripe for Smith's partner to pluck." Eva sucked in air. *She'd even criticized Adam for not going after Smith.*

Adam parked in front of the house. "Nice place. It would be a shame to give it up for a coffin or worse. Smith is after you. He wants to do more than put a bullet in your head and that's scarier than hell. What did you say to him yesterday?"

"Ever see the old movie *I Saw What You Did*?"

"Yeah. And?"

"I basically said that to Smith. Told him there was a special place in hell where he'd burn and suffer exactly what he did to Kaylee. I told him I'd make sure he got there."

"*Damn*, you don't pull any punches. As unhinged as Smith is, you might as well have painted a target on your back and stood naked in an empty field." He set his hand on hers where she had it resting in her lap. Her pulse kicked and her mouth went dry. "Promise me, you'll be careful."

Eva sat stunned. Her gaze centered on his intense expression and the perfect shape of his mouth, almost expecting more from the moment.

Shaking her head, she slipped her hand from Adam's and opened her car door. "I'll be careful, Frasier. Go catch your plane. Don't forget to dig into Smith's adoption and see if the surveillance video can ID his gun. Let me know if you have any luck on Facetime with the Reverend Smith."

"I'll be in touch. And when this is all over we'll talk about *Hayden's Hell*."

Eva shut the door and dashed up the double staircase, wondering at what point in the past forty-eight hours she'd lost her mind. She couldn't blame anyone but herself for Smith's attack, but this situation with Adam was Devin and Iris's fault and they were going to hear a thing or two right now.

Out of the corner of her eye, she caught the shadow of a man wearing a familiar hat and the tangy scent of pipe tobacco tickled her nose. *Paddy*. The man was waiting up like a father worried over a daughter's first date. Eva waved at him before she entered the house geared for battle.

Lannie met her in the foyer with tears shimmering in her dark eyes and punctured all the hot air out of Eva's outrage. "Thank God you're safe. Paddy told me about the flat tire thing. Then Iris and Paddy up and left you with a stranger? I gave them a piece of my mind and deprived them of my pecan pie. Both swore the FBI agent was Superman incarnate and you were perfectly safe."

Eva crossed the marble and hugged their housekeeper. "Frasier's not quite Superman, but he did manage to hold his own."

Lannie sighed. "Coming from you, that's a five-star compliment. You should have brought him in with you. Like I said, I've pecan pie and there's chicken pot pie in the oven, too. Are you hungry?"

More calories after McDonalds? Eva didn't have the heart to tell Lannie no. "Sure. A little bit would be great."

Lannie smiled. "Warm food and a hot bath can work wonders."

After eating and reassuring Lannie that she was well, Eva went looking for her siblings. She rushed through the pristine white hallways, ignoring the many pictures and portraits of St. Claires at numerous family events—weddings, baptisms, birthdays, and Christmas gatherings. To look at them, one would never know the cursed darkness hidden within their forced smiles—but she did, which is why she tried to pretend the pictures weren't there.

The one picture she couldn't help but glance at, hung at the top of the stairs. It was of her parents on their wedding day at an Italian castle. They stood on a tiny bridge amid a lush garden with the deep blue waters of Lake Como behind them. The love shining in their gazes out-sparkled the diamond-like crystals covering her mother's wedding dress and held no hint of the tragedy to come.

Love became a bridge too far, was the sad epitaph Eva's Aunt Zena had chosen for her parents' shared mausoleum. Why had her mother made most of their funeral arrangements just before their deaths? It was as if she'd known what was about to happen.

The St. Claire's were masters at hiding and avoiding things. She found Devin on the phone talking to a college buddy he hadn't spoken to in years. Iris had locked herself in her bathroom with the music blaring.

Eva wanted to shoot down their delaying tactics, but decided to take Lannie's advice and get a hot bath first.

Afterward, she tackled the internet, wanting to settle some of the questions in her head after speaking to Mason Smith's mother. Remembering the pen Mrs. Smith had given her, Eva went searching. She'd stuck it in the back pocket of her jeans when Adam had tugged on her arm to go. She had to admit the Reverend's booming voice still chilled her blood.

She found the pen. It was black. One side had a phone number. The other side had the words Repent or Perish. She shivered. The prison guard, Tom Hatchett had a pen like this one. Did that mean the man had a connection with the Reverend Smith?

She went to the internet. From a social media perspective, Tom Hachett appeared to be fairly normal. He had a Facebook page with posts touting his sons' sports accomplishments on a team he coached. There were occasional posts about stopping crime and supporting the Second Amendment. She didn't see a wife in his pictures and he'd listed his status as single, so she assumed he was divorced. She'd likely overreacted to the pen connection between Officer Hatchett and the Reverend Smith's Holiness Congregation. A prison was the ideal place for a church to distribute "Repent or Perish" pens. She set the pen aside.

With the image of the sick clown in her mind, she did a Google search for upside down crucifix makeup. The pictures she got seemed to be a contest for the most twisted and profane. She did come up with some bands from Heavy Metal to Doom Metal like Kilslug, and Pentagram, to Thrash and Death Metal like Lamb of God, Legions of the Damned, Marilyn Manson Band, and Testament, even to rap with Amber Rose's tattooed forehead. Fathered by early bands like Black Sabbath, Megadeath, and Iron Maiden, the albums and songs pretty much centered on being the antithesis of everything Biblical.

In Eva's opinion, the extreme bands and their subject matter gave irrefutable fuel to Mrs. Smith's condemnation that any music aside from gospel music would lead a person to the gates of Hell. Music and artists should stand on their own merits rather than basing their entire existence on being anti-God, but then she supposed that *was* their reason for singing.

Moving on, she hunted for any possible leads to Smith prior to his adoption at seven. She found many horrific reports of abuse, even one of a young girl sexually mutilated by her mother. But she didn't find any old articles from the Rockdale County area about a boy and two sisters being orphaned or taken from negligent parents that matched Smith's age range. Based on her experience, the search had been a long shot. After her parents' murder-suicide, news of the St. Claire's orphaning hit every paper across the country.

She did, surprisingly, locate who she hoped was the right Randy Bell in Louisville, Kentucky fairly quickly. He'd partially followed the Reverend Smith's footsteps by pastoring a controversial religious sect, but had traded snakes for guns. He matched her bald profile. It was hard to tell from his picture on the website, but Randy looked as if he shaved his head in a Neo-Nazi-like way.

While the man's militia-oriented doctrine screamed issues at her, it zeroed him out as being Smith's accomplice. She emailed the contact address for the Advent of the Holy Tabernacle asking for a response from Bell. Hopefully she'd get answers to her questions without flying to Kentucky.

Locating Miss Carroll proved harder because the woman seemed to have disappeared. As it turned out, Virginia Carroll married and became Mrs. Virginia Jones. Eva found her by doing a search for the Rockdale County Sunshine Band. In the article mentioning the band, the woman featured had taught music before stopping to raise a family. Then years later, she started a band at her retirement home. Eva reluctantly sent Adam an email update on her progress with a reminder to access Smith's adoption records as soon as he could. She really wanted to locate Smith's siblings. Armed with a plan to see the band teacher tomorrow, Eva left to battle her siblings before going to bed.

Within the rambling Victorian house, they each had their own areas upstairs apart from the common rooms such as the kitchen and the entertainment room. And then there was the room that they rarely ever went to—their parents' bedroom, where nearly twenty years ago her father killed her mother.

10:30 P.M.

THIS TIME DEVIN HAD the music blaring. Eva found him in the exercise room on the treadmill, running from demons he could never escape. He'd had a vision before their parents' tragedy, but hadn't understood what it meant. What eight-year-old would? He'd kept silent about it at the time then blamed himself afterwards. Eva thought he needed to let the whole damn thing go. She doubted anything Devin could have said would have stopped their father. The police investigation had concluded her father thought her mother had been unfaithful. Eva thought her parents were in love, but what did a nine-year-old kid know? The reports Eva later read gave no evidence to substantiate her father had acted in a jealous rage and no man had been named as her mother's lover. That her mother had made funeral arrangements only added to the confusion. While the false allegations angered Eva, she'd let the case go rather than delve into the painful ugliness all over again. Grace DuMond continued to be a thorn in Eva's side. The reporter never failed to resurrect her parents' tragedy.

Shaking off her thoughts, Eva killed the music and moved to stand in front of the machine where Devin could see her. "Tell me what your premonition is. Why is Adam essential?"

"You don't want to know," Devin said, a little breathless from his breakneck pace.

"Yeah, I do. Going into this blind isn't an option. What have you seen?"

He slowed to a stop and shook his head as if Armageddon was at the gates. "I told you yesterday that the price of justice would be high when you said you had to write Kaylee's story. In my vision, there is a horrific storm. Through the lightning and the rain, a dove and a hawk race neck and neck, fleeing from a flying, fire-breathing, two-headed serpent. Lightning strikes close. The dove falters and the two-headed serpent attacks. The hawk rushes in saving the dove, but is ripped open by the fangs of one of the serpent's head just as lightning strikes the other serpent's head. The serpent dies from the blow, but too late to save the hawk. My vision fades with the dove weeping next to a bloody, motionless hawk."

Eva narrowed her gaze at Devin. "Are you saying Adam dies saving me?"

"I'm just telling you what I saw. You're the dove. He's the hawk."

"Then he needs to stay in D.C. I can't believe you pulled him into this."

"Hey, I have my priorities. You come first."

Eva threw her hands up in exasperation. "At his expense? Absolutely not."

"I didn't drag him into it. He came looking for you. Now the wheels are already set in motion."

"That doesn't mean we have to sit back and wait for the train wreck."

"Are you going to drop Kaylee's book and forget Smith's accomplice?"

"No."

"Then it is inevitable." Devin cranked up the treadmill and ran harder.

"Forewarned is forearmed." Eva muttered and went looking for Iris. Devin's premonitions were allegorical images of the future, which made them difficult to interpret. Just because the dove had wept didn't necessarily mean the hawk had bit the dust. Adam Frasier would not die in her stead or on her watch. She refused to consider it. She already had enough burdens to bear.

On her way to Iris's art studio in the turret, Eva heard the tea-kettle whistle and made a beeline for the kitchen.

"What do you want? Earl Grey or Bavarian Wild Berry?" Iris called out even before Eva reached the kitchen. "The shouting in your head is giving me a headache. Why are you so upset about a dove and a hawk?"

Eva drew a deep breath, entered the kitchen, and tried to calm her thoughts. "I'll take Earl Grey. It's Devin. In his vision, the hawk supposedly dies saving the dove from the serpent. Adam's the hawk."

"What?" Iris snapped her head around, eyes wide with shock. Distracted, she poured hot water all over the counter rather than the tea cup.

Eva rushed forward. "Careful! Don't burn yourself!" She eased the tea kettle from Iris's hand, but managed to knock the teacup off the counter when she set the kettle on the stove. "Lannie's going to fuss," Eva said as she popped two dishtowels over the puddle of water and threw away the broken cup.

Iris gave a half laugh. "She's been fussing at me and Paddy all day about leaving you with Adam. And to think, I pushed him closer to his fate." She caught Eva's hand. "We can't let that happen, Eva. We can't let Adam die."

Eva squeezed Iris's hand before letting go. "We won't. He's gone back to D.C. He's out of the picture. I'll put more water on for tea."

"I knew I should have read his mind."

"Adam's?" Eva set the kettle on the stove before turning to Iris.

"No. Devin's. When Paddy brought me home, Devin gave me the third degree then avoided me the rest of the day."

"Speaking of which, what happened at Dimensions? Was it the same as what happened before when that killer's thoughts flooded your mind? Were you unable to stop the connection?"

"Heaven's no. No tsunami wave. I heard the threat against you and went after it. But I couldn't identify who it was from his thoughts. I do know he wants to eliminate you."

"Hell, Iris. You mean you chose to lose it while Adam was with you?"

"I wasn't about to ignore a threat against you."

"I don't know what upsets me more. You foisting me on him for the day, or you risking exposure of our psychic junk to an FBI agent."

"You'd have done the same if someone was after me. The only harm done is he thinks I have spells of some kind."

"Don't underestimate him. He's sharp and looking for answers for more than just Kaylee's case and finding Mason."

"To what then?"

Eva explained what happened to Adam's sister and how responsible he felt. "It marked him. He can't get truth and justice for his sister, but he can exact them from the world around him every chance he gets."

"No wonder he was drawn to my swing set paintings. Poor man. He's like us, trapped by tragedy."

Eva shook her head. "Empathize with his pain, but don't let your guard down. And no more psychic surfing when he's around. What was the specific threat against me?"

"'St. Claire knows. Must find out how. Must kill her before she talks.' This guy isn't like others I've tapped into. Words that come to mind are cold, calculating, with a chilling lack of emotion. Pure evil."

Eva frowned. "Evil describes Smith but the rest doesn't. Maybe it was Smith's accomplice. They set Angel Banning's house on fire just up the street from Dimensions this afternoon, which is why you tapped into them. I shouldn't have lost my cool with Smith yesterday. He knows I know what he and his partner did to Kaylee and wants to shut me up before I can tell all."

Iris drew a shaky breath. "I don't like this. I really have a bad feeling about the whole situation."

"It's because this is just different. We've always dealt with cold cases. Smith's escape and accomplice has changed that."

"Different? That's an understatement. You're the target of two killers and Devin gave Adam a death sentence. I'm not leaving your side until this is over. If Smith or his partner come close, I'll know it."

Eva started to argue with Iris but then the tea kettle whistled. She decided to relax for now and battle it out with Iris in the morning. While Smith's bullet had shaken her today, she didn't want her sister connecting with the minds of killers any more than necessary, and she didn't want her in harm's way either.

DAY 3
MONDAY, MAY 12TH

5:30 A.M.

BLEARY EYED AND DRIVING a rental sedan from the airport, Adam parked at the entrance to Eva St. Claire's driveway, off the road and hopefully out of view of the sweeping security camera mounted on a high pole at the guard house. He'd seen some kick-ass set ups before and Eva's ranked. Probably cost as much per month to keep operational as he made in two.

He'd received her email update. If he didn't miss his guess, she'd leave as early as possible to speak to Smith's band teacher. He considered presenting himself at the gate then ditched the idea. Not only was it early, but giving Eva the opportunity to reject or avoid him didn't seem prudent.

It had been one hell of a night. His mad dash to collect his father, his luggage and make his flight last night had gone smoothly, despite his father's ribbing about Adam's speeding. Once Adam reached the airport, his gut kicked in and wouldn't leave him alone. The farther he flew from Atlanta, the greater his conviction that he should have stayed became. He hit D.C. and caught the next flight back.

Maybe his mother's psych doctors needed to examine him.

It wasn't logical. It wasn't practical. It made zero sense. Eva had all the resources money could buy, but he couldn't walk away from her and the situation she was in. His belief that she was a key factor in apprehending Smith ASAP was only an excuse. There was just something about her and the threat facing her that had his gut wrapped in knots around her finger.

Three hours from now, he'd call Quantico and explain the unexplainable. He'd have someone dig into Smith's adoption records, locate his siblings, and check out Randy Bell's Kentucky militia. In the meantime, he'd take a much needed snooze as he waited for Eva to start her day.

"EVA! DEVIN! WAKE UP! He's here!"

Barely asleep, Eva rolled out of bed and ran into the hallway. Iris flew her way, eyes wide with fear. Wearing a bright pink *Hello Kitty* nightshirt, she had her cell phone to her ear. "Have Zeb search the grounds, Paddy. Somehow he's giving Eva a taste of Hell."

Iris hung up the phone as Devin stumbled from his room, barely having jerked on sweat pants. "What did you hear?" he demanded.

"A lot of laughter and 'Let's give this writer bitch a taste of Hell with her coffee.'"

Eva winced. "Now *that* sounds like Smith. What can they do? The security team is on high alert. The perimeter alarms will sound if there's any breach."

Devin scrubbed his palms over his face, clearly trying to wake up. He'd likely taken a sleeping pill. "No place is one hundred percent secure. If there's a will, there's a way."

"Well, he definitely found a way," Iris replied. "Now we have to find it before it finds us."

Eva pressed her fingers to her temple. "I told Smith I'd make sure he got to Hell and burned. After the inferno at Angel Banning's yesterday, odds are it'll be fire."

Devin grabbed the fire extinguisher from the wall mount in the hall. "You two go downstairs. I'll search up here. Call Paddy and security and let them know."

A loud whooshing sound came from the direction of their parent's' bedroom at the opposite end of the hall.

"What the hell?" Devin ran toward the noise. "Both of you get downstairs, now!"

Eva clamped her mouth shut. No way she'd ever leave anyone to handle trouble alone, much less someone with diminished sight. Flipping on the lights, she followed Devin. Iris was on her heels.

"I'm calling 911," Iris cried, jabbing at her phone.

A vapor of smoke oozed from beneath the bedroom double doors. Devin placed his hand against the wood panel, checking for heat. Eva did the same to the other door, her stomach clenching with dread. She almost hoped it was too hot to open.

Entering her parents' bedroom was like running a psychic gauntlet of failure and shame. Not because a vision of her father killing her mother haunted her, but because it remained the one murder she couldn't see, no matter how many times she tried.

Face grim, Devin eased open the double doors to the bedroom. Smoke billowed out. He went in with the fire extinguisher blasting. Coughing, Eva turned on the lights to see past the smoke. Part of the ceiling was on fire and burning debris dropping down had ignited the bed. Her silk T-shirt and shorts absorbed the heat, irritating her skin as much as the smoke stung her eyes. Devin put out the bed fire in a flash and started on the ceiling.

The fire faded and Eva saw the bedroom as she had that day after school when she and Devin had run up the stairs all excited about a fall festival at their school that night. The first thing she noticed when opening the door were tiny, bloody footprints on the white carpet. "Iri," she cried, fearing her sister hurt.

Devin pushed past her and stood, staring at the pitter-pat of blood.

A whimper drew her attention to the bed where Iris, covered in blood, crawled from beneath. Then she saw her parents on the bed. The knife embedded in her mother's chest. Her father's head, bloody and gaping. Devin screamed, over and over. She grabbed Iris and pulled Devin from the room.

Iris's yelling jerked Eva from the past. "Fire department and paramedics are on their way. I'm reading Paddy's thoughts. He's coming this way panicked for us. He's also dismissing his chest pain as heartburn from Lannie's cooking, but I think it's worse."

Eva grabbed Devin's arm as she had all those years ago and pulled him toward the door. Though the room had been redone afterward—new everything from furniture to carpet to paint—no one had slept there since that day. Seeing the room burn now left her feeling it should have burned twenty years ago.

She snapped her focus to Devin as he tried to pull away from her. "There's no way to know how much of the house above us is on fire. It's not worth our lives. We need to get out."

"I can handle this," he yelled, making her heart ache for him and the disability he fought with every breath.

She dug her nails into his arm, ready to drag him out. "The fire department is on the way and Iris says Paddy is having chest pain."

Devin glared at the sputtering ceiling and cursed as he lowered the fire extinguisher then turned to the door. "Where's Paddy?"

"Coming," Iris called as she ran down the hall toward the stairs.

Eva hurried after her, dragging Devin along. Reaching the railing, she saw Paddy, pale and short of breath, halfway up the curved stairway. Then she gasped. Iris was on the stairway straining to lift their parents' large wedding portrait from the wall.

"The roof is on fire in several places!" Paddy cried. "Don't worry about pictures. Just get out."

"I'm not leaving them to burn," Iris said firmly and Eva's heart squeezed again. The look in her sister's eyes wasn't much different from her confused, hurt, and worried gaze when Eva had found Iris under their parent's bed.

Devin cursed and tossed aside the fire extinguisher to help Iris with the picture.

"We're coming," Eva assured Paddy and hurried down to him. He didn't look well at all. "Where's your pain?"

"I'll be fine once you three are safe. Lannie's in the back by the pool."

Smoke from the bedroom finally reached the fire alarm in the hall upstairs and the siren blared in ear-splitting blasts. Eva cursed that safety systems weren't programmed to detect fires originating on the roof. How had Mason done it?

All of them exited through the back doors to the pool area. Lannie, hair spiked wildly and tears streaming, grabbed each of them in a bear hug. "There's a firing squad for the bastard who did this. Even if lightning had struck in a freak storm, it wouldn't set a fire in four different places."

The sirens of the fire truck and ambulance blared louder and louder, bringing back memories of another time she'd waited for help. Back then, she'd wrapped Iris in a blanket, and carrying her sister, had pulled a shell-shocked Devin down the stairs to wait.

Zeb and Carson from security ran up. "Fire trucks are here. We've had no breach of the perimeter's security and we've searched the estate. There is no trace of anyone on the property."

Yet Mason had penetrated their security. Looking back at the roof line, Eva saw patches of fire from almost every direction. Dawn had hit the horizon, shedding light into the darkness. The area over her parents' bedroom was the worst. Three other places, at opposite corners of the house, appeared to be new, smaller fires. How had Smith done it? Shooting burning arrows from outside the large perimeter would be impossible. If Smith had fired some sort of incendiary rocket, surely someone would have heard or seen that.

Paddy continued to breathe heavy and Eva caught his arm, directing him to a chair. She waved at Lannie. Being an ex-army nurse, Lannie knew how to handle everything. "He's having chest pains, Lannie."

"Did you take your medicine, you stubborn old coot?"

"What medicine?" Eva demanded, glaring at Paddy.

"It's nothing, but gas from your cooking," Paddy told Lannie.

Lannie cursed like a sailor and started patting down Paddy's pockets. "Doctor gave him nitro pills. He's been having a twinge or two every now and then."

Eva found a seat before her knees gave out. Tears of confusion and hurt burned her eyes. "And you didn't *tell* us?"

Iris and Devin placed their parents' photo safely on the outdoor dining table and moved to Paddy's side, glaring and muttering their own upset.

Paddy scowled at them all. "The doctor is wrong."

Eva sucked in air about to argue, but swallowed her response when Iris cried out in horror. "Look! The stable roof is on fire, too!"

Iris ran toward the stables. Zeb followed, shouting into the radio to the others on the team.

Devin made a quick turn, clearly going after Iris, but didn't see the lion-footed planter on his left. He fell over it, landing hard onto the stone pavement. EMT's came around the corner of the house and a fire truck rushed down the road towards the stables.

Devin quickly rose to his feet. He didn't say anything. He just stood very still, breathing harshly. Eva knew her bother waged a hard battle with a knife-sharp sense of failure because of his growing blindness.

Blinking back tears again, she looked at the men running to the rescue and thought maybe this whole event had to be a nightmare, because she surely wasn't seeing right. What the *hell* was Adam doing here?

WITH THE WINDOWS DOWN, the early morning birds and cool air had lulled Adam to a restless sleep...*A woman with misty eyes and ebony hair stood tied to a cross. Her diaphanous dress billowed in the moonlight. Surrounding her, enraged men and women brandishing pitchforks and torches as they screamed, "Burn witch, burn."*

The crowd lit the woman afire. She arched and twisted, trying to escape the rising flames. Adam rushed to save her, but the harder he ran, the more distant she became.

Adam jerked upright from his sleep and caught sight of a fire truck and ambulance whizzing by him, their sirens blaring.

What the hell? He threw off the windbreaker blanketing him, hit his not-so-funny bone on the steering wheel in his hurry to crank the engine, and cursed a blue streak at his negligence. Something big had happened while he'd slept. He floored the gas pedal and followed the emergency vehicles through the compound's iron gate.

At the first curve of the drive, just before the house came into view, Adam saw in the review mirror a guard running behind him with his AR15 pointed. Adam slammed on his brakes and stuck his head out of the window.

The wide-eyed guard was the same one from last night. Breathing heavy, he stopped about ten feet from the car.

Adam raised his hands. "I'm FBI. I brought Eva home last night. What's going on?"

"Roof fire."

"How?"

The guard shook his head.

"I'm going in." Adam didn't have to say 'over the guard's dead body,' the man read his intent loud and clear. He lowered the AR 15.

Adam raced after the ambulance and fire trucks. He parked in the grass, far out of the way. When he opened the car door, he froze, blinking in disbelief. Positioned over the fire trucks, barely silhouetted in the dawn sky by flashing lights, hovered a black quadcopter drone with something attached beneath it.

Son-of-a-bitch! Some sick bastard had to be watching or filming Eva's house burn. Adam grabbed his windbreaker and hurried toward the fire trucks. Staying out of possible camera range of the drone, he caught the attention of a fireman at the back of a truck, pulling out axes and other equipment. Adam pointed at the drone and then mimed capturing it with his windbreaker.

The fireman caught on fast. He pulled out a long pole and a heavy, fireproof jacket. Keeping far to the perimeter, the fireman circled behind the drone to Adam. Using the pole, they lifted the heavy jacket and netted the drone. The quadcopter came down fast. Adam pounced on it, feeling its whirring blades crack beneath the pressure. Once he'd disabled the UAV and uncovered it, the noxious fumes of gasoline immediately burned his nose and eyes.

A thick gel oozed from the split package attached to the bottom of the drone. Adam reared back as his brain made the connection seconds before the quadcopter ignited. He threw the fire jacket over the intense flames and turned to the firefighter. It didn't take much to melt Styrofoam in gasoline. The gel that formed, burned super-hot and stuck to its target or victim like glue.

"Napalm! The son-of-a-bitch. Drones with payloads of homemade napalm! Warn everyone. And watch out, this could be a first-responders' trap." Adam's gut told him Smith and his unknown partner had to be behind this attack. As badly as the Banning's mansion burned yesterday, odds were, Napalm had been used there, too.

Eyes wide with shock, the fireman ran back to the truck, yelling at his team who already had water pumping onto the roof of the house and the front doors broken open.

Adam dug out his phone and called Brad Warren, fully confident his friend could galvanize whatever reinforcements were needed. Adam explained in crisp sentences as he took off for the back of the house since he didn't see Eva and her family out front.

"It's only a matter of time until UAV's become our worst nightmare," Brad said, then advised Adam to be careful. Adam hung up. Every technological advance made opened another gaping hole in humanity's safety net. But then, safety was an illusion that could disappear in an instant anyway.

Two EMTs hurried ahead of him on the path, carrying their equipment. Turning the corner, Adam saw Devin rising to his feet at the edge of a stone patio. The EMT's stopped at Devin, but he waved them on. "Paddy's having a heart attack," he told the men.

A dozen feet or so behind Devin, at the poolside, stood Eva. Next to her, Paddy sat on a lounge chair with an older woman who had her fingers pressed to his neck. "I gave him nitro," she said to the approaching EMTs.

A man wearing a security guard uniform, paced as he spoke low into a Bluetooth. He stopped and turned to Eva. "Drones. Drones are setting fire to the roofs."

Adam hurried toward them and saw another quadcopter swoop down. The world slowed as if a twisted hand warped time. His heart pounded painfully. The harder he ran, the further away everyone became. Just like in his dream.

He screamed and pointed at the drone.

Eva looked up. The quadcopter hovered over her for a moment more then quickly darted toward Devin, coming at him from the side. He didn't move. He couldn't see the threat.

Eva ran forward, crying in fear. "Watch out, Dev!"

"Everybody get down!" The guard went to one knee and aimed his 9 mm at the drone.

"Noooo!" Adam yelled. "Don't shoot!"

He warned too late. The guard fired and hit the drone. It exploded. Fiery debris rained like lava on Devin's bare skin.

Devin screamed as his shoulder and back ignited. Adam, already at a full run, went low. He dove into the raining fire, and lifted Devin onto his shoulder. Adam's back arched with pain as droplets of fiery gel burned through his shirt. He yelled at the pain, straining to run faster, managing to plow them both into the pool less than ten feet away. Water swallowed him, instantly cool and suffocating.

Adam held onto a writhing Devin as he powered to the surface, worried Devin would inhale water in his pain and shock. The moment air hit Adam's face, he felt Devin's weight easing. An EMT had jumped into the water to help. The other one waited on the side of the pool with his emergency case open.

Devin moaned as the EMT lifted him. Devin wrapped his fist around Adam's wrist and jerked him closer, his face a grimace of deep pain. "Save Eva," he whispered. "Promise me."

"I promise," Adam whispered back, the surreal feeling that Devin didn't mean this moment in time stuck in Adam's gut. He swung around to see Eva in the pool, too. She stood, shivering, staring at the EMTs helping her brother.

Tears streamed down her deathly pale face, clumping her thick lashes into dark circles. Adam went to her and slid an arm across her shoulders, feeling the wet silk of her pajamas and the vulnerable shake of her shoulders. His own pain faded and his chest squeezed tight with emotion and concern. The guard who'd shot the drone, sat with his head in his hands, groaning.

The first responders placed Devin face down on a lounge chair, hooked him to a vital sign monitor, started an IV, and ripped open Water-jel dressings, covering—Adam noted with relief—a relatively small area of Devin's shoulder and back.

"Is he going to be okay?" Eva asked.

"Right as rain on a dove," Devin said from the lounge chair. The strain in his voice told a different story.

Eva gasped as if hurt.

Adam shook his head at the odd reply and tightened his arm around her shoulders. "He's in pain, but I don't' think the burn will be critical," he said softly.

What had Devin meant with the dove line and why had his words upset Eva? More importantly, were there anymore drones out there? Though no flames and very little smoke rose from the roof of the house, it would be impossible to hear the whirring hum of a drone above the noise of the firefighters.

Smith had to be within half a mile of Eva's home and up high enough to operate the UAV's in the dark. Even flying with a camera on board, some visual was needed to be effective. He searched the sky, looking for the tiny telltale flashing light of a drone in the emerging dawn and any high ground where Smith might be lurking. Was Smith up there gloating? Had they been watching Eva's fear as the drone flew at Devin?

Eva eased closer to his side. Feeling her scrutiny, he looked down at her, sliding his gaze over her disheveled appearance, taking in the wild wave of her dark hair, and the enticing way wet silk clung to her breasts. For the briefest of moments, heat arced between them then she shut it down with a frown and smacked him on the chest with her palm. "Damn it, Frasier. What are you doing here? You're supposed to be in D.C.! Not hovering like a mother hen."

He scowled and muttered. "Thank you, Adam, for saving my brother from an even worse injury. You're welcome, Eva." He scooped her up into his arms, getting a whiff of Ivory soap and lavender before he deposited her on the edge of the pool. Tempted to walk away, he forced himself to join her. He had thicker skin than that. Yet her words stung on par with the minor burns to his back.

A mother hen? *Really?* What happened to knight in shining armor analogies? Devin snorted and groaned. "Believe me. I'm grateful, Adam."

EVA'S HEART THUNDERED WITH fear. She stood on shaky knees and urged Adam up as well. If another attack came, she wanted to be mobile. The exploding drones were too close a match to the fiery serpent in Devin's premonition of Adam's death. And the idiot was here! Devin's dove comment didn't help matters at all.

"He'll need a hospital, but the burns could have been much worse," one EMT said.

Even though he'd been hurt, Eva wanted to smack Devin, too. How could he be so accepting of Adam's possible death? And how could she explain her fear to anyone?

She scanned the horizon, feeling vulnerable out in the open. Until the firemen cleared the house, the only nearby cover was the gazebo at the opposite end of the pool. But it didn't offer much more shelter and it would hinder their view. She wanted to see what came at her.

"James, take the monitor and check the other gentleman," one EMT said to the other.

"I'm fine. Pain's all gone," Paddy insisted. The EMT went to Paddy, urged him to lie down and hooked him to the monitor.

"He's had two nitro," Lannie said.

"Sinusbrady of 40 with a BP of 160 over 94. You're coming with us as well, sir," the EMT said as he pulled out an IV set up.

Eva couldn't believe how things were playing out. Smith had penetrated her security defenses in the blink of an eye with piss-ant drones. He'd set fire to her home, injured Devin, and triggered Paddy's previously unknown heart problem. And Adam had "Sir Galahaded" himself into harm's way.

He suddenly grabbed her arm. "Where's Iris?"

Eva pointed down the drive to the stables. "She went to the horses when she saw smoke coming from the roof."

Adam tightened his grip, his gaze urgent. "We don't know how the drones are triggered to ignite. I suspect they're camera equipped and maybe set off by remote control. What if Smith had intended to seriously harm Devin with the drone? I may have been wrong. By shooting the drone before it hit Devin, the guard could have saved your brother from something worse?"

"Did you hear, Carson?"

"I heard," the guard said grimly, not sounding relieved.

"Smith might try and hurt Iris, too," Adam said. He pointed at a distant knoll rising just about the tree line to the left of the estate. "That seems a likely place for him to be."

"That's Shirley's place," Lannie said.

"Who?" Adam asked.

"One of the women who helps Lannie clean several times a week," Eva said, recalling the quiet, forty-something petite blonde who always had a cheerful smile. Eva hadn't known Shirley lived on the knoll—the highest point in the area besides the St. Claire home. In fact, since she only saw Shirley in passing every now and then, she didn't know anything more about her even though she'd worked at the St. Claire house for several years.

Writing and her cursed "gift" kept Eva isolated, but they were no excuse for being so disengaged from the lives of those outside her family circle.

Eva knew in her gut that Adam was right. Smith would target anyone around her. She fought the urge to run for Iris, already seeing Adam chase after her and fiery drones attack them both. If she did that, she'd play right into Devin's vision. Instead, she sent her sister a strong mental warning then turned to the security guard. "Carson, call—"

"I'm on it." The man had already gained his feet and called the stables. After a couple of long minutes, he turned back. "Iris's inside with the horses. The fire is out with minimal damage to the roof. Zeb and Hank headed out the back entrance to check on Shirley. She didn't answer her phone," he said grimly.

Eva's spine shivered with dread.

COFFEE IN HAND, EVA stood in the checkout line at Northside Hospital's snack bar, staring at the chocolate covered donuts. Dressed in a hoodie—one of Devin's college throwaways—and old jeans she'd dug from the bottom of her closet, they brought her little of the comfort she sought. Though the damage to the Victorian could have been worse, after the fire investigation and inspection were finished repairs would be needed before they could live in the house again.

The firemen had accompanied her, Iris, and Lannie back into the house to change clothes and get some essentials before coming to the hospital. Their parents wedding portrait had gone to Paddy's for safe keeping.

Other than standing outside her bedroom door when she'd changed from her wet pajamas, an alive and well Adam had yet to leave her side, which meant the fire-breathing serpent of Devin's premonitions still loomed ahead.

Worse, Eva's confidence that being forewarned and forearmed could avert disaster had nose-dived. It hadn't meant squat this morning.

Tears burned her eyes and nausea churned at the sight of the donuts. Was it just yesterday morning she'd sat envious as Devin and Iris vied over chocolate iced donuts?

Yeah and so what? She bit her lip and mentally smacked herself for her pity party. She needed to buck-up and focus on the next nightmare waiting for her—Shirley's cottage. She also needed another pair of sunglasses to shield her from the world. She'd been so rattled when she left the house to follow Devin and Paddy to the hospital that she'd left them behind.

Ahead of her in line, Adam pulled out a wet wallet and handed a limp five-dollar bill to the cashier.

"Since Devin and Paddy are stable and settled in their rooms with Iris and Lannie fussing over them, I'm going to Shirley's before my Aunt Zena arrives," she told him. That guards were now posted outside of Devin and Paddy's rooms, she left unsaid.

Adam's exhale rivaled the Big Bad Wolf's. He looked as ragged as she felt—bloodshot eyes, rumpled hair, and grim expression. She was sure the minor burns they'd treated on his back didn't help. The worn jeans and faded shirt he'd grabbed from his suitcase when they'd arrived at the hospital in his rental car, made him too comfortable looking for her own good. The urge to relax into him and his steely strength in the midst of the chaos kept niggling at her. She straightened her shoulders, searching for strength.

"Do you ever give yourself a moment to breathe?" he muttered. "And why must we leave before your aunt arrives?"

"Once you meet Aunt Zena you'll know. She's a hurricane in motion that sucks everyone in."

"There isn't anything to see at Shirley's yet. When I spoke to Warren fifteen minutes ago, they were still processing the crime scene. It will be a while before anyone can—"

"Shirley, Zeb, and Hank were my employees and came into harm's way because of me. I'm going. Period. Even if it's just to stand on the street."

Adam accepted his change and swung around. "How about I go, check out the situation, and report back while you relax here until the investigation finishes?"

"Ms. St. Claire! A moment please!"

Startled, Eva twisted so fast, her capped coffee sloshed, burning her fingers. Standing a mere foot away, dressed like a shadow in black and filming her with Adam, was DuMond's camerawoman.

How much of her conversation with Adam had the woman taped?

Eva winced and frowned at Grace DuMond. The perfectly coiffed blonde wore power red as usual. That it could be a Prada suit didn't escape Eva. The reporter wielded the microphone like a sword as she closed in, joining the intrusive camerawoman. Adam inched in front of Eva, looking as if he'd throw his coffee at the camera.

"You know I don't do interviews, Ms. DuMond. Have a nice day." Eva urged Adam to leave in the opposite direction with a nudge. She really wished for her sunglasses now. She hated being caught vulnerable for the world to see.

True to form, DuMond's voice rose in volume, a tactic meant to intimidate. "Rumor has it that fugitive Mason Smith attacked you and your family this morning. Is it because you're writing about Angel Banning?"

"No comment," Eva said firmly, moving away from the spotlight. The half-dozen people in the snack bar and the nearby hospital employees directed their gazes at the disturbance.

DuMond persisted. "Where are Angel and her family now? What have they said about their house burning yesterday?"

"The lady said no comment," Adam replied forcefully, his green gaze dagger sharp.

"What did you say to Smith during the interview on Saturday that sent him on a murdering rampage?"

Eva flinched and snapped her head around, shocked at DuMond's accusation. How had the reporter learned of her meeting with Smith?

Green gaze shooting fire, Adam pressed his coffee cup into Eva's hand and whipped around. He marched right at the reporter but then went for the camera first. He grabbed the lens and pointed it downward. Eva saw the camerawoman's wide-eyed surprise behind her Elton John-like pink glasses. She shot Adam a bird and turned, cuddling the camera in her arms as if comforting an injured baby.

"How dare you!" DuMond cried, outraged.

"No, how dare you," Adam said quietly as he flipped out his FBI badge in front of DuMond's face. "The lady did not consent to be filmed and by stalking her in the hospital, you're invading her privacy. Shall my boss call yours?"

DuMond read Adam's badge and turned off her microphone. "Let's go, JJ. Need to find out why St. Claire has a FBI watchdog."

"Show's over," Adam told the staring audience then took back his coffee. Eva fell into step with him as they left the snack bar. "You win," he muttered. "We'll both go to Shirley's. With vultures like her around you'll be picked to death in an hour."

"Vultures retreat and hover when attacked. Grace DuMond is like a crocodile. Once she locks on she doesn't let go and you just put yourself in her death grip."

"I can handle it, but I do need to make a call to the office on the way and explain why I'm here and not there."

"I knew you'd miss your flight last night. Don't get me wrong. I appreciate all that you've done this morning, but why didn't you just catch the next flight out?"

"I didn't miss my flight. I landed in D.C. and took the next flight back. Call it gut instinct or whatever, but I'm here until Smith and the UNSUB are stopped and caught."

They stood in an empty hallway outside the snack bar. Eva didn't know how to respond to Adam. He'd flown all the way back here just for her. Knowing what he had done warmed her heart even as fear for his safety waved red flags in her mind.

Her cell vibrated, saving her from having to respond. She answered Iris's call. "Is everything all right?"

"That's my question to you. I felt…something. I don't know how to describe it other than a mix of anger and strong belligerence. No words or thoughts, just a dark cloud of emotion."

Eva lowered her voice. "*From* me or *at* me? I just had another run in with DuMond. While I have you on the phone, Adam and I are going to Shirley's."

"I'm coming with you."

Eva wished like hell she could talk privately a moment. But with Adam in tow, she couldn't just tell Iris out-right why it was more important for her to stay here. She needed Iris's telepathy protecting Devin and Paddy from another attack. She sent Iris a very strong mental plea. *I need you here, Iris. Devin and Paddy are vulnerable and Smith could be anywhere. Tell me you understand.*

"I read you," Iris said through the phone then sighed. "Promise me you'll stay safe."

"I will. Frasier is with me."

"His name is Adam and not saying it won't make him any less appealing. This really sucks. I have a love-hate relationship with Devin's abilities. While part of me is so thankful he sees you'll be all right in this disaster, another part of me is screaming in protest over anything happening to Adam. How does Devin do this?"

"I don't know. I do know that what was to be, won't be. I won't let it happen. I'll call you later." Eva disconnected and found Adam studying her.

"Care to explain?"

She wished she could explain the unexplainable as much as she wished she could just be Eva so Adam could be Adam. Instead she was a St. Claire and that didn't leave room for anything else in life. She turned away from him. "Just sister stuff, Frasier. We've got killers to catch."

9:30 A.M.

DARK CLOUDS OVERCAST THE sky, tinting the world in a sickly green hue that matched Eva's stomach. A safe place. Far away from her. Where Smith couldn't reach. That is where everyone in her life needed to go. Her arrival at Shirley's drove that fact, knife-sharp, into her gut. Adam's keen eye had nailed the spot from where Mason and unknown company had launched the drone attack.

The killer's actions had ripped away home, health, and any scrap of well-being from the St. Claire's and their employees, leaving her neck-deep in badges. Men from practically every one of Georgia's law enforcement departments and related agencies, including Detective Rollins and Detective Curly, prowled over Shirley's place.

Keeping the St. Claires's secrets while navigating this investigation loomed over Eva like a swim through sharks with chum dangling around her neck.

History had proven over and over again that anonymity was a psychic's only protection against exploitation and stake burnings—literally in the past and figuratively now. If what she, Iris, and Devin did became known, it would destroy their lives. Just as it had other St. Claire existences. Only Aunt Zena had managed to turn that truth on its ear with an over-the-top, larger-than-life persona.

Eva sucked in air. Thank God for sunglasses from the hospital gift shop. She doubted she had the strength to hide the horror passing before her eyes. And thank God she'd called Zeb's wife *before* she'd left the hospital, because she wouldn't be able to speak to Aubrey now. Eva either had to leave the vicinity of Zeb and Hank's murder or fully succumb to the vision clawing at her mind. Trying to keep it contained, had created a migraine coming on like a freight train.

Her taste of hell from Mason didn't lie in the damage to her home or in the hospital beds with Devin and Paddy. It started here in Shirley's driveway beside the bullet riddled Escalade Zeb and Hank had driven. She didn't have to wait for ballistics or a crime scene analysis to know what happened.

Mason's twisted laughter rang loud and clear. She dug her teeth into her cheeks until pain and the acrid tang of blood filled her senses. She had to keep a degree of awareness during the vision. Pain would keep her from going too deep.

For the first time, the deaths before her stemmed from a choice she'd made. Devin had warned her, but she'd determinedly marched on. Waving a banner of injustice, completely blind to the consequences her brother had known waited on the horizon.

Nausea churned, knotting her stomach into a ball of angst. She sat down on a log and wrapped her arms tightly around her jean-clad legs, closing herself off to everyone.

She prayed that somewhere in the death and destruction she'd discover the identity of Smith's partner or a clue as to what the evil duo's next move would be.

Fortunately, Adam didn't think it odd for her to sit and stare at the congealed pool of blood where Zeb had hung upside down, paralyzed from a bullet.

Zeb hadn't re-upped with the marines, but had stayed stateside after his son's birth five years ago. To be safer; to be there for his kid. A bone-cracking chill gripped Eva.

I'm sorry, Zeb. I'm so sorry. She fell into his nightmare, seeing what must have played over and over again in his mind as his blood poured to the ground.

"Roll down your window, Hank. I'm going to park near the road and we'll go on foot." Windows now down, Zeb cut the headlights and the engine, letting momentum ease the car into Shirley's driveway. He studied the quiet house about fifty yards ahead. The tiny cottage looked as if it had been built during the depression era—minimal amount of space and no style. Shirley's blue Volkswagen sat parked in the driveway

halfway between them and the house. Nothing about the grey morning appeared out of the ordinary.

"You really think the bastards are here?" Hank whispered, adjusting his grip on his AK.

"Assume the worst then you'll live through the rest," Zeb replied. "Hopefully, Shirley's sleeping soundly and just hasn't heard the phone ring. We'll check the perimeter first. Me left, you right. Then we'll go together toward the clearing in the back. That's likely where they are with the drones. It's the only clear view around of the St. Claire's estate."

Zeb grasped his St. Christopher medal hanging from his neck, kissed it, and shouldered his AK. "Ready?"

Hank nodded.

Keeping an eye on the house, Zeb eased his head out the window and grabbed the car's roof to slip silently to the ground.

The ambush of bullets came from each side, shattering windows, tearing upholstery—and ripping through flesh. Half in and half out of the window, Zeb screamed. He twisted, thrusting the muzzle of his AK toward the attackers hidden in the woods. He squeezed the trigger.

"Dear God, no! I'm hit bad," Hank cried, his anguish pierced Zeb's heart.

Pain exploded across Zeb's chest as bullets slammed into him then a searing fire burned through his neck. His body spasmed and went flaccid. He fell, hanging from the car window. He tried to move, tried to do anything to save himself or fight back, but could do nothing.

His ears roared. His heart thumped painfully, slower and slower as blood poured over his face and dripped to the ground. Silence followed. Nothing came from Hank's direction.

After everything he'd survived, he couldn't believe that it would all end here.

Aubrey! I'm sorry, babe. I love you. God, take care of my Jack.

Laughter rang out. "Whew, that rocked. Freaking A plus movie review."

"Best rush in fucking forever. This one's still alive, but not for long. Should I put him out of his misery?"

Something pressed into the back of Zeb's head. His head fell to the side and the gun barrel slid to his cheek. He saw boots. Black, not shiny. Or were they just wet and muddy? Jeans.

"What? You get soft while I sat in a cell? Let him die slow and let's go play This Little Piggy again. St. Claire will suffer like hell over the video."

"I've got work at eight, remember? Crime never sleeps."

More laughter. *"Funny. What the fuck am I supposed to do all day?"*

"Had you listened to me before, you wouldn't have gotten caught. You should have never left our place and you never, ever hunt without a plan."

"You're always working and leaving me with nothing. Our cabin is boring. I went for a ride and Angel scootered onto the sidewalk just as I passed. It was meant to be. I planned to share her with you when you got back in town."

"I believe you. Do whatever the shit you want today. Watch the movies. Play with the woman. Just stay inside and you damn well better keep her alive until I get back. She's our only leverage with St. Claire."

"What makes you so sure she'll trade herself for the woman?"

"She will. Tonight will be special."

That Shirley lived, sent Eva's heart pounding even as her stomach roiled. *Trade herself tonight? How could she? How could she not? Would Devin's premonition be the endgame, then? Somehow, Adam would either die or be injured trying to save her. She had to figure out who Smith's partner was before tonight.*

"You and your FBI lap dog think you're special, don't you."

Eva blinked at Detective Curly's rude interruption and shivered as she stared at his wet, muddy boots. He stood between her and Zeb's blood. While Zeb had wondered if the boots he saw were black, Eva had no question. Curly's boots were black and shiny. She lifted her gaze. Wearing antagonism like a battle flag, jeans, and a black T-shirt under a blue blazer, Detective Curly glared down at her.

She stood on shaky legs. "Excuse me?"

"No, I damn well won't. Just because you write crime books and have money to grease FBI palms, you think you've got VIP leverage. None of that buys you shit. This isn't the movies but a real fucking crime scene and your asses shouldn't be here."

"Do whatever the shit you want today. Watch the movies. Play with the woman. Just stay inside and you damn well better keep her alive until I get back. She's our only leverage with St. Claire. Tonight will be special."

Same vocab. A Dexter-like detective would make the perfect partner in crime. Eva narrowed her gaze at Curly, looking him dead in the eye. If he wasn't with

Smith then he'd picked the wrong day to come after her. The drones had already blown her fuse and this man had stepped over the line. She kept her voice low and soft, but pushed back hard as hell. "Are you hiding something, detective? It's Psych 101 that whoever attacks without provocation is usually guilty of something, very insecure, or both. Do you suffer from SPS—Small Penis Syndrome? Got kiddie porn on your phone?"

Curly's eyes bulged and his jaw dropped.

"Whatever it is, I'll figure it out," Eva added. "Now get out of my face and put your energy into finding Mason Smith and the son-of-a-bitch who helped him murder my friends."

"Eva?"

Turning toward the familiar voice, she found Sheriff Doug approaching. Behind him, Adam was in heavy conversation with a man unknown to her. She stepped away from Curly, but he grabbed her arm.

Jerking free, she glared at him. His face flushed a purple red and he opened his mouth to speak, but she beat him to it. "You have work to do, detective. Crime never sleeps."

She watched for a spark of reaction to the phrase, but didn't get it.

"Is there a problem, Detective Wright?" Sheriff Doug asked as he joined her, looking sharply at Curly.

"No problem," Curly replied with disgust and walked away.

Sheriff Doug's familiar presence soothed. He'd been one of the first officers to arrive when her world had fallen apart twenty years ago. During the investigation into the storm of her parents' death, he'd been a life raft of calm. Over the years his waist had bulged, his hair had gone from black to salt and pepper, and he now wore a tuft-like toupee that fell short of Mohawk status. His wife of forty years liked the Elvis effect it created with his existing hair and that's all that mattered to him.

He opened his arms, and she entered his embrace, blinking back tears. She almost told him what Smith and his partner planned, but didn't. If Sheriff Doug even remotely thought she'd trade herself for Shirley, he'd lock Eva in a jail cell. "This is all my fault."

"You can't take responsibility for Smith's evil."

"I can when I'm the one who drew his attention my way."

"Anyone exposing evil becomes its target. Do you stop the fight?"

Eva sucked in air and stepped back from his comfort. She didn't deserve it.

Sheriff Doug arched a graying brow, deepening his wrinkles as he glanced about the area. "We'll talk later."

Her phone buzzed. She glanced at the screen and shuddered. Then took off her sunglasses and read the screen again. She'd seen it right the first time. The text came from Shirley Pearl's cell phone. "Oh, God."

"What?"

Eva just held up her phone for him to see, her hand shaking. "You read it."

Sheriff Doug took the phone from Eva's numb fingers. "Hey, Warren. We've got contact. Rollins, we need a GPS on Shirley Pearl's cell ASAP."

Adam hurried over and placed a steadying hand to her back. "What is it?" The man he'd been speaking to moved next to Sheriff Doug. "Eva, this is Major Brad Warren. Brad, Eva St. Claire."

The Major acknowledged with a nod as did she. Then they both directed their gazes at her cell phone.

Sheriff Doug did as she had. He held the phone for them to see Shirley's name on her screen.

"Damn," Detective Rollins came up behind her with a sour Detective Curly in tow.

Sheriff Doug opened the text. It said, "This little piggy…" A video accompanied the text. Doug activated the video. Loud music immediately blared, nauseating similar to the heavy metal music in visions of Kaylee's torture. The image of Smith, holding a hatchet over what had to be Shirley's trapped foot panned into view. Shirley fought helpless against her captors. Her muffled screams ripped Eva to shreds. Mason sang. "This little piggy went to the market." The cleaver sliced down.

Eva turned away and stumbled to the woods, losing the coffee she'd drunk. The sound of Smith singing continued. "This little piggy stayed home…and this little piggy will go wee wee all the way, all the way…we'll be in touch."

"Shit," Adam muttered.

"One toe was found in the kitchen," Detective Rollins said.

Eva's gut wrenched again. She was so mad and so sickened that her vision blurred and a cold sweat covered her from head to toe. What would be next if she didn't trade places with Shirley tonight? The Hokey Pokey? Would she get videos of Shirley being hacked to pieces?"

"I'm getting you out of here. You shouldn't have come," Adam said grimly, shoving a handkerchief into her hand.

She grabbed the soft linen and wiped her face. "Do you think getting that video at the hospital would have made it any better?"

"No. The sick son-of-a-bitch. Even the death penalty doesn't cut it."

She met the rage in Adam's gaze head-on and connected with his desire to obliterate evil with his bare hands. "Yeah, I feel the same way. Makes me wonder where God is right now."

"I always come back to that question when shit like this happens."

Brad Warren joined them, handing Eva her cell phone. "If you two are interested in my two cents on that question, I'll buy you a cup of coffee someday. We've sent the text and video in for analysis and deleted it from Eva's phone. Odds are he's already burned Shirley's cell, but we'll at least get an area from a cell tower ping. They'll set up a trace for incoming texts and calls to your phone. He didn't kill Shirley outright which means he wants something from you, Eva, and he'll use her torture to get it. Be prepared. He will contact you again."

"I doubt anyone can prepare for evil like that." Eva slipped her sunglasses back on, wondering exactly what Warren had to say about one of the world's most inextricable questions. Though not quite Adam's height or build, the man packed an equally determined punch, but differently. Come hell or high water, he too would get the job done, but with cool assurance as opposed to Adam's haunted drive

"You misunderstand me," Warren said. "By prepared, I mean figuring out what he wants from you and how can we use that to save Shirley."

Eva clenched Adam's handkerchief in her fist. She already knew what Smith—or more accurately—what Smith's partner wanted. He wanted to know how she knew the details of Kaylee's torture. Shirley was forever scarred because Eva had said too much. "How do you propose to save Shirley from them then, Major Warren?"

"They want something. They'll act to get it. Once that happens, we'll be ready with a wide tech net and enough man power to back it up." Warren narrowed his eyes. "Do you already have an idea about what he wants?"

Did she look guilty? Eva clenched her teeth, wishing she could help and wondering if she should dare to rely on the authorities. Did she even have a choice about it? Devin had foreseen just her and Adam fighting a two-headed serpent. Would introducing an army of law enforcement stop the prediction of Adam's death, or by involving them, and him, was she playing into fate's hands?

She didn't have to decide any of that until Smith made another move, or if she found him first. She answered Warren's question with a half-truth. "I know he'd rather be chopping *my* toes off."

Adam cursed, turning to Warren. "She's been through enough this morning."

"Just telling her the truth, bro. Let's pray we find Smith soon."

Eva was already praying for that. "If he follows his MO, he'll head north to a rural area with cabins to rent. Easiest routes from here are up Interstate 75 or 400 North."

Warren arched a brow. "Troopers went out in force with that in mind the minute I arrived here after Adam's call this morning. Any other ideas on Smith?"

Eva bit back her "sick clown" partner and heavy metal music clues, not seeing a way to feed them into the investigation yet or that they revealed anything important enough to risk exposure. She glanced at Shirley's cottage. Detective Rollins had returned to the front door with Curly at his side.

"Not yet." She couldn't wait any longer. She had an agenda on hunting Smith last night and needed to get back on track. Stopping Smith was wrapped up in solving the puzzle of who partnered with him in crime. She settled her gaze on Adam and her chest tightened with anxiety. He didn't have to come back from D.C. to help her, but he had and he'd done it on gut feeling alone.

She doubted anything she could do would make him return to D.C., either. That meant to keep him alive, she had to glue him to her side until tonight. Then she had to figure out how to outwit Devin's vision of death. "Ready to tackle Detective Rollins? Surely by now they can let us inside?"

Adam narrowed his gaze. "Are you sure?"

"Yeah, I'm sure." Bolstering herself, she headed for Shirley's front door.

10:30 A.M.

EVA HAD YET TO understand the limitations of her psychic gift. She didn't walk down the street and see every crime ever committed. Most of the time, she saw nothing at all. Only crime that ended in violent death hit her radar screen. And not always then. Her mother's murder and father's suicide being proof of that. Because Shirley was supposedly alive at this point, Eva doubted she'd see what had happened inside, but she'd try.

If she only saw murders from the victim's point of view then she could surmise her mind tapped into the unresolved spirits of people who'd had their lives violently cut short. Like with Zeb's vision where he she saw a replay of his actions and thoughts upon his arrival at Shirley's to the moment of his death. But sometimes in the vision, she was in the killer's point of view. Either way, she'd always been an innocent observer.

Not now. What happened to Zeb, Hank, and Shirley sat squarely on Eva's shoulders. She shuddered then faced the detectives.

"Detective Rollins, has your team reached a point where I could go inside a moment? Shirley worked for me. Maybe there's something I'll see that will help."

"Like you're gonna see what trained experts can't," Curly muttered with disgust.

"Word of advice, pal," Adam said dryly. "Don't under estimate a woman, especially this one."

Eva clenched her fist. She didn't need Adam throwing her punches. Slipping off her sunglasses, she directed a glare at the sour detective. "Seems to me, stopping Smith should be more important than anything else, even inflated egos, detective."

Chuckles from behind told Eva that Sheriff Doug and—she glanced back—Major Warren had joined her and Adam.

"Eva and SA Frasier are with me," said Sheriff Doug. "Major Warren and I will take responsibility."

Detective Rollins held his hands up. "I've no problem with it, Grant. It'll be fascinating to see how Ms. St. Claire does her work. Point of entry was Shirley's back door. The bedroom is unscathed. She must have heard them and surprised them in the living room. The trail of violence starts there and leads into the kitchen." He opened the door to Shirley's and the scent of blood and baby powder hit Eva's senses.

Remembering baby powder from Kaylee's visions, Eva expected a vision of Shirley's torture to slam into her. It didn't. Five more steps inside, she realized no vision would be coming. That meant the strong smell of baby powder had to have a source. "You guys recognize the scent?" Eva asked.

"Baby powder," Warren said.

"Yep," said Sheriff Doug. "It's been a while since the diaper stage in my house, but I remember it well."

"It lingers like incense here and it's not a scent a single woman of forty would choose to burn."

"It'd be more in the wheelhouse of child predators wanting to evoke a certain atmosphere for their fantasies," Adam said.

Eva nodded. "If Shirley bought it then she'd have a stash here. If she didn't, then Adam's dead right."

Moving across the great room, she registered the crime scene investigators and the knocked over furniture—bench and coatrack by the front door, side table by the couch— then focused on Shirley's home. Folk art with tidbits of wisdom decorated the walls, blue checkered curtains framed the windows, and potted plants breathed fresh life into the worn furnishings.

Nice TV in one corner. Mac computer and iPad with a sound system on a desk. The great room immediately gave a view of the kitchen and the bloody, once white, floor. Reminiscent of the Manson family murders, they'd written in blood on a cheery, yellow wall. She knew the horseshoe symbol instantly. "Omega," she whispered. "The end."

Adam joined her. "Reverend Smith repeatedly yelled 'I am the Alpha and the Omega' from the pulpit last night.'"

"He's the root of Mason's grandiose delusions, but I doubt he's aiding and abetting," Eva replied.

"Is there something you haven't told me?" Warren asked.

Adam explained their trip last night to see Mrs. Smith. "In my opinion, the Reverend Smith shouldn't be ruled out as an accomplice."

"We questioned the reverend and his wife, just after Smith's escape," Curly said, smugly.

"Yeah," Rollins said. "But we need to redo that interview."

Eva turned from the view of the bloody kitchen and focused on the living room. She came up short at the coffee table where a black "REPENT OR PERISH" pen sat amid a collection of crossword puzzles, and romance novels. The end of it had been chewed. "That pen on the table. A guard at the prison where I interviewed Smith on Saturday had one like that. I autographed a paper for him with it. They're distributed by Reverend Smith's Holiness Church. Mason Smith's mother answers the salvation hot line. She gave me a pen last night."

"What was the guard's name?" Rollins asked.

"Tom Hatchett." Eva seriously doubted solving the puzzle of Smith's partner would be as simple as connecting the dots by a peculiar pen.

"Hatchett?" Curly asked incredulous. "Sounds like something you'd read in a crime spoof."

"Real life is unfortunately stranger than fiction," Eva replied.

"Bag that pen and get me prints ASAP," Rollins ordered a tech.

"On it," replied the tech.

Eva nodded to the desk. "Smith had music playing in the video. Have you checked the iPad's play history? What were the recent searches?"

Detective Rollins motioned to an investigator near the desk.

"We've fingerprinted everything. Last internet search came up for a joint in midtown. We told Detective Wright. We haven't done the iPad yet," the man said.

"Got it written right here for us to check out sometime. A piano bar doesn't sound relevant to the case," Curly said, holding up a pad.

"How many times do I have to say it? Share when you hear something, Curly. I don't care if you think it's important or not," Detective Rollins muttered. He nodded at the tech, "Give the iPad a look-see."

Eva heard a strong note of frustration in Rollins's tone. Seemed that Curly had a habit of keeping information to himself—an easy way to manipulate investigations, perhaps? She studied Curly a second, wondering what he'd look like in black and white makeup and a wig. His size and shape were similar to Mason's. Nose and jaw line were off, though.

"Here goes," said the investigator. Using the tip of a pen, he turned on the iPad and played the last song in the queue. Eva recognized the noise. "That's the song from the video." *And Kaylee's vision.* "What is it?"

"'Cake and Sodomy' from Marilyn Manson's *Portrait of An American Family Album*," the man said. "Before that was another Manson song, 'Kiddie Grinder' from *Smells Like Children* Album. Then before 'Kiddie Grinder', looks as if they played an album *IRRev 18* by a group named Balaam's Horn. Some of the songs were 'Synagogue of Satan,' 'Unrepentant', 'Little Jezebel in Hell', and 'Beginning of the End—the Death of Omega'."

Eva sucked in air at the nauseating chills running up her spine. The men broke into a conversation about Manson's name being a hybrid of Marilyn Monroe and Charles Manson. The shock rocker first came onto the music scene in the mid-nineties. Eva pulled out her phone and Googled the words to the two songs. Shuddering, she placed a few more puzzle pieces into the sick psychology of Mason and his partner. Phrases like *I am the god of fuck*, which she'd heard directly from Mason's mouth when she'd interviewed him in prison. To *Here we are, children! Come and get your lollipops!* and *I wear this fucking mask because you cannot handle me.*

Finally, Eva had a window to share her sick clown information with investigators. "Smith lived off the grid for years and has stonewalled investigators on where he was. A lot of the Goth and Death Metal scene stay underground. That may be where Smith went after leaving his parents' house at seventeen. The culture hides behind painted masks and pseudonyms, but somebody always knows something for the right price."

"I've seen the weird punks at the Jungle's DV8 in Buckhead," said Curly.

The men started talking about what they knew about the warehouse-sized nightclub.

"Well, as I live and breathe, Adam Frasier. They didn't mention D.C. had been called in. Grant, Warren, Rollins, Wright, you boys ready to play show-and-tell with a GBI girl today?"

Eva swung around to see a very tall, athletic woman with short blonde hair, ice blue eyes, and a kiss-my-ass walk. Some women aged. This one didn't look as if she did. Eva put her between 35 and 45, but only because of her attitude. She hit the room like a storm that had every man frowning—except Curly. He appeared star-struck.

"Geena, you look...well," Adam said. "I heard you're now the SAC of region ten."

"That I am. How's Vince?"

"Having the time of his life. You did him a real favor by forcing his retirement." Adam's smile held a deadly edge that Eva hadn't seen before. "I'll give him your regards. Have you met Eva St. Claire? She's—"

"Yes, I know. The crime novelist." Geena reached out.

"Actually, true crime writer," Eva said, absorbing Adam's revelation, as she shook the woman's hand. "Novelists write fiction."

"Yes, I know. I'm Geena Winters. As Adam said, I'm Special Agent in Charge of this region. It's intriguing to meet you. But in all honesty, after reading *Hayden's Hell*, I can't say it's a pleasure. Tony and his wife were part of our family. Your book is dumping salt into old wounds and making them bleed."

Eva blinked at the woman's bluntness and returned the favor. "It's still a free country. No one forced anyone to read the book, and I make it clear from the start the graphic nature of the content. *Hayden's Hell* delves into the *facts* surrounding the Hayden murders and their alleged killer, John Carlan. Did you expect the book to be a cakewalk?"

Geena's smile didn't reach her eyes. "Of course not."

Eva forced a smile. Before she could say more, Adam stepped to her side. "Hate to cut the conversation short, but Eva and I are already late to an appointment. You ready?"

She slid on her sunglasses. She needed to have a talk with Adam about intervening into her every confrontation like a knight in shining armor, but this time she took him up on his offer. She didn't want anyone to see how deeply she bled, especially the GBI's Ms. Un-con-Geena-lity. The leads she'd gleaned from the crime scene, had her antsy to get moving.

"Yes, I'm ready," she caught Adam's arm. "Lead the way, Galahad."

ADAM WINCED. HE EXITED the crime scene with Eva, glad to escape before Geena dug her claws any deeper. On one hand, hearing he'd graduated from this morning's Mother Hen moniker was good—having it broadcasted to the Motley Crew inside, not so much.

He wasn't surprised at Eva's insight into the case and the information she'd puzzled together in minutes. She knew her prey, had spent months studying him. It was part of why he'd flown back from D.C. to be with her, but not the *whole* reason. He'd yet to examine his motives completely, other than to realize they weren't all professional.

He had no doubt the investigation would have produced the same leads Eva had hit on, just not as speedily. They had to conduct every aspect of an investigation to the letter of the law and they didn't know Smith like she did.

Eva let go of his arm. "How did Ms. *Un*-con-Geena-lity force your father into retirement?"

"Un-congena-who?"

"The beauty queen with attitude."

"Ahh." He laughed, recalling the Sandra Bullock movie. "Funny. Geena has a big mouth and knows how to use it to her best ability. She expertly bent the director's ear and inflamed resentment among the other agents about my father's views on the Hayden murders. She kept a constant, negative tide flowing, effectively eroding years of good service. I can't put the full blame on her, though. My father did his share of irritating when it came to Tony Hayden's case. Despite the evidence, my father didn't buy into Carlan as the killer and he never stopped questioning the verdict. But we'll talk about that later."

"Okay. Any idea when we might hear about Mason's siblings?"

Adam frowned. Eva wasn't one to drop a subject easily. He knew she had questions on why *Hayden's Hell* had drawn him to her doorstep, yet she quickly left the subject whenever he brought it up. *Why?*

He glanced at his watch. It'd been two hours since he'd called D.C. and put the gears in motion to unlock Smith's adoption records. They should have heard back. "I'll call them on the way. Shall we hunt down goths in Buckhead?"

"No. Let the detectives chase that thread for now," Eva said picking up her pace. "We've a lunch date."

Adam nearly tripped over his own feet.

"Hey, Adam? What happened to 'leave no man behind'?" Warren called out. Adam turned to see that both Warren and Sheriff Grant had vacated the Geena-infested crime scene.

"Unless it's life or death, it's every man for himself," Adam shot back and found his footing. They had to meet someone for lunch about Smith.

"Watch for the payback," Warren said then laughed. "You want to tell me where you and your Top Gun are heading?"

"I'll get back to you on that," Adam said, glancing Eva's way. It felt really weird having her in the driver's seat on this investigation, but she'd yet to steer them wrong. He knew what he was doing, but hell if he'd take flak from others about it.

"We're having lunch at a retirement home in Rockdale County, Major Warren."

"Because?" Warren asked, just as puzzled.

"There's a band playing that I want to hear," Eva said.

Ah, Smith's band teacher. Adam gave Warren a thumbs up and hurried Eva past the bullet-riddled Escalade to his rental parked on the street, managing to catch the media—still minus the DuMond shark—off-guard. A good thing. He'd had his fill of reporters for the day. He hit the gas. "So we're seeing Virginia Carroll Jones?"

"Yes. My gut tells me the key to Mason's partner lies in Mason's past." Sliding up her sunglasses, she reached for the radio. "You mind?"

He shook his head. "Suit yourself."

She scanned the channels. "It's about time for the news. Call me masochistic, but I have to know how much DuMond taped this morning. She's not circling Shirley's which means the shark is up to something else." Eva tuned into WGGS mid-weather report that forecasted severe thunderstorms with possible tornadoes for the next twenty-four hours.

Eva inhaled.

Glancing her way, he saw her looking at him with real fear in her misty gray eyes. "Don't tell me you're afraid of thunderstorms."

"Didn't used to be," she muttered."

"What makes—" she held up her hand and increased the volume.

WGGS's own Grace DuMond has a live update on the hunt for escaped killer Mason T. Smith.

Grace's grating voice cut through the car. *There's a serial killer on the loose and this time we can thank author Eva St. Claire for it. This morning she pretty much confirmed what Officer Tom Hatchett told us in our exclusive interview last evening. She is complicit in driving Mason Smith into his killing spree.*

Zeb Cole and Hank Duffy, St. Claire's security guards, were gunned down this morning by Smith during an attack on her mega estate. This is what the poor-little-rich-writer had to say about it. 'Shirley, Zeb, and Hank were my employees and came into harm's way because of me.' Shirley Pearl is in the hands of the killer as we speak and Eva St. Claire is under FBI protection with Special Agent Adam Frasier, a local boy who's made good at Quantico. To refresh your minds, here are a few clips from Officer Hatchett, an eye-witness to St. Claire's part in this horror.

"I haven't seen rage like that in a while. One minute Smith sat smug, leering at St. Claire and the next he went berserk trying to get at her. She put the fear of God in him, she did. When I asked her what she said to Smith, she said, 'I told him he couldn't escape justice. He's a dead man on his way to being every man's bitch in hell!' St. Claire has this way about her. One look into her mysterious gaze and you see fate staring you in the eye."

Eva snapped off the radio, anger steaming from her every breath. "I never said that! Just wait until Hatchett sees *his* fate! We're taking a detour to my house, Adam."

Adam chuckled in part because in her upset, she'd used his first name for the first time. Secondly, because Officer Hatchett had hit the nail on the head about seeing fate with one look into Eva's eyes. It had happened to Adam.

She smacked his shoulder. "This isn't funny, Frasier."

"I know. You've got to realize nobody will believe you said those exact words. The vernacular is completely out of character. And so what if you had? DuMond is trying to sensationalize something cops often say to scare perps. What's at your house?"

"Officer Hatchett's phone number." She snapped her sunglasses in place, ready for battle.

He wanted to smack the man, too. But knew they'd be trampling over a bunch of sensitive feet, especially since he wasn't in charge of the investigation. "Later. You just tagged Hatchett in a double murder-kidnapping. If you go after him before homicide verifies his prints on the pen and questions him, it'd be seen as interfering with the investigation. Especially if he runs."

"I couldn't ignore the pen connections. They keep popping up. But if Hatchett is our guy, seems pretty careless for him to leave a pen behind after being smart enough to escape detection throughout the investigations into Angel Banning's kidnapping and sexual assault."

"More bold, means less careful. In my opinion, their purpose in killing is devolving. After escaping, Smith and company could have stayed hidden until the search for them eased then resumed hunting young girls. Instead, their focus is revenge. First the Banning's mansion then coming after you. If anything, your interview with Smith derailed them."

Eva shook her head. "That doesn't ease my guilt over Zeb, Hank, and Shirley."

He set his hand over her clasped fist. "I know. I didn't mean to imply it should. What I'm saying is your involvement in this case is driving them to take chances, which increases their odds of making a mistake and our chances of stopping them sooner."

She inhaled and directed her gaze to the horizon as if looking to find something new. Unfurling her fist, she slid her palm to his and squeezed before letting go. "I pray to God that is so. How is your back?"

"Right as rain," he said with a grin, trying to lighten her burden.

The corners of her mouth lifted in a half smile and she shook her head. Instead of the dark lenses she hid behind, Adam wished he could have seen into her eyes the moment she had clasped his hand. As desperate and dire as the hunt for Smith and the USUB with him had become, he couldn't ignore her in the mix. Had she felt the same jolt of heat that had zinged through him? Clearing his tightened throat, he focused on driving. Rain and wind moved into the area, making the roads hazardous and the impossible traffic even more horrendous.

Eva called to check with Iris on Devin and Paddy while Adam silently *blessed the hearts* of more than a few idiots on the road. He blessed a few at Quantico too, where they'd yet to access identifying information about Mason's siblings. There'd been a medical emergency with the judge on one sibling, thus delaying the process. With the other sibling, in a different judicial district, the adoption records along with any identifying information had been destroyed. The researcher promised to call as soon as she found anything out. He explained to Eva.

"Destroyed? In 1987? Can that be done?"

"Yes. Under certain circumstances if the information is deemed harmful to the child or if the child is a victim of a crime, records can be destroyed, redacted, and a pseudonym substituted for the real name. It's along the lines of expunging juvie records."

"Interesting, but if there were three of them why only destroy one?"

"Good question. I'm afraid only the judge and the adoptee know the answer."

"So we're SOL."

"Not completely. Information on the other sibling is delayed." Once he hit Interstate 85, Eva gave him the directions to the retirement center. The forty-five minute drive passed quickly as Eva Googled more information on the music from Shirley's iPad. Balaam's Horn, once known as just Horn, was a local band that found its roots in the nineties spread of death metal. Eva also learned Marilyn Manson portrayed a character named Omega for the release of his *Mechanical Animals* album in 1998.

"How local is Balaam's Horn? I've never heard of them, but any kind of heavy metal or techno anything isn't my scene," Adam said.

"They've never hit my radar either, but I bet they can give some insight into their fans. There's an agency contact number on their website for bookings." Eva dialed and left a message for the agent to call back. He called back shortly. He introduced himself as Mange. Eva asked for an interview with the band and the man heartily agreed, but it would have to be via webcam later this afternoon—as the band was still touring in Europe. He'd get back to Eva with the time soon.

12:30 P.M.

ADAM PARKED AT THE retirement center as Eva hung up the phone. "It feels like we're making progress," he said.

"We are, but not enough fast enough. Every time I think of Shirley and what might be happening…" She sighed. "I've never had to deal with that pressure. My work has always been research after the fact."

"It's rough and it never gets easier. Most active cases are a race against time with dire consequences hovering like a Guillotine over everyone's head. All you can to do is keep moving forward."

She leaned forward and eyed the turbulent clouds roiling overhead before drawing a deep breath, seemingly preparing for a battle. "Full speed ahead then."

Eva didn't say 'Damn the torpedoes,' but Adam sure as hell felt that sentiment charge the air. She exited the car and he followed.

Dashing through the blinding rain, they arrived inside the center in time to hear a senioresque band, called VC's Gang, in the midst of playing *Cherish*. It was just after noon. Lunch dishes scattered the tables reminding Adam that it'd been a while since that coffee and power bar at the hospital. His stomach rumbled at the aroma of roasted chicken.

Bright flowers of yellow, purple, and red decorated the room and a big banner that said, PUT A SPRING IN YOUR STEP plastered the wall behind the band. About thirty elderly men and women filled the room. Half of them were up slow dancing and the other half sang along with the band from their chairs, nostalgia etching their life-weathered faces.

The talented woman singing, whom he assumed to be Mason's band teacher, Virginia Carroll Jones, could easily double for Betty White and the men on guitar, keyboard, and drums might be seventy-something, but they still had it going on. The body may age, but the music in the soul proved timeless.

Cherish the life. Cherish the love.

The scene had Adam thinking about his mother, his abducted sister, his burdened father and how much of his own life had passed by *uncherished* because Adam had been too driven lately to think about cherishing anything—or anyone.

Was that the connection he felt toward Eva? Did part of him recognize in her the same haunted drive that fueled him, controlling every aspect of his life?

He cut his glance her way. She stood quietly at his side—minus her sunglasses, her thickly-lashed gray gaze focused on the woman singing. Without makeup and designer suit, Eva's vulnerability grabbed at him. Something about her in jeans, a faded shirt, and threadbare hoodie made him want to hold her close to him for more than just a moment in time.

*Hell…*he shook his head and shoved whatever was going on with him down a deep rabbit hole in his mind and slammed the door shut. Lack of sleep had to be messing with his objectivity. He had to stay totally focused on running Smith to ground and keeping Eva safe.

Devin's pain-filled plea in the pool this morning rang loud in Adam's head. It was as if Eva's brother knew something was coming down the pipe and wanted Adam ready to meet the challenge.

Warren was dead-on that Smith wanted something from Eva. After the shooting yesterday, Adam had surmised as much. Now that Smith had sent a video of Shirley's torture this morning, it was evident Smith wanted Eva.

Not good. Eva's guilt had her ripe and ready to sacrifice herself to save Shirley.

The song ended and the band struck another tune that snapped Adam from his reverie. Every senior in the center stood to clap and dance or rocked from their wheelchairs. "That's the Way" by KC and the Sunshine Band.

He and Eva were the only non-dancers in the room. Even the kitchen staff came out to party. Adam leaned Eva's way. "They move better than I can."

She nodded. "Me either."

He smiled. The song ended and the lead singer announced they'd play again tomorrow. He motioned for Eva to take the interview lead since this was her set up, but she'd already headed to the woman. Adam quick-stepped to catch up.

"Mrs. Jones? I'm Eva St. Claire and this is Special Agent Adam Frasier. I wondered if we could have a moment of your time to ask some questions about—"

"Mason Smith, I know. I've been listening to the news. Call me Ginny please. Mrs. Jones is for Marvin."

Adam laughed at her play on the old hit Marvin Gaye song.

Her blue eyes twinkled his way before she looked compassionately at Eva. "I'm sorry to hear about this morning's attack." She glanced around. "If you don't mind, let's go to the kitchen. The cook saved some lunch for me. There's likely extra too, if you haven't eaten. Even after all these years, I'm still too nervous to eat before I sing."

"You shouldn't be," Eva said. "You and the band are very good. We'll join you but—"

"Lunch would be amazing as well," Adam interrupted, making extra sure Eva wasn't about to turn down food.

Ginny smiled. "Good. I lost my Ernie last year and hate eating alone."

Eva murmured condolence as they followed Ginny into the commercial kitchen. Chef Brett, who looked ten years younger but as sweet as sugar on Ginny, set them up in a room with a minimal amount of fuss.

After a few bites, Ginny set down her fork. "I've been waiting for someone to question me about Mason ever since I saw what had become of him on the news. Mind you, if I thought I'd had anything important to say about him, I'd have gone to the authorities myself. As it is, all I know about him is water that passed under a bridge years ago. I wasn't surprised to learn what he'd done, though."

"Why is that?" Eva asked.

"With a Jekyll and Hyde mother who abused the hell out of him physically and mentally, and a father who labeled him the devil incarnate, Mason was a powder keg primed to blow."

Adam snapped his gaze to Eva's shocked expression. "Did you say his mother abused him? As in *the Reverend Smith's wife?*"

"The one and only. I tried to get DFCS involved a number of times, but Mason and the Reverend always adamantly denied it. Swore he'd gotten into a fight, or he'd fallen, or he'd crashed his bike. There was always an excuse. They were so outraged by my continued suggestions of abuse that they went to the principal and accused me of religious persecution." She frowned. "I might have muttered something about snake handlers being crazy after the Reverend lectured me on interfering with God's work, but that had nothing to do with his wife and her abuse. I was told to cease and desist my 'witch hunt' or leave the school. I wasn't a teacher at Rockdale Middle School, only a volunteer. And the Sunshine Band was a free extracurricular activity for children interested in exploring music together. I had to let it all go."

She shook her head. "Mason first started coming when he was eleven. He was gifted with a fiddle. If he heard something, he could play it. His problem was that, he was forbidden to play anything other than hymns. Everything else was 'of the devil'."

Eva frowned. "Then how did he play in the band?"

"I made sure we always played a hymn or two and he sat on the sidelines for the rest. Which is one of the reasons I think he was drawn to the Dreadful Jaynes. They played anti-hymns, almost satanic in worship. But I'm getting ahead of myself."

"Dreadful Jaynes?"

"A Heavy Metal band led by Daisy Jayne. They never made it past local garage parties. Let me backtrack here. I don't want to ruin your lunch, but what I have to say isn't pretty. Mason's mother didn't break bones or use a belt. She pinched him where it hurt the most until he was black and blue then boxed his ears purple. One time when she caught him looking at a girl after a concert at the school, I heard her yell that he'd better get the devil out of him right that minute. They were outside and I was just inside the doorway. She had her back to me and Mason stood facing her. Seconds later he was on the ground moaning, holding his crotch as if he'd been kicked by a mule. I charged at her, snatching her away from him, demanding to know what she'd done. She replied that she hadn't done anything. That her boy knew she loved him. Mason said he'd gotten a sudden leg cramp. Leg cramp my ass. His last year of middle school, he stopped coming to band practice. He told me he quit. I later saw him hanging around with Daisy Jayne at a local music festival.

She went by the name Dreadful Jayne, wore black, had purple hair and piercings everywhere. Towards the end of the school year, Mason's mother came looking for him at practice. She was irate to discover he wasn't there. I heard through the gossip-vine that she found him playing in the Jayne's garage. She went insane. She used his violin to obliterate every instrument there, screaming 'Satan be gone' at the top of her lungs. Police were called, but in the end, the Jaynes didn't file charges."

"And nobody believed he was a victim of abuse after that?" Adam shook his head at how many times important shit fell through the cracks.

Ginny shrugged. "Nobody with the authority to help him saw fit to intervene into the Reverend Smith's *righteous* household."

Eva sighed. "It makes me sick to hear it. If someone had listened to you back then and figured out how to reach Mason, maybe he wouldn't be what he is today."

"I've thought the same myself." Ginny resumed eating.

"This Daisy Jayne, is she still around?"

"Heard she started drugs in high school. Her parents sent her to a boarding school for rebellious girls and she ran away. Don't think she ever came back, either. Even when Mr. Jayne passed away from a heart attack late one night at their hardware store. Mrs. Jayne didn't find him until the next morning. Mrs. Jayne's still going strong, though. She and an assistant live in an apartment over the family's hardware store in Olde Town Conyers historic district."

Adam managed to clean his plate as Ginny talked. Eva had barely touched hers, but sucked down two cups of coffee with extra sugar and cream.

"What year?" Adam asked.

"For the hardware store? I think it was built in the late eighteen hundreds."

"No. What year do you think Daisy Jayne ran away?"

Ginny frowned. "Not sure. You'd have to ask her mother."

Eva pushed her plate away. "Hopefully, she'll see us now."

"She will. Most days she sits in the rocker on her balcony and people watches. But with it storming today, she won't."

Adam eased Eva's plate back in front of her. "No food, no go."

"*Seriously?*"

She looked at him as if he'd morphed from Galahad into Mother Hen and he almost backed down. After all, she was an adult and capable of deciding what she wanted. But then, he'd learned the hard way during hot investigations it was either eat, or chance defeat. Caffeine and sugar only fueled the brain for so long. Taking one for the team, he dangled the car keys. "Driver rules. No food, no go."

Ginny chuckled. "It's nice to see young people together who are meant for each other."

Adam's jaw dropped as he glanced at Eva. She sat frozen with her fork half-way to her mouth. She peeked at him from beneath her thick lashes with those incredible eyes. "We're not—"

Ginny laughed harder. "Maybe not yet, but life is too short not to love."

Adam's cell vibrated. Eva jumped as if she'd heard a ghost and dropped her fork. It was Quantico. He answered as he stood and moved to the door. "I'm watching," he mouthed to Eva before stepping into the hall. She glared and picked up her fork again.

The news stunned Adam.

Ten minutes later, Adam pushed open the door and Eva exited the retirement center shaking her head. It was raining lighter than when they'd arrived, but the wind had picked up and the skies roiled with ominous blackish-green clouds. Tornado weather.

"I feel as if I've been blindsided. Mason's mother was Mason's main abuser? She had me completely snowed. Question is, why even give us Ginny's name? She had to know what the band teacher would say about her."

Adam arched his brows. "Good question. Unless, she sees herself as having done no wrong. Keep in mind, she likely doesn't know Ginny's knowledge of Mason's involvement with Daisy Jayne or her clearing the Jayne's garage of 'Satan's influences.' People with such a righteous mindset see themselves above the law, both man's and God's."

"And here I was feeling sorry for her situation."

"My bet is she is the one orchestrating Reverend Smith's whole ministry. They make a very dangerous pair. We've interesting news from Quantico. I'll tell you in the car." Adam made a dash into the rain.

"What? Frasier, you're a…a…brat," Eva shouted, following on his heels.

They piled into the car out of breath and laughing. Splattered with rain, she looked stunning with rosy cheeks and spiked lashes framing her misty eyes. He couldn't help but touch her, gently brushing the moisture off her chin with his finger. "I believe tease is the word you're looking for Ms. Saint. And yes. I can be a very good one."

Her eyes widened with awareness and her lips parted then she shook her head, breaking the spell. "You said you have news?"

He could see the painful reality of the day's awful events return to her eyes. They'd both forgotten themselves for a moment. Now, the walls were back. But that brief glimpse at an unburdened Eva had him hungry for more.

EVA'S HEART POUNDED AS sensations zinged life into places she couldn't afford to acknowledge existed. Images of Adam teasing her tried to flash through her mind. Instead, she bit her lip and forced herself to remember what had happened today and that she had too many secrets to protect.

But she'd never met a man so…tempting in so many ways. His keen gaze studied her intently and had her almost wishing for the impossible between them. "The news?" she asked again.

The interested fire in his eyes dimmed to worried concern.

She fisted her hand, regret at what could not be gripped her.

"Eva…I want you to know, I understand the heavy weight of what has happened, but you can't be afraid to let yourself breathe. Every now and then, when air comes your way, you have to breathe it in or you will suffocate. I've been living life and death circumstances too long. I know what I am talking about. It's why Grant and Warren were joking with me as we left Shirley's. Stress is a killer, too. Especially if you keep it all bottled up inside you."

Eva closed her eyes a minute. She'd heard Lannie's "live-love-laugh" from everyone it seemed. "When the bad stuff happening is your fault, you don't deserve to breathe," she finally said.

"Is it your fault? Truly? Or is it Smith's and those who helped form the monster he became? If you promise to breathe, I'll share my news." He winked at her.

She glared at him, knowing he was deliberately teasing her again. "I promise I'll breathe but you will cease breathing unless you tell me now."

He laughed and she smiled.

"I have news on at least one of Mason's siblings. She's older than Mason. Bounced around foster care for a few years then was adopted by Jerry and Nora Grace. When she began a career in journalism in her early twenties, she changed her name to none other than…drum roll please…Grace DuMond."

The news slapped Eva in the face, but she still couldn't get a handle on what he'd said. "You're telling me the shark reporter who circles my ass looking for a bare patch to bite is Mason Smith's *sister*?"

"Do you have a bare patch?" He slid his gaze down and then back up.

She shoved his arm. "Answer me."

"Yes. According to adoption records, Grace DuMond is Mason Smith's sister."

"Do you think she knows it? Do you think she's involved with Mason?"

Adam shook his head. "According to the researcher, only non-identifying information has ever been released in both Mason and Grace's adoption records. So I'm going to say DuMond doesn't know. The biological parents never signed a release form, so their identity is sealed. The researcher did find out that the mother was institutionalized—for life. We already know the other sibling's records were destroyed years ago."

"I think it's time to give DuMond that interview she's been hounding me for."

"A tricky move, but okay. I think I'll hold off telling Warren and the detectives until after we meet with her and I can assess if the information is important to the case or not."

Eva called DuMond's broadcasting station. She was put through to DuMond's producer who quickly scheduled an interview at the station's broadcasting office in Vinings, a suburb of Atlanta, at five o'clock. As she ended the call, she could hardly believe she'd signed up to do what she'd sworn she'd never do.

Adam interrupted her thoughts. "What will you say to her? We have to be careful not to compromise the investigation if by some wild chance she *does* know Mason is her brother and she is complicit in his escape. I just don't see her as a killer, but then Mason's mother had me snowed as well."

Eva thought for a moment. "I'll play tit for tat with her. I'll answer one of her questions, if she'll answer one of mine. It will be interesting to see what she remembers of her childhood, her parents, and her siblings."

"What will you say about Mason?"

"I'm not. She'll have to bring him up. And no, I won't tell her they're related. If she wanted to know who her siblings were, she would have sought the information for herself."

"Even after she's made of point of targeting you and your family, you'd show her that respect?"

"It isn't 'Do onto others as they do onto you', but 'Do onto others as you would have *them* do unto you'. Now don't ask me that when she's in the middle of invading my privacy, I might not be as altruistic."

"I feel you on that. So which way? Back to Atlanta, to DuMond and the Balaam's Horn interviews or over to Mrs. Jayne's first?"

"Mrs. Jayne. I'm curious about Daisy."

"Can you imagine being named Daisy Jayne?"

Eva shook her head and breathed as Adam suggested. "It'd be dreadful," she deadpanned.

Adam laughed. "She thought so. But hey, at least it wasn't Daisy Duke."

"Or Daisy Duck."

He rolled his eyes. "You win. To the victor go the spoils. What is your dearest wish?"

She spoke without thinking. "What every person who's ever experienced the horror of tragedy and loss wants. To go back in time."

The smile fell from his gaze. She'd spoken the truth. Her dearest wish at the moment was to go back to Saturday and do things differently."

He caught onto her wavelength with a surprisingly avid and emotional response. "To go back and fix what went wrong? To make a different choice than the one made? I know what that's all about. As a kid, I read every time-travel story and saw every time-travel movie I could, hoping and praying I could go back to that day in the park and make my sister be okay. Make my mother whole again. Wanting to go back in time eventually destroyed my mother. She couldn't let it go and live." He paused, drew a breath and shrugged. "Truth is, I've never really let it go myself on some level. As an adult, I still read every time-travel theory proposed."

"I did the same thing after my parents…died, only dorkier. I watched an old Superman movie over and over and over. The one where he flies around the earth so fast that he reverses its rotation, turns back time and saves Lois Lane from dying. I kept praying for God to send Superman to me."

"Sorry, I'm late," Adam said and started the car, keeping a straight face.

Eva burst into laughter. "I opened the door wide for that one."

"Yeah. It felt good walking through it, too. Seriously, though. All we can do is move forward."

"Then I'll amend my Daisy prize. On the way back to Atlanta I want a hot fudge sundae. It's been years." Eva knew she'd pay the price in pounds later, but comfort food was just what she needed at the moment.

"Years?" Adam shook his head. "Someone needs to teach you how to live. Hot fudge sundae it is.

Eva blinked. Adam said the same thing that Iris and Lannie had. She also realized he was right. That even though Mason had attacked and killed. And even though Shirley was in dire circumstances, she did have to "breathe" and Adam made breathing possible. Adam eased the overwhelming horror. Most times, when writing about the horror and tragedy evil perpetrated, she didn't let herself be… alive or human. It seemed almost wrong to be living when the victims had suffered so much. *How screwed up was that?*

Ten minutes later they dashed into Jayne's Old Fashioned Hardware Store, which turned out to carry a lot of old-timey products that could still be bought. The clerk at the register had a smile as sweet as the packed candy counter surrounding her.

Eva picked out Clove and Beeman's gum and five candy sticks. Adam was still looking over the goodies. Digging in her purse for her credit card, she saw out of the corner of her eye a mini ice cream parlor at the back of the store with a picture of an amazing hot fudge sundae on the wall. *Providence?*

The clerk rang up her items, her eyes twinkling. "It's usually the men who are decisive and the women who can't make up their minds."

"There's an old fashioned store not far from my house, my dad—" Eva swallowed the lump in her throat at the good memory she hadn't realized she had. "My dad always bought exactly this every time we went. A candy stick for everyone just because…he loved us. The gum he gave out later if we were good."

Adam set a bag of Boston Baked Beans and a box of Bit-O-Honey on the counter. He slid a hand to her back and leaned into her side, effectively giving her a supportive hug. Then he eased away and drew out his wallet. She stayed his hand and paid. "You got breakfast. I'll get this."

The clerk took her credit card.

Eva smiled, hoping her request would go well. "We were just at the retirement center talking to Ginny Jones. I'm a writer doing research and wondered if Mrs. Jayne would be up to seeing us. Is there anyone we can call and ask?"

"Sure thing. I love Mrs. Jones. She meets with a group of ladies in the ice cream shop the first Friday of every month. I call them the Sunshine Girls." The clerk lowered her voice. "Do you know what they do?"

Eva shook her head. "They choose one person in the community who is in need and then make that person matter. Whatever that person needs doing, they plan it all out over banana splits. Then each of them leaves here with a list of things they either have to do or get someone in the community to help do."

"She didn't mention it," Adam said.

"That's the way she is. Outlooks were pretty bad around here due to the economy. It's amazing what a difference the Sunshine Girls have made." The clerk handed Eva back her credit card.

"By making one person feel like they matter, they brought hope," Eva said softly.

"Exactly. Let me give Missy a call. She lives in the apartment upstairs with Mrs. Jayne."

The clerk picked up the phone, stepping to the end of the counter. Eva turned to Adam. "I'm not surprised. Ginny seems to have spent her life trying to help others."

"Helping and giving hope, too. Very special," Adam said. "I help, but more often than not, I deal in cases with no hope of a good outcome."

"And I deal with cases where the only hope left is one for justice. I thought what I did helped, but this morning showed me how much harm I could cause as well."

"Not you."

"Not directly, but indirectly." He shook his head and she drove her point home. "Can anyone convince you that even as a child you didn't indirectly contribute to your sister's abduction?"

"No," he said curtly.

"So no matter what logic determines, emotions rule our perceptions?"

"Exactly."

The clerk returned. "Missy says to meet her at the stairs out back. The door is to the left of the ice cream counter. She'll take you up to see Mrs. Jayne."

"Thank you," Eva started to turn away then stopped. "How do the Sunshine Girls fund their ministry?"

The clerk beamed. "Through fundraisers they hold every few months. There's a special account at the Community Bank for donations."

Eva thanked her again and followed Adam outside.

2:00 P.M.

MISSY, A THIRTY-SOMETHING woman dressed in jeans, a plaid shirt, and smelling of oil paint, met them. Introductions were made.

"You're an artist?" Eva asked.

"I dabble. How did you know?"

"My sister paints. I can detect oils a mile away."

The stairs led to a sun porch where an easel and the disorder of an artist at work reigned. Missy walked through the French doors into the apartment. Eva followed with Adam behind her. It was like entering a time warp. The antiques and décor would be right at home in a nineteen twenties or thirties upper middle-class parlor. Framed on one wall were two portraits. One of a very handsome man and elegant woman in their thirties, dressed to the nines, he in a tux and she in sequins and a boa. They were smiling as if the world was their oyster. The other portrait was the opposite in every way possible. Compelled, Eva stepped closer. Purple hair with an uneven cut framed a face of sadness. Though a girl of not more than twelve or so, there was nothing young about her. She looked as worn and hopeless as her tattered jacket. She was extremely overweight.

"Mame, the guests are here."

"Bring them on in. Any friends of Ginny are welcome."

Eva swung her gaze to the corner shadows. The woman from the portrait was years older now. Petite with silver, beauty-parlor styled hair, weathered cheeks, and a pink lipstick smile. Her flowered dress looked like a vintage classic. She sat primly at an antique table set for tea looking like a postcard from a by-gone era.

Eva smiled and moved toward Mrs. Jayne. "Thank you for seeing us. Forgive me for intruding on your day. I don't want to misrepresent myself, I'm not a friend of Ginny's but after meeting her today, I hope that I will be. My name is Eva St. Claire and this is FBI agent Adam Frasier. I am a writer and he's helping me investigate a person who once lived in the area. From what Ginny said, your daughter Daisy knew him. I'd like to talk to you about that if you agree. If you don't, then I understand and we'll leave."

Her weathered face crumbled. "You want to talk about Daisy?"

"Yes ma'am."

She sighed. "I haven't seen her since we dropped her off at boarding school in 1996. You might as well sit and have tea with me. I don't get many opportunities to share Southern Hospitality these days. It's a forgotten tradition."

"Truly, we can just have tea, if that's what you'd like. I don't want to force you into this."

"No. Perhaps talking about Daisy will help. Not a day doesn't pass that I don't wonder if I could have done something else to help. If I could go back, I'd have done everything differently." She motioned to the empty chairs at the table. "Missy, why don't you go ahead and paint for a bit. We'll be fine without you."

"Just call me if you need anything." Missy went out on the sun porch and shut the French doors.

Adam pulled out a chair for Eva then moved to Mame's other side. "We appreciate your willingness to help us, ma'am."

Mame handed Adam a plate of sandwiches. "I haven't exactly agreed yet, boy. First, I need to know what publication Ms. St. Claire writes for and why she's in need of a strapping agent to help her. I'm not interested in plastering Daisy's story all over the news."

"I'm about your daughter. I don't write for the media. I write books about victims of crime and I'm trying to piece together an escaped killer's past, in an attempt to find him. There's no simple way to say this. Daisy knew a boy named Mason Smith. Do you remember him?"

"Not likely to forget the Reverend Smith, his kid, and his crazy wife. Not surprised Mason went bad, either. Not with parents like that. They bamboozled my husband with their righteous right, betrayed his trust, then sent Daisy into drinking and drugs with all their stone throwing. What if I don't want anything I tell you put in writing anywhere?"

"Then it's just between us three. As I said, we're trying to find Smith before he kills again. Understanding his past and the people in it may be the key."

Mame slowly stood. Using a cane she had tucked under the table, she moved to an old fashioned writing desk, picked up pen and paper and returned. Adam helped her sit back down. "Put that in writing for me and both of you sign it. I'll decide later if I want what I say to go into a book or not."

Eva complied with Mame's wishes, wondering what had the woman so burned and suspicious. She passed the paper for Adam to sign. He handed it to Mame. Mame tucked the letter in her pocket and poured tea. "Don't ever doubt how easy the path to insanity or hell is. It happens one step at a time. The tunnel you enter disappears behind you and you can't see anything around you except going down the road you're already on." She paused and Eva glanced at Adam. He appeared as puzzled as Eva over what Mame said.

Mame continued. "Before I get to Mason and his destructive family, I need to tell you a little about Daisy. What do you know about hermaphroditism?"

"Having both male and female sex organs."

"Yes. Daisy was born with both to a sick mother who abused and mutilated her over a period of years. She came to us so scarred that the doctors couldn't ever truly make her male or female. She struggled with the memory of abuse and her identity with her every breath. We spent years in counseling to help Daisy deal with what had been done to her. It wasn't until she discovered that horrendous noise they called Metal music back then and began playing it herself that she found some purpose, acceptance, and even enjoyment in her life. She stopped overeating. Stopped cutting herself and her dolls and seemed to finally be on a path toward healing. I didn't care if she was Daisy Jayne or Dreadful Jayne, I just wanted to heal the damage done to her. Through the music she connected with a couple of local girls who were into that stuff. They'd be all fangirl over bands named Megadeath and Overkill. They'd often go to local clubs in Atlanta to see a band named Horns.

Daisy had finally found friends and acceptance. Then she adopted Mason into her circle of and everything fell apart."

"He was a bad influence on her?"

"I can't say that. In my opinion, Mason suffered psychological abuse from his extreme parents and their ideology. I think Daisy and Mason clicked because of the abuse they'd suffered. They were opposite in many ways. He was skinny as a rail and Daisy was almost two hundred pounds. Maybe more. She didn't want people to know how much she weighed, so she'd sabotage the scales every time we bought one. Mason's hair was practically shaved from his head. Daisy had long, purple hair."

"What went wrong then?"

"Mason mother was the first step toward hell. She found Mason playing music with the Dreadful Jaynes one day towards the end of middle school and destroyed every instrument in the garage, screaming for the devil to flee from the place. The police arrested her. That night the Reverend Smith came to our house. He and my husband went into the study. I'm not sure how it was even possible, but one more step to hell was made. The Reverend Smith convinced my husband that Daisy was possessed by evil spirits and needed exorcising. What needed exorcising was the Reverend's wife."

Eva felt her phone vibrate in her purse she'd set on the floor next to her foot. It had flopped against her leg when Adam helped scoot her chair in. Dread curled in her stomach. *Had Mason sent the next installment?* She wasn't about to interrupt Daisy's mother right now to see.

"My husband wouldn't listen to reason when I tried to stop the insanity. He felt nothing we'd done over the years had helped Daisy. It was time to call on a higher authority. A nightmare of sessions began. The devil's music was taken from Daisy. She wasn't allowed to see her 'evil' friends. She was forced to sit through hour after hour, day after day, week after week, of the Reverend's fanatical screaming, admonishing her wretchedness, and telling her to denounce Satan in all her ways. Daisy turned to drugs and the human being I saw beginning to emerge from the horror of her past disappeared. She stole to get money for drugs to numb her pain and make her feel good. My husband developed heart problems. I got breast cancer. She became violent. She attacked my husband. She attacked me. And we sent her away to that school. She ran away. And I didn't try and find her until after my husband died and they declared me cancer free. I paid an investigator thousands to locate her but he never did. He ended up getting murdered in Atlanta and I let it all go. I know you're going to ask, where was Mason in all of this? During the exorcisms he was at the Reverend's feet, on his knees with his eyes shut, praying for Satan to release Daisy. If he stopped, if he opened his eyes, if he so much as relaxed a muscle his mother was right there to pinch him hard under his arm. Outside of that, Daisy and Mason never saw each other as far as I knew or heard. I'll never forgive myself for not finding a way to stop it all. Sometimes life catches you up in a storm and nothing you think of doing at the time stops the nightmare."

Adam cleared his throat. "What year did Daisy run away from school?

"Nineteen ninety-six. She was sixteen years old."

Eva stirred the tea she'd yet to drink. "So Daisy was adopted? When is her birthday?"

"Her birthday is July 17, 1980. Since I couldn't have children, we'd taken in troubled children on and off over the years. Daisy was in the foster care system and came to us when she was ten. We adopted her the next year. I believed that if she was shown unconditional love and knew no matter what, she belonged with us, it would heal her. I failed."

Eva touched Mame's arm. "You truly loved Daisy."

"I did. I tried."

"Then you didn't fail. Failure is to never try. Did Mason and Daisy have any friends they might have stayed in contact with?"

"At one time I would have said the other kids in the Dreadful Jayne band. But they've all grown up now. They have families and upstanding jobs in the community here. Only one moved to Atlanta to be near the Horns band. She wanted to become a rock star. Her name was Ivy Benton. I haven't heard anything else about her over the years. I hope I've said something to help, but I doubt it."

"You have," Eva assured Mame, feeling the connection to the Horn's band, now known as Balaam's Horn wasn't just a coincidence. Ties between Mason and Daisy in the past and Mason and his unknown partner grew stronger. "Any insight into a person's past is important. I'm sorry for the way things turned out with Daisy. I can tell you cared."

"If I could do it all over again, I'd have taken her and ran. We might not have had a roof over our heads or food on the table, but at least she maybe would have realized she was more important than the stone throwers who tried to destroy her."

"You keep saying stone throwers," Adam said. "You mean—"

"Condemners. There's a story about a woman caught in adultery and about to be stoned to death for her crime in accordance with the law. Jesus was a stone dropper, not a stone thrower. He didn't condemn the woman for her crime. His one question had the self-righteous accusers dropping their stones and walking away. He set her free."

"I understand the meaning behind the phrase. I was asking *who*. Who were the stone throwers? Do you mean the Reverend Smith and his wife?"

"They started it. Convinced my husband to cast stones and then others in the community joined in. Daisy couldn't even walk to school without someone shouting she would burn in hell for being a child of the devil. She was persecuted and bullied. I should have put her in the car and left. I didn't." Mame picked up her tea, took a sip and set it back down. "If you don't mind, I think I need to rest a while. There isn't anything else I can tell you."

Eva placed her business card on the table. "If you think of anything, please call me. Two last questions. Do you know who Daisy's biological parents are? And did you and Daisy have any fun moments?"

Mame smiled. "No idea of her parents. Considering what was done to Daisy, we didn't want to know. And yes, Daisy and I had a number of fun times. She had such a quirky sense of humor."

"Then remember those times and the love you have for her. I lost my parents under tragic circumstances and I can tell you it helps to do that."

"Thank you, dear."

Eva stood. Adam rose as well. He reached for Mame's hand and clasped it in both of his. "I feel compelled to commend your strength. Not every person can go through the trials you have and still face each day with grace." He bent and kissed her hand.

Mame blushed and fluttered her lashes. "A real Southern gentleman. You're a rare breed these days. If only I were forty years younger."

Adam laughed. "Or I, forty years older."

She shook her head. "It doesn't work that way. Older men go after the young chicks. Not women their age." She looked at Eva. "Better nab him now while he's looking your way."

"I'll keep that in mind. Thank you for entrusting me with your story. I will be in touch if I need to write about anything you've said today. And I'll stop by and say hello, when I'm out this way again."

"You do that. Next time we'll really have tea instead of just pretending."

"When you leave, tell Missy I'm ready for a nap."

Eva relayed the message to Missy on the way out. Upon seeing the woman's talented landscapes, she made a mental note to tell Iris.

At the bottom of the stairs, Adam turned to her. "Are you thinking what I'm thinking?"

"I'm still reeling that Mason and DuMond are siblings. You're wondering if Daisy is Mason's accomplice?" Eva kept toying with the idea, but couldn't wrap that around images of Mason's partner from her visions. She saw two men who looked alike, and from Daisy's portrait as an overweight teen, she didn't see a lot of resemblance between them. "I don't know. Besides, Daisy ran away a year before Mason left home. For some reason I pictured his partner as being a man. Not a woman."

"Yeah, but couples have been known to kill. Here's a wild idea. Daisy was in the foster care system. What about that missing sibling slot? Do you think it could be Daisy?"

Eva shook her head. "Mason was born on July first and Daisy the seventeenth of the same year. I'm going to catch the restroom."

"I'll see what Quantico can dig up on Daisy and on Ivy Benton. And order those hot fudge sundaes."

Eva frowned. As much as she wanted the treat, now that they had leads to follow, she wanted to move on them as soon as possible. "We should leave for Atlanta before rush hour traffic hits."

He shook his head. "I'll get them to go. Then you can indulge and not feel guilty about the time."

He already knew her too well, Eva thought as she ducked into the restroom. She dug her phone from her purse to see who had called. The unknown number had left her a voice message. Mason's voice desecrated the air as he sang. She could barely breathe.

"Hickory Dickory Dock
A bridge too far at nine o'clock
Come alone
Or she's undone
Hickory Dickory Dock"

Eva shuddered. How deep into her life had Smith and his partner invaded? She didn't have to think twice about where to meet them. The mausoleum holding her parents' remains. *Love became a bridge too far*, engraved the stone monument.

3:00 P.M.

WHEN EVA EXITED THE restroom, she found Adam in the ice cream parlor. Two hot fudge sundaes sat on the table in front of him. He was on the phone, his expression grim. The police's technology wheels in monitoring her calls must have moved fast. He hung up. "When were you going to tell me that Smith called?"

"Considering I just listened to the message in the bathroom, maybe in the next minute." She grabbed a sundae off the table and left him in her dust. The last thing she felt like doing was eating and she almost tossed it in the trash on the porch outside, but the smell of fudge hit her and she shoved a spoonful into her mouth. Then another and another.

Comfort food. Try not to be pissed off food. Guilt food. Whatever. She devoured it faster than she'd ever eaten anything in her life. Adam exited the hardware store a few minutes behind her just as she finished the last bite. She tossed the empty cup into the trash.

He looked at her. His brows drew into a frown as his gaze settled on her mouth. "Years? What else have you deprived yourself of?"

She blinked, refusing to address that question even in her mind.

Though the gleam in his gaze told her he had no problem entertaining the answer in his mind, he didn't wait for a response. "I'm sorry. That Smith has Shirley and is terrorizing you like this pisses me off. I hadn't had time to process the fact that we'd been busy with Mrs. Jayne when the call came in. Warren called while you were in the restroom. He asked what you and I thought Mason's message meant. I didn't know what he was talking about. You can take it from there. New development is prints on the chewed pen at Shirley's house were a match for Officer Hatchett. They've brought him in for questioning and are checking out his alibi for this morning."

Eva furrowed her brow. "Not that I don't want him squirming in the hot seat for his comments about my interview with Smith, but it seems too easy. Although you did say the bolder a killer gets, the more apt they are to make a mistake. So maybe he did."

"If Hatchett is the partner, it would mean Mason plans to meet you by himself. Warren, Rollins, and Curly are scouring Atlanta, looking for any World War II monuments besides the one at the Georgia's War Vet Memorial at the veteran's complex. They aren't finding anything more, which is sad. They are a little stumped as well. Why would Mason choose a downtown complex to meet?"

"This time a bridge too far has nothing to do with World War II."

Adam drew a quick breath and exhaled hard. "Your parents' grave."

She stepped back, shocked that he knew.

He winced. "Saturday night after hearing DuMond's spiel on the radio, I did some research on what happened to your family. I wasn't cyber-gawking. I was seeking to understand. We'd just met and…quite frankly, you're the most intriguing woman I've ever encountered."

She stood stunned, grasping for something to say to his bald-faced honesty.

He handed her his fudge sundae and spoon. "Eat up while I drive. We've a hell of a lot to get done before tonight. I'll call Warren and the detectives to let them know the location. They want to meet us at six-thirty to go over the trap they have planned."

Eva looked down at the fudge melting the ice cream and started eating as she followed Adam into the rain. Years had been a damn long time and unfortunately, no amount of fudge diminished his appeal to her. It did help though—a little.

ADAM EASED THE CAR into his father's empty driveway and cut the engine, leaving only the sound of splattering rain and Eva's steady breathing to fill the void. His father was likely up at the nursing home seeing his mother. With Eva's house out of commission, they needed an operating base. He could have gone to a hotel, but chose the safer option—for now. They had forty minutes to spare before the web interview with Balaam's Horn. At some point during the drive back to Atlanta Eva had fallen asleep and lay propped against the car door.

He wanted to pull her into his arms and have her melt against him. She was a vulnerable puzzle. He feared that once he pieced the mystery of her together, he'd never be the same or be able to walk away.

Years? As eagerly as she'd devoured the hot fudge sundae, he could just imagine what hunger a kiss would spark. A thought he should be smacking himself for, but didn't. He did put it on the back burner, though. First, they had to get through tonight. Then there was the little matter of finding out how she knew the killer had positioned Melissa Hayden's doll beside her, then nailing the son-of-a-bitch without crucifying his father in the process. Yawning, he set his iWatch alarm and shut his scratchy eyes for a power nap.

Vince rapping on the window cut the twenty-minute nap short. Startled, Eva snapped awake with a cry, glanced fearfully, saw him and immediately relaxed. He got the distinct feeling that she was specifically worried for him. *Interesting*.

Adam opened his car door. The rain had become a drizzle, but from the storm clouds whirling, that was only a momentary reprieve. "You have the finesse of an elephant. Ever hear of a light tap?"

"Yeah, Yeah. You said this morning at the hospital that you'd keep in touch, then bupkis."

Grabbing his bag from the backseat, Adam exited the car. Eva did the same, coming around to meet them and move to the shelter of the porch. "It's been a busy day and it's about to get even busier. Can we borrow your computer? We've a web conference and your screen is bigger than my laptop. Be polite and say hello to Eva."

Vince scowled. "I was getting to that. Ms. St. Claire, it is a pleasure to *see* you at *least*." He held out his hand.

She laughed and shook Vince's hand. "Same here, Mr. Frasier. Please call me Eva, though."

)

Really? Adam arched an amused brow. He's was the one putting his neck on the line for her and he couldn't call her Eva, but his father could?

Vince unlocked the front door. "Come on inside. It's not much, but its home and I've got hot coffee."

"On a day like today, hot anything works."

Adam bit his cheek to keep his mouth shut on that line, but the images she had innocently evoked had him breaking into a sweat. He started to follow her too-curvy-for-his-peace-of-mind backside into the house when his cell rang. Answering it, he moved back to the porch.

It was Warren again. Adam ducked back onto the front porch and connected the call. "Do you all have news?"

"Do you?" Warren asked.

Adam frowned. "Somewhat. Progress feels too slow, though. I want to be chasing the killers and not dust bunnies. We've interviewed two elderly ladies associated with Mason's past and are getting ready to talk to a band one of Mason's friends hung around. Eva's meeting with Grace DuMond at five before we come to the station."

"Because?"

Adam bit back spilling DuMond's connection to Smith just yet and gave Warren a half truth. "Eva feels DuMond's broadcasts about Smith are slanderous. Guess she wants to tell the woman to cease and desist."

"Good luck. We just left DuMond. Questioned her about her interview with Hatchett yesterday and got very little cooperation. The woman has a chip as big as Everest on her shoulders. So far Hatchett's alibis for last night and this morning are solid. But his girlfriend could be lying. We'll only be able to hold him until morning unless stronger evidence than the pen rises or the woman changes her mind."

"Is it possible Hatchett left her and returned without her knowing it?"

"She says he was there the whole time. Claims she's a light sleeper and heard him snoring. Also says he's a devoted dad on steroids. He would have never left his kid for even five minutes without waking her up to assure she'd watchover his son. He's crying innocent at the top of his lungs and demanding to take a poly to prove it. We're digging into his past hard and not finding any connection to Mason apart from working at the prison where Mason was being held for sentencing."

"What about with the Reverend Smith and his wife?"

"No connection so far. Hatchett says there are dozens of those pens lying around at the prison, which is where he got his. He doesn't remember when he last had the pen and has no idea how it could have ended up at Shirley's. What's this about a band?"

"Balaam's Horn, an Atlanta band who used to be called the Horn. Their music was on Shirley's iPad. Years ago two of Mason's friends were avid fans of the band."

"Interesting. One of them named Hatchett?"

"No. Daisy Jayne aka Dreadful Jayne and Ivy Benton. I have the office looking into both of them. I'll let you know what pops."

"We've made little progress here ourselves. Shirley's phone and another toe were found in a plastic bag outside of the local farmer's market. We found the burner phone he made the call from with another toe outside an Arby's in Atlanta. No witnesses. They're working on surveillance cameras."

"'This little Piggy went to Market. This little piggy stayed home. This little piggy had roast beef…' The bastard is sick. I'll never see nursery rhymes the same way again."

"Me either. No luck on tracing the drones either. Most of the evidence was incinerated with them."

"Every thread we pull on this case comes loose. I'd hoped one of them would unravel the identity of Smith's partner before the meet tonight. I don't like the set up."

"Me either. Nine at night in a graveyard makes it hard to put undercover men close by. I have a dead-end feeling about this whole thing."

"I'd laugh at that if I didn't feel the same. There's no way Eva won't go. She has to do everything she can to save Shirley. We'd both do the same."

"I know. I just wish we had more to go on. See you soon."

Adam hung up the phone and found Eva inside with his father, making coffee in the kitchen. He left them talking as he readied a place in front of his father's computer for him and Eva. Once they each had a hot mug in hand, Eva called Balaam's Horn's agent from the house's land line and put it on speaker phone.

"They're set for the interview," the agent said. "I need to know what publications this will come out in."

"I explained earlier that I don't work for the media. I'm a crime writer and I'm investigating a crime."

"I got that. But at some point you'll put this interview in writing and I want to know when we can expect to see it."

"You do understand I'm investigating a serial killer who may be a fan of Balaam's Horn. Surely you aren't looking to connect the band to that."

"Why not? Punks these days get off on shit like that. Look what *Portrait of an American Family* did for Marilyn Manson. You do know that he originally titled it *The Manson Family Album* with Charles Manson in mind? I'm still not sure why you want to talk with them, but I don't care. Getting Balaam's Horn heard is my angle and any publicity is good publicity."

Was this guy for real? No wonder the world kept spiraling into *Idiocracy*—a movie he'd never forget. Adam was about to interject into the conversation when Eva gave the nut what he wanted.

"The book will come out within the next twelve months. I will cite my interview with the band and include a pre-approved picture as well as a list of several songs related to the case. Now can we do that interview?"

The agent smiled. "Glad we reached a deal. The lead singer, Java Heat will introduce you to the rest of the band. I'll be in touch with the photo."

The screen switched and five men appeared, sitting in a semi-circle with beers in hand. He got what he'd expected tattoos everywhere visible, and piercings so many places, it was painful to see. Hair covering the spectrum. Dark red lenses to odd shaped sunglasses. And grunge clothes that had to be a homeless person's rejects. Adam thought it would be easier to see through a Mardi Gras mask than to read these men. The only thing he knew for sure was which end was up—maybe.

"So Mange says we gotta talk with you. I'm Java. This is Grease, Iggy, Ram, and Mace."

"I appreciate this. I read you're local to Atlanta. Tell me a little about yourself first. Why you play what you play. Who are your fans."

"What you want in our heads for?" One of the guys said, shaking his head.

"Chill," said Java. "I got this. Either of you ever been angry at life fucking you over? Parents? Cops? And especially the religious do-gooders who send you to hell when their fleece is black as dirt. They all become part of the screw over. That's the message we started out with. That shit brought us together and brought us the fans. We gave them a voice to scream about all the shit that had happened to them. Now, we play…because the money ain't nothin' and the chicks may not be free, but they're free flowing."

"True that," said the guy to Java's right.

"I heard that," came a woman's voice from off camera.

"Ah, sugar. You know I love you best," Java replied.

"How long have you guys been together?" Eva asked.

Java grinned. "Depends if you count time off for rehab and issues—" Eva laughed and then they all laughed, too. "We go way back. Started out in the nineties as The Horns playing local dives. Hair dye and sunglasses hide the years."

"I wanted to ask you about your early days. This is a long shot, but do any of you remember two fans from the Conyers area. Daisy Jayne and Ivy Benton?"

"What the fuck? Was this just a ruse to get to Wild Ivy?"

"Who is Wild Ivy?"

The band members' jaws dropped. "For real?" one of them muttered.

"She's like the Lady GaGa of Europe."

A woman with green hair and tattooed vines wrapping around her arms and neck walked into camera view and sat on Java's lap. "Who's asking about Daisy?"

Eva leaned forward. "You're Ivy Benton? You're from Conyers and used to play in a band named Dreadful Jaynes?"

"I wouldn't call it a band, but yeah. And you are?"

"Crime writer Eva St. Claire. I'm doing research on serial killer, Mason Smith."

"I knew that creep show was bad news," Ivy said. "He only played with the band a few months before his Jesus-screaming mother came and cleared our rock temple in the garage. I never saw him after that."

"How was Mason bad news?"

Ivy shrugged. "Just was. At least for John."

"Who's John?"

Ivy's brows lifted in surprise. "Sorry, I meant Daisy. A year after she came to Atlanta, *she* decided to become a *he*. Shaved her head and called herself John Jayne. Said Daisy Jayne/Dreadful Jayne was dead and everyone she knew was dead to her. It was really weird. Looking into his/her eyes I didn't see anyone I knew anymore.

I never saw him after that."

"And no one in the band remembers Daisy?"

Ivy kicked one of the band member's leg. "Fess up, Grease."

"What the *hell*. I didn't know what her name was. She was just a fat friend of Ivy's. We were all off on drugs at a party one night and hell she was just there. Everyone was having sex but us. We got to kissing. I dove for her crotch and she slammed my head with a whiskey bottle. I didn't wake up until morning. After that, I stayed the hell away from her. So did everyone else. Creeps me out now to learn she decided to be a he, but at least it makes sense of what happened."

"Ivy, you never tried to see John again?"

"I went looking a few times, but it's as if he/she disappeared. Nobody Daisy knew ever saw or heard from her again. Why? What's with all the questions?"

"As I said, I'm researching Mason Smith."

Ivy gasped. "Do you think he killed her? I heard he left Conyers, but I never saw him in Atlanta."

"What makes you think John could be dead and Mason killed him?" Adam interjected sharply.

Ivy startled, her eyes widening. "Nothing. Honest. Other than Mason is now a known killer, and John seems to have disappeared."

"How much of what we said are you going to write?" Grease asked.

"Only that you were helpful in providing information during my investigation." Grease sighed with relief.

Another band member elbowed Grease in the side. "You going homophobe on us?"

"Nah, man. I just like to know who I'm kissing."

"Can you all think of anything else? Anyone who Daisy hung out with in Atlanta?"

Ivy shook her head. "As I said, Daisy turned John and disappeared. Nobody heard from her again."

"Thank you all. Ivy if you think of anything else, Mange has my contact information," Eva said.

Adam disconnected the conference. "Interesting. I'll get the FBI searching for a John Jayne. But as often as this Daisy changes her name, it could be Tom, Dick, or Harry as well."

Vince shook his head. "Seems if that guy was really worried about who he kissed he'd lay off the drugs and booze."

Eva sighed. "Daisy/Dreadful/John and Mason both fell off the map in 1997. I'm betting they moved somewhere together and the killing started. We know more than before, but unless John Jayne has a local footprint we're still at square one."

"Maybe. Maybe not," Adam said. "I don't know about you, but I'm catching a quick shower before we meet up with DuMond in forty. There's a bath down the hallway if you want to do the same."

"That sounds like heaven." Eva stood smiling.

Nope, Adam thought. *Heaven would be taking the shower together.* Then he mentally smacked himself back in line. *Get a grip, man.*

"What are you two seeing that shark for?" Vince asked.

"It's complicated," Adam said. "Hopefully, I can explain it later. Right now we've got to move."

"I'll hunt up to-go cups for the coffee. While I'm at it I'll order a wheelchair since I'm too old and decrepit to handle an investigation anymore."

"Pops! Don't start any crap. I said I'd fill you in later and taking you along now just wouldn't…work."

"Yeah, yeah, yeah," Vince muttered walking away.

5:00 P.M.

THOUGH REFRESHED AND RECHARGED, Eva still didn't feel ready to face DuMond as Adam swung into WGGS's parking deck in the upscale suburbia of Vinings, Georgia. Isolated on a hilltop with a long drive up Elm Street, aptly named for the numerous trees and thick foliage, the brick broadcasting station almost felt like a resort.

She was yet to be able to see the reporter as Smith's sibling, which showed her how off her skills were and the doubt kept spreading. In Kaylee's visions she'd seen two bald Masons. Was one of them a shaved Daisy/John Jayne? She didn't see a resemblance between Daisy and Mason's younger selves.

Adam cursed and killed the engine.

"I'm not looking forward to this either."

"I haven't even thought about DuMond yet. My dad is on our tail. I spotted him half a block from the house. He pulled down into the truck entrance just now. I need to call and send his ass back home."

Eva laughed, desperate for the relief. "He's really following us? Too funny."

"Hilarious," Adam replied, his tone anything but.

"What harm can it do to let him follow us around? We're only going here and then to meet Warren and the detectives."

He exhaled. "I suppose you're right. Have you thought any more about what you'll say to DuMond?"

"I've run so many circles my mind is butter."

He opened the car door. "Let's just go do this then."

Eva braced herself and followed. Inside, the station buzzed with activity. Broadcasting for both radio and TV, the place must never slow down. She and Adam were escorted to a studio with floor to ceiling black curtains on three walls. Center stage was set up with video camera, lights, and two chairs backed by posters of infamous criminals and shattering crimes. Plastered over the top of the collage was a large black and white eye with the words, Crime Never Sleeps written under it.

Eva's spine tingled. Mason's partner's exact words! She almost turned to Adam in her surprise, but remembered at the last moment that she'd heard it through Zeb's vision. Having Adam with her constantly was undermining her safety barriers and she had better watch her step. Adam may be attracted to her but he wasn't her friend.

Seeing the motto had her mind scrambling. This was yet another connection between Smith and DuMond. Did Smith's partner watch DuMond's show? Was Smith's partner associated with the show?

"You okay with her taping this?"

Adam's question snapped Eva back to the present. "No. Hopefully when she hears my terms then she won't be either."

Adam spun in a circle, scanning the room. "If there's a surveillance camera, it's hidden."

DuMond, her camerawoman, and two others—a woman carrying an iPad and a bald man wearing makeup—entered the room. DuMond looked Eva's way. "Did hell freeze over?"

"Something like that," Eva replied.

"Then let's get this show going before it melts." DuMond waved to the man. He carried a professional make up kit. "Johnny, fix her up fast."

"You got it, luv." Johnny smiled warmly.

Eva was about to refuse, but here she had a slightly overweight, bald, effeminate man named Johnny and she needed a closer look at him. He wasn't the same height as Mason though.

"The god of fortune is looking my way. What a beauty we two could make of you. Smoky eyes, a touch of auburn to your midnight hair, and just the right shadowing to thin your cheeks. You'd be a new Sophia Loren." He motioned for her to join him at the corner of the room.

"Create later, Johnny. Interview starts in five," DuMond said then went on to bark orders at the others.

"He just called me fat," Eva whispered under her breath to Adam.

"He's a blind fool then. You're perfect."

"Now who's the blind fool?" She moved to meet Johnny. He sat her in a chair and went to work. Pinning her hair back, he brushed a heavy beige powder on her face commenting on what he called amazing skin.

"So, have you always lived in Atlanta?" she asked.

"Most of my life. Moved to LA for a few years but came back broken-hearted. West coast lovers run too hot and cold for my blood. I've read your books. Don't know how you sleep after facing the evil out there."

Eva studied Johnny's expression as he applied blush to her cheeks and shading beneath her chin. He seemed sincere and cool as a cucumber. "Doesn't Grace's show do the same?"

"Nowhere close to the detail you cover in your books." He shuddered. "And then, I only do makeup here in the studio where it's safe. Never in the field where she confronts the monsters."

"So, who do you have come here? I confess that I've never watched the show."

"Witnesses. Victims. Family, professionals and others related to investigations like the prison guard last night. He was very impressed with how you dealt with Smith."

"Times up, Johnny. Ms. St. Claire, please come join me. I have waited years for this."

Eva stood and approached the set where DuMond, dressed in a red skirt, blouse, and heels sat like a predator ready to pounce. Eva shrugged. "Well, Ms. DuMond, you may have to wait even longer, unless you agree to my ground rules."

The woman with the iPad gasped. "There were no conditions attached to this interview."

Eva smiled at DuMond's producer. "I recall every word. No conditions were attached because they were not discussed."

"What are your demands?" DuMond cut in, glaring hard.

"Simple. For every question you ask, I get to ask one in return. You answer mine, I'll answer yours. And no taping, but you can put my answers into an article should you decide. I, too reserve the right to put your answers into anything I should choose to write as well. If you don't answer truthfully, the interview is over."

"Why did you come in the first place?"

"Is that one of your questions?" Eva sat in the chair

"No. Kill the lights and the camera, JJ. We'll do this her way." Eva could practically see steam rising from DuMond.

The bright lights died, enabling Eva to see the others in the room. Adam looked relaxed in a nearby chair, grinning. The dreadlocked camerawoman had her arms crossed as if in a pout and the producer paced, anger swishing with her every step. She didn't see Johnny. While bald and adept in makeup, Johnny's demeanor didn't match Mason's partner from Kaylee's visions.

"We'll get to Smith in a minute. I've always been curious as to why you've never written about your mother's murder. Is it because there is more to the story that the St. Claire family doesn't want revealed?"

Eva curled her toes painfully in her shoes. DuMond had hit hard, fast, and somewhat accurately, too. There were so many unanswered questions about the tragedy, beginning long before her father committed his supposed crime of passion. Of all the years her parents were married, why had her mother chosen to make their funeral arrangements just months before their deaths?

"Yes," Eva replied. "I have chosen not to write about the murder of my mother and my father's suicide because I don't want to know what brought the love between them to so tragic an end. I want to remember them as they were before that awful day. Now for my question, Ms. DuMond. What are your earliest memories of your childhood?"

DuMond paled then blinked and shook her head almost in slow motion, as if she couldn't believe the question. "I—" she started to speak, swallowed hard then frowned. "Why do you want to know?"

"Is that one of your questions?" Eva smiled.

DuMond cursed. "My earliest memories are a blurred nightmare of an abusive father, a screaming mother who only shut up when he beat me, my sister, and brother or he knocked her out."

Eva heard a commotion in the room but kept her gaze locked with DuMond's. This was much harder than Eva thought it would be. Blindsiding DuMond and making her dump the demons from her past this way felt wrong until DuMond drove her next question home.

"According to the investigation your father stabbed your mother in the heart because of another man whose name was never revealed. Did you ever see your mother with anyone who might be the man she had an affair with?"

"No. I also read over the case reports. There was never any evidence to support that conjecture. Her children were her life. My mother never left us. Even when my father traveled for business, she stayed home with us. What about your family? Where are they now?"

Eva looked for a tell or any hint of deception in DuMond's face. Her complexion paled and her jaw tightened, but her response remained steady.

"My mother killed my father. They put her in an institution and sent us to DFCS. We went into foster care and I never saw my brother and sister again. Didn't want to, they were vicious brats. So, even when it comes to tragedy you and your family come out like a shiny penny. Who is the focus of the book you are working on now?"

Eva finally understood DuMond's obsession and anger. If, and when, the woman discovered Smith was her brother, it would only add to the reporter's antagonism. Eva hoped the FBI and police would be merciful with their knowledge. Empathy had Eva revealing what she could about her upcoming book.

"One of Mason Smith's victims, Kaylee Waters, but the book will not release until the DA and the courts decide how they intend to proceed with the case and the trial."

"Then Smith will be retried for the death penalty?"

"You'll have to ask the DA that question."

"You say 'one of Mason's victims' as if there are more than two."

"There are more than Angel and Kaylee already. You need to add the transport guards, my security people from this morning and the realtor from yesterday. But aside from those, I believe we will find more of Smith's victims over time. My question to you is, having known tragedy, how can you be so merciless in your reporting of it? And what made you choose the 'Crime Never Sleeps' motto?"

DuMond stood. "I don't expect you to understand me. Unless you're born with a silver spoon, aggression and dogged persistence are the only ways a woman can carve a place for herself in a man's world. As for the motto, some say the phrase is a play on the Pinkerton's "We Never Sleep" slogan. It aptly reminds everyone to stay alert and ready to fight. I'll ask you to wait a few days before printing anything about my pre-adoption family. I'd like to make the announcement first."

"No need. I won't be saying anything or writing about your past. I just wanted you to know what it felt like to have something so painful, that is beyond your choosing or control exploited over and over again."

DuMond met her gaze. "You made your point. How did you find out?"

Eva smiled. "I have great resources."

"Mr. FBI?"

Eva glanced Adam's way and discovered that the three of them were the only ones left in the room and he had his attention on her. "Operational support. He makes a great chauffeur."

"I get it," DuMond said, she turned Adam's way and frowned. "Where did JJ and Gloria go?"

He shrugged. "Don't know. Camerawoman left and the other lady followed."

"So you drive her everywhere she wants to go?" DuMond's tone turned the question sexual.

Adam arched a brow, a devilish twinkle lit his eyes. "Anytime. Anyway. Fast or slow. All she has to do is call."

DuMond laughed, exposing a genuine side beneath her shark bite.

Eva tripped as she swung to fully face him, barely catching her balance. Adam nodded. "Ready to ride, Sally."

Blushing until her ears burned, Eva made a beeline for the door.

"Let me know when hell freezes over again," DuMond called out.

"Don't hold your breath, but I can honestly say I will keep it in mind this time."

"Thank you," DuMond said, her soft tone as unexpected as the appreciation.

Eva stopped a moment and sent DuMond a genuine grin. She had no illusions. When it came to reporting, DuMond would always be a shark, but getting a glimpse of the woman beneath, made her bite a little less painful. "Thank you, too."

The downpour outside splattered rain into the parking deck, adding a misty chill to the evening air, but Eva was still hot under the collar. She elbowed Adam. "'Anytime. Anyway. Fast or slow, all you have to do is call', my ass, Frasier."

"Hey, you're the one who went down that road. Ms. Operational Support Saint." He shook his head. "Better charge my cell phone or I'll miss your call. It died during the interview. It was killer by the way. Excellent way to handle a shark."

Before she could respond, her cell rang and her stomach clenched even though she'd yet to see the screen—knowing Mason had her number had turned a safe lifeline into a pipeline for evil. It was Iris.

"Where are you?" Iris's tone ratcheted Eva's anxiety.

"With Adam. We just finished an interview with DuMond. Is Paddy all right? What's wrong?"

"Hell froze over?"

"Yeah, now what's wrong?"

Nothing maybe. Everything maybe. Paddy's fine, just grumpy as hell that Lannie's camped out in his room. It's Devin who's wrung out. When the burn specialist saw him, he decided to clean debris from the wound. No big deal. They knocked Devin out to do the procedure and he's been sleeping on and off since, asking about you frequently, but doing all right. Then a few minutes ago he woke up in a cold sweat, confused about where he was, and shaking so badly he could hardly speak. He pulled out his IV and stripped off his monitors, insisting he had to see you immediately. It took me, Aunt Zena, and two nurses to calm him down. They think he reacted adversely to the pain meds. We both know he didn't. It's been a long time since a vision held him captive. He has to talk to you."

"Okay, put him on." Eva glanced at Adam. "I'll be just a second." She moved further away from the car and lowered her voice.

"Eva." Devin's voice sounded like scraping glass. "Something's changed. You're not safe."

"What do you mean? What did you see?"

"Darkness. Suffocating darkness. I didn't see anything, but it felt like death."

"I don't understand. Did you have a vision or not?"

"I'm telling you, *I don't know*. I don't remember the vision. All I have left is this sense of overwhelming doom."

Eva inhaled, searching for a way through this dark cloud. Devin has always remembered his visions. They haunted him. Why was now different? Unless it wasn't a vision. "Dev, please take this the right way. Could it be the drugs? Truthfully, I'm likely safer than I have ever been during this investigation. Tonight, when I meet Smith, I'll have the full force of the APD, the State Troopers, and the GBI with me."

"*You're meeting Smith?*"

"It's fine. You need to focus on healing. You wanted Adam in the mix and the man hasn't left my side. Until you see differently, we'll stick with the vision you had and not what could be a drug-induced sense of doom."

"Don't go."

"I have to. He has Shirley. You should be ecstatic I'm not lone-wolfing this."

"That's only because you're hoping to keep Adam safe by increasing the numbers. Now, I'm telling you it's not safe for either of you."

"Can you swear it's not drugs talking? When have you ever *not* remembered a vision?"

"Never."

"Exactly. Listen, I will call Iris as soon as I know the details of tonight's plan. If you remember anything, or have another vision, you call me, okay?"

"Eva. No. Don't do this."

"Trust me. It will be all right. I've gotta go now." Blinking back tears at the raw fear in her brother's voice, Eva disconnected the call and joined Adam in the car. He had his cell charging and offered to hook hers up, too.

Turning the headlights on, he exited the parking garage into the heavy rain. "We'll see how good my father is at tailing in pea soup provided he stuck out the wait while we were inside."

"I don't see him." Eva strained to see outside. It was a shame that most of the spring blooms wouldn't survive the punishing storm. Rivers of water ran along the gutters of the hilly road. The thick green foliage only added to the darkness of the evening. "Didn't it strike you as odd that all three of DuMond's staff abandoned her?"

"Maybe not. You were with the makeup dude and didn't hear how she spoke to the women. I swear if DuMond had been male, the women would have reported her for harassment."

"She was demeaning to them?" Eva was about to regret being nice to DuMond.

"Not demeaning, more impatient and not politically correct in her expressions. But if they were angry at her, it wouldn't make sense for them to become upset when you took a bite out of DuMond, would it? They stormed out when you brought up the reporter's childhood."

"The producer, like DuMond, was likely worried about damage control. But I'm not sure exactly why DuMond felt it would be damaging to her image if she didn't release news of her past first."

"Me either. Speaking of upset, you don't look unscathed yourself. Everything okay at the hospital?"

She forced a smile and explained Devin's possible reaction to a medication. "He's worried about me."

"Can't blame him for that. I'm worried, too. Other than you're to meet at your parents' grave at 9:00 or Shirley will be undone, we don't have anything to work with. Will you get instructions on what to do next there? Will Shirley be close by? This whole day has felt like a slow motion walk to a guillotine."

"I couldn't have described it any better." She shuddered. "And Shirley's been under that blade all day."

Adam reached over and clasped her hand. Eva met his quick glance and something inside her heated, chasing back the cold after her soul. Suddenly, through the driver's side window, she saw a white van with its lights off barreling at them from the truck entrance.

"Watch out!" Eva screamed.

6:00 P.M.

ADAM SNAPPED HIS GAZE, saw the van through the rain, and wrenched the steering wheel hard to the right. Eva, still clutching his hand, jerked him her way, pulling him further from the imminent impact. He relaxed, ready to go with the flow. It happened in a bone-jarring, muscle-wrenching flash. Pain exploded. Metal screeched. Glass splintered in a web of cubes impossible to see through as Adam felt the car flip. Seat belts cut then ripped. The air bags erupted almost too late to help.

He tried to hold on to Eva, but the violence ripped her from him and a fire-storm of pain ignited in his right shoulder. His arm went weak and his fingers turned numb. A hundred things flashed through his mind, but uppermost was the truck that hit Smith's transport yesterday. The officers who'd survived the crash, had been executed in the wreckage.

Adam had no doubt the van had deliberately struck him and Eva.

Smith and/or his partner had somehow known he and Eva met with DuMond at the broadcasting studio and had lain in wait for them. *Was DuMond in collaboration with Smith?* Nothing he'd seen yet had made him a believer of that theory. What if Smith had located Adam's father's house and had followed them from there? DuMond had all but given out Adam's personal information this morning on the radio. It wouldn't have taken much research to find the home Adam had grown up in.

Adam had to admit, he'd been ticked his father had followed them. *Had he been too distracted and missed another person on his tail?*

Son-of-bitch! Vince had taken the truck road on the way in. *Had he encountered the killer?*

Eva screamed then went silent just before the car settled upside down.

Dear God, had she been thrown from the car? Hanging from his hips, he fought against the airbag, frantic to get his knife from his pocket and call for help before the killer appeared. Unbearable pain throbbed from his right shoulder and his right arm wasn't working anywhere near right. He had to fight against a dizzying black mist clawing at his consciousness. The seconds stretched longer with every thud of his heart. He couldn't find their cell phones. They'd been plugged in on the center console before the crash.

Cursing hard, he gave up using his right hand to search for his phone, and dug for his knife with his left hand. He cut himself loose before puncturing and deflating the airbag, searching immediately for Eva.

"Eva. *Dear God*, Eva!" His stomach wrenched with dread. She lay unmoving, her head hanging out the broken passenger window, her legs still inside the car. The heavy rain splattered everywhere.

Still no sign of the killer. Had the son-of-a-bitch been injured in the impact?

Scooting forward, Adam reached for Eva, afraid to move her. He placed his fingers around her ankle and focused on calming his pounding heart enough to feel her pulse. The strong and steady beat nearly brought tears to his eyes. A hand to her ribs told him her respirations, though shallow, were even and unlabored.

Through the cracked windshield and rain, all he could see was dark green leaves. Their phones were nowhere in sight, even the charger had been ripped from the dash.

"Eva, please, luv. Can you hear me?"

Adam heard thrashing from outside. "Adam! Adam! Jesus, are you all right?"

Thank God. "Pops! Call 911 and watch out for a killer!"

The burst of strange laughter from outside chilled Adam's soul. He stuffed his pocket knife in Eva's shoe and dug for his Taurus at the small of his back.

"Run, Pops!" Adam lunged forward, praying like hell, he didn't injure Eva more as he covered her limp body with his and tried to get a view out of the window.

With the car upside down, they were partially lodged on thick bushes about three feet off the ground. He couldn't see anyone, just the bushes and the rain and the foliage. "Run, Pops!"

"Keep your hands up, old man! Too bad you don't have time to make that call. You'll need it," the stranger said.

"Who the hell are you?" Vince yelled.

Adam strained, his rage white hot. "I'm going to kill you!"

Another laugh. "I'm everyone's nightmare on Elm Street tonight." The gun shot and a cry of horror ripped Adam's heart apart. "Pops! Pops!"

A satanic, black and white painted face appeared in Adam's sight. With his right arm worthless, he fired left-handed at the bastard clown.

Ducking back, the man laughed. "You have to the count of five to throw your gun out the window or I'll blow her head off."

"One."

Christ, he couldn't get Eva back in the car. Nor could he get out of the car to protect her.

"Two."

God. Eva, honey. I'm sorry.

"Three."

Adam slipped the magazine from his Taurus 9mm and stuffed the ammo down his pants. He searched for anything else that could help save them and saw Eva's purse. "Who are you?" Adam yelled loud enough to cover his lunge for Eva's purse and the Glock inside. He also shoved her mace in one sock and a pen in his shoe.

"Four."

Cringing, Adam tossed his Taurus out the window.

"Five." The sicko shot out the back passenger window, right next to Eva.

Trying to shield her from the flying glass, Adam fought the urge to fire back. He slid the gun up Eva's side, inside her shirt and hoodie to secure it beneath the elastic of her bra under her arm. He might be a dead man, but she'd hopefully have a chance in hell.

"Next time don't make me wait for what I want. Push her out of the car and then you come out nice and slow."

"She's hurt."

The man fired again, blowing out the back window. "Do you want her dead? Last warning; don't make me wait for what I want."

Shit. Praying he didn't injure her more, Adam worked Eva out of the car, by lifting up on her legs and then pushing her slowly out until she lay on the bush. The car rocked precariously. Would it fall more and crush her?

Instead of moving slowly, Adam dove out the window, caught Eva in his arms and rolled. They hit the ground. Pain from his shoulder wracked his body and stole his breath. He kept rolling them to safety as the branches of the bush broke and the car tilted and sank deeper. It would have crushed Eva.

When he came to a stop, he found the man with the painted face had KISS-like hair. Two upside down crosses framed his eyes. The red contacts he wore were sickening in their evil glow. He hovered over them and smiled as he placed the muzzle of a double barreled pistol against Eva's head. "Roll off her. Spread eagle and put your hands behind your head."

Nearly passing out from the pain, Adam complied as much as he could. "I can't move my right arm."

The man did a quick pat down. He found the mace and kicked Adam in the ribs as punishment. Thankfully, the man missed the crotch ammo. He only patted Eva's pockets. So far, her gun in her bra and his knife in her shoe were safe.

"Where are your cell phones?"

"In the car," Adam said.

"Get up and carry her to the van."

Adam gained his feet and searched through the pouring rain for his father as he lifted Eva's weight with his left arm and clutched her to his chest with his weak right arm. The pain burning in his shoulder was unbearable, but nothing compared to seeing his father lying face down in the rain and unmoving about ten yards away. Adam's knees nearly gave out from the wave of grief crashing into him. All he could do was pray his father was alive and that help would come. But there was little traffic on this private drive. The van had knocked him and Eva off the road and down an embankment. In this rain, the crash wouldn't be seen from the road. His father's Batmobile and the white van were up on the roadside.

Adam's rage kept him going. As soon as he had Eva in the van where he could make a fast getaway, he'd take the bastard out. He couldn't determine who the man was. With makeup, wig, and a black trench coat, he could be any number of people. If it was Daisy/John Jayne then she/he had lost a good amount of weight since her teen picture. Instead of grossly obese, she/he was somewhat overweight.

Adam focused on Eva, searching for signs of severe injury in her pale face. She had a hell of a bruised egg on her forehead. The bleeding from the blow appeared to be superficial instead of inward. That was a good sign. A few minor cuts on her face oozed blood which the rain kept washing away. He didn't see or feel any other injuries and prayed hard she'd just been knocked unconscious, but the longer she was out of it, the more he worried.

"One wrong move and I put a bullet into your spine so you live long enough to see what I do to her."

He wanted to annihilate the bastard behind him in word and deed. He didn't care what traumatic experiences had led this sicko to this point. When evil reigned like it did with this killer and his partner, obliterating it became the only option. Any redemption could be worked out at the pearly gates, not among the innocent where more lives were at stake.

Adam slid twice in the mud climbing back up to the road, and each restart cost him. He kept waiting for that bullet and kept praying for Eva to wake.

For the first time in his life, he seriously doubted his ability to survive the situation, which pissed him off even more. His rage went from white hot to icy cold, a level he'd never known.

The back doors to the van hung open. Now, on level ground, he readjusted Eva's weight. He heard the sound of sirens and prayed his father had called 911 before coming down to the car. His gut wrenched again. He had to hold onto the hope that his father was alive.

"Where are you taking us?" Adam asked, hoping to distract the killer while he grabbed the gun he'd tucked beneath Eva's bra. He'd have one chance and he'd have to shoot with his injured right hand. The moment he laid Eva down on the hard metal floor of the van, he twisted and fired the Glock without standing upright.

The man's eyes widened in surprise, but he didn't drop dead. Adam's aim for the heart hit six inches too low. A split second later the man fired one of the two weapons in his hands.

Adam expected a bullet. Instead, he got tased. The projectiles hit his back and side. He fell on Eva convulsing, his entire body on fire, unable to control any of its movements.

Was the man wearing a bulletproof vest? He seemed unaffected by Adam's bullet as he quickly zip-tied Adam's hands behind his back, wrenching his right shoulder hard. *Dear God!* Adam screamed. A cold sweat covered his body, his vision dimmed, his hearing warbled and the world went black.

EVA WOKE TO SUFFOCATING darkness. She could barely breathe. A ton of warm bricks pressed her back painfully against cold metal. Her head throbbed with nauseating intensity and the vibration of a moving car thrummed, jarring her every muscle with needles of pain.

She remembered the accident. *Was she in an ambulance? Was she blind?* She knew her eyes were open, but she could only see blackness. Devin's warning came flooding back. *Darkness. Suffocating darkness…it's not safe for either of you.*

That would mean she wasn't in an ambulance. She tried to move, seriously feeling each breath become harder and harder to draw. She couldn't budge an inch. Her hands and feet were bound. She was trapped in a vise. Desperate, she bucked hard at the weight on her, which made her head throb with dizzying stabs of pain. In her panicked confusion, it took her a few minutes to register it was Adam on top of her.

"Adam?" she whispered. Nothing.

She bucked again, trying to shift him to one side. Her thigh accidently slid between his legs and rammed upward where she hit hard metal rather than soft flesh.

His body stiffened and he groaned as if in dire agony.

"Adam? Where are you hurt?"

"Everywhere now."

"Sorry. You have to move. I can't breathe."

"And I can't move now that you shoved my clip to the North Pole. *Damn.*" He shuddered then rolled with an *umph* and groaned.

"Your clip?"

"What I could salvage of my Taurus. I'll explain later."

"Where are we?"

"Back of a van with a painted-faced perp who's wearing a KISS wig and a trench coat."

"It's Smith's partner. It has to be Jayne."

"Eva?"

"What?"

"Why don't you sound surprised in the least over the makeup and wig?"

"We already uncovered the goth theme that Daisy/John Jayne was into."

"Beneath the makeup, wig, and trench coat, it could be Ronald McDonald. I don't know if it is Jayne or not. If it is, he's lost weight. Right now, we need to get loose. I'd rather die than face what's coming after I shot that bastard."

"You shot him?"

"Tried to. He must have on Kevlar. Tased me and tied me up afterward like a pro. There's a knife in your shoe. Can you get to it?"

"How did it get there?" Eva scrambled, trying to get the knife from her shoe with hands tied behind her back.

"Me."

The van slowed and hit gravel.

"Fuck," Adam said. "Get free. When the van doors open, you run. You hide. And no matter what happens, don't turn yourself in. They're going to kill everyone. You living will make it infinitely less painful. And Eva, I want you to know that after years of...existing...you've made me feel alive these past three days."

"Adam, I...shit. Don't tell me stuff like that when hell is about to unleash. We're going to get out of this. And we'll do it together. I'm not leaving you behind." She almost clasped the knife with her fingers, but the van jerked to a stop and she lost her hold. "It's too late now. We'll escape together."

"No! You don't understand. The way he operates, there are no options. He's already shot—maybe killed—my father, I think. Jesus, I need you to take care of my mother. There is no one else. You have to escape, Eva."

"Your father? Dear God, Adam!"

The van doors wrenched open, splattering cold rain over her. Eva blinked at the sudden light streaming in. KISS-hair stood silhouetted against a bright flood light. She and Adam were in the back of the van along with loads of camera equipment.

"Fucking A, John John! I've been calling you all day. The bitch threw up on herself when I drugged her. I can't find the key to let her loose to clean up nor can I find my blue pills. I've had no fun at all today." Mason Smith's voice rang out from somewhere behind KISS-hair.

Despite the desperate circumstances, relief that Shirley was alive and hadn't suffered greater horrors flooded through Eva.

"The pills expired and I've got the key. Couldn't risk you deciding to find another cabin to play in. That's what screwed us to begin with, and now it's worse. There's been a change of plans. After we finish them off, we're leaving here."

"Why?"

"They got too close. I had to take them and this bastard shot me."

John John raised his left arm. Eva saw the flash of a pistol. She twisted and kicked him in the stomach. The shot sounded like thunder in the van. Adam jerked, groaning in agony and John John doubled over, disappearing from Eva's sight. Blood spread from the fresh bullet wound in Adam's right shoulder. He was a whiter shade of pale, unmoving except for the rise and fall of his chest. *Dear God!*

"John John!" Mason screamed, a wrenching sound of complete anguish.

She knew who Mason's partner was. DuMond's dreadlocked camerawoman, JJ. Who was most likely Daisy Jayne. Officer Hatchett had done an interview with DuMond. Jayne would then have had an opportunity to take Hatchett's pen and plant it at Shirley's, too. While Mason knelt to John John, Eva dug for the knife in her shoe. She clasped it and hit the opening trigger as she pulled it up.

Mason wailed. "Wake up, John John!"

Wedging the blade against her shoe, she snapped it into place then slashed at the zip-tie holding her ankles.

It took three stabs to cut the plastic. One stab nicked her ankle.

"Mason. Get the bastards into the cabin. We're going to make them pay."

"You're hurt. You can't die. You just can't."

"Just do it."

Eva hooked her ankles together and tucked the knife into her waistband. Mason grabbed her by the hair and jerked her toward him. "This is all your fault, bitch!" He slapped her hard. She reeled, held up only by her hair, eyes stinging. Blood flooded her mouth as her teeth cut the inside of her cheek.

"Hurry, Mason."

John John sounded bad off. Mason lifted her from the van and carried her through the rain to a rundown cabin. She saw only woods beyond the flood light. She didn't hear anything above the storm. A quick glance behind, showed John John walking slowly to the cabin. Relief flooded Eva, she had feared he'd shoot Adam again.

As soon as Mason entered the cabin, the scent of baby powder hit her and flashes of multiple murders on hyper speed assaulted at her. Screaming girls, knives, axes, torture, death. Twins holding hands crying. *Forever Cissy. Forever Macie.* This was their main killing zone. The noise of the horror clawed at her mind, demanding to be heard. It was overwhelming. Eva felt death. She heard death. She breathed death. She'd never experienced a site of mass killings. The cold stabbing her was paralyzing.

She gasped for air, feeling as if the very life of her was being sucked away. Nausea and pain warred in her gut. She couldn't give into the visions or Adam and Shirley would die. She fought to shut out the victims, biting her injured cheek, she focused on the pain ramming into her awareness and grabbed Mason's arm. "John John isn't telling you the truth because he doesn't want you to worry or miss out on what you two planned. But he's hurt bad. You hurt me, Shirley, or Adam and I won't help you save him. He will die."

"He'll be okay."

"No, he won't. Remember, I know things. He *will* die if I don't help him."

Mason grabbed her by the throat, squeezed and shook her. "How do you know shit?"

"He'll die without me," she gasped. "God tells me things," she whispered. "Like you two killed twin sisters here named Cissy and Macie."

Thunder shook the cabin and lightning flashed. Mason threw her away from him and stepped back, fear bulging his eyes.

Jayne staggered into the cabin. "What the fuck is taking so long? Get the bastard out of the van."

"She's a witch, John John."

"It doesn't fucking matter what she is. They're both going to pay."

Mason hurried outside. Jayne stumbled to a large chest, leaving a trail of water and blood on the floor. The man wouldn't be walking for long. Eva took the opportunity to free her wrists then pretended to be tied. The cabin was rustic with a bare minimum of clutter. Notably, against one wall stood a table piled with drones and electronic paraphernalia. She looked for Shirley, but didn't see or hear her. She prayed the woman was in one of the rooms visible down a short hallway. She didn't think she'd gotten through to Mason and her mind scrambled on what she could do to save everyone.

She gambled. "Grace doesn't know Mason is her brother, and Mason doesn't know she's his sister, does he? But you do, right Daisy?"

Jayne whipped around and cried out as he grabbed his stomach. He had an axe in his hand. The makeup on his face had smeared, deforming the crosses and his red eyes glowed in the dim light. Eva wanted to wipe his face clean and yank his wig off. Seeing Mason and Jayne together brought their similarities to the forefront. Though their posture was different and Jayne was heavier, they were the same height. "Don't call me that. Daisy is dead."

"Mame wouldn't say that."

Jayne threw the axe. Eva rolled, keeping her hands and feet together, pretending to be helpless. The axe embedded into the wall behind her. She stared at it a moment then saw, just beyond the axe, a rifle in the corner of the room, not far from a cold hearth.

"Who the fuck are you? How do you know shit?"

She forced her gaze to the man. "I'm God's messenger. He's how I know things. He sees everything you do. Mason's going to be very upset that you've lied to him for years. If you two leave here now, I won't tell him. You can ride for the Mexican border, find a doctor and save your life. You won't live through the night unless you stop the bleeding."

He rushed toward her, stumbling. "I'll just kill you now, bitch. Then you can't tell him anything."

"Tell me what?" Mason asked from the doorway.

Jayne turned to face Mason. "Nothing. Where's the FBI piece of shit?"

"He's still in the van. He's too heavy. I need help."

"You can't fucking do anything yourself," Jayne yelled.

"Help! Somebody, help me!" Shirley's slurred cry came from down the hallway.

Eva wished she could run to her, but not until she'd taken Mason and Jayne down.

"You're bleeding bad," Mason said. He frowned at Eva. "What did she tell you, John John?"

"Let's make the shit easier to carry." Jayne jerked the axe from the wall. Eva's heart raced with dread.

8:00 P.M.

MASON FOLLOWED JAYNE OUT the door and Eva scrambled for the rifle. She fought against dizziness and her balance was as wobbly as her knees. The room spun twice by the time she'd lifted the rifle and checked the barrel. Damn, it wasn't loaded and she didn't see any ammo.

Dear God. Keeping the rifle and praying, she ran to the chest Jayne had left opened. No ammo there either, but from the mini-torture arsenal, she grabbed duct tape and a long-ass knife. Working as she ran to the door, she anchored the knife to the end of the rifle with the duct tape. Something had to outreach the axe.

Mason and Jayne stood at the back of van. "Where the hell is he?"

"He was right here, John John, and unconscious. Son-of-a-fucking-bitch, I bet that witch inside did something to make him disappear. She's got powers. She knows shit."

"Shut the fuck up and find him. He can't have gotten far. Here's the pistol."

Taking the gun, Mason ran toward the woods and Jayne bent down to look under the van. One second he was kneeling, the next he was jerked forward until his head smashed into the bumper. He fell to the ground and cried out. Adam's legs swung from beneath the van, looped over Jayne's head, then twisted and squeezed, choking the killer.

Mason ran back, pointing the pistol at the men writhing on the ground. "Let my twin go! Let John John go. Don't hurt him."

His twin? One more piece fell into place. Eva bulleted from the cabin aiming her makeshift bayonet at Mason's back. She sank the blade in the soft area between his hip and his rib cage. She might as well have hit a hornet's nest. Mason roared with rage. He swung around and charged at her, waving the pistol wildly.

Lightning struck and Mason looked up in fear. It was the break she needed. Eva thrust the knife into Mason's neck. "This is justice for Kaylee," she said fiercely.

His eyes widened as blood gushed from the wound and his legs gave out. He fell to the ground. Now that he was down, she thought about applying pressure until help arrived, but he wildly aimed the pistol in her direction and fired. Except he didn't have the strength to keep the barrel tip up. The bullet hit him in the thigh, more blood gushed in spurts. His hate and evil intent had made her decision for her and hastened his own death.

A quick glance showed Jayne down and unmoving, Adam's legs still wrapped around his neck.

Twins! Daisy Jayne's birthday had likely been altered from the first to the seventeenth. Adam had been right. Daisy was the missing sibling. Eva had recently read where semi-identical twins had been born, one born fully male the other with both male and female organs—one egg, fertilized by two sperm which then split in half.

Whatever the circumstances of their upbringing that was beyond these men's control and the cruelty they'd suffered, it didn't justify the evil they'd perpetrated. Their violent death didn't seem enough of a punishment to bring justice to their victims. *Did that mean she was as depraved as they were?*

She left Smith there, bleeding out alone. She'd wanted him to get a death sentence. She never imagined it would be by her hand. And if she could do it all over again, she would have shown him less mercy than she had. Some people might have a problem with that, but after the visions of the vicious torture they'd perpetrated on young, innocent girls, she didn't regret it. She dreaded going back into the cabin and realized that the death Devin had had a premonition of was the overwhelming nightmare of so many victims grabbing at her psyche all at the same time. She honestly didn't think she was strong enough to sift through the morass of death. At least not today. Not tomorrow either. But she would have to at some point. Their spirits had a right to be heard. At least she and Iris wouldn't have to chance exposure by sending multiple drawings through the mail.

Reaching an unmoving Jayne, she saw his red-contact-covered eyes open and found no pulse. Whether he'd died from strangulation or blood loss from being gut shot, it didn't matter. He was dead.

The killers were exposed and beyond earthly justice. The case was closed, but it wouldn't be over until all of the remains of the girls murdered by Mason and his twin were returned to their grieving families.

She pulled off Jayne's wig to find he was balding like Mason. Nothing that played out had matched Devin's vision of Adam's death. Though it was raining and there'd been an occasional flash of lightning, there'd been no yawning field and lightning hadn't struck Mason or Jayne. Adam was lying in the rain, somewhat, but he wasn't dead. Devin was never wrong, so she wondered what that implied.

Taking Adam's knife from her pocket, she cut the zip-tie on Adam's ankles. "Adam, you can let go now. He's dead."

Nothing.

Eva got down on her knees in the rain to look under the van. Adam lay unconscious, his shirt soaked with blood. *Had she discounted Devin's vision too soon?*

"Adam!" She crawled under the van and cut his arms loose. After finding a steady pulse at his neck, she let herself breathe a prayer. It was hard as hell maneuvering under the van, but she used her belt and her rolled up hoodie as a pressure dressing for his shoulder. Then, placing her palm along his rough jaw and her body next to his, she pressed against him, trying to warm the icy cold from his body. "You have to be okay. You can't make me feel alive then die on me. Do you hear me, Adam?"

Groaning, he cracked his eyes open and locked his left arm around her back, squeezing her tight against him. "Am I in heaven?" He sounded slightly delirious.

"Not quite," she said shaking her head.

"You feel like it, but everything else is hell." He groaned and glanced around then shuddered. "Smith? Jayne?"

"Dead. Shirley's alive. I heard her cry out in the cabin."

"Thank God. I pray my dad is alive, too. Go find a phone while I crawl out of here."

"I'm on it, Frasier. But you need to stay put until the paramedics come. You're either in shock or close to it."

She tried to pull away from him and he pressed her closer. "This mutual 'alive' feeling is just beginning, Eva. That's a promise."

He'd heard her plea. Heat stung her cheeks and her pulse *zinged* and *zanged*.

Hot fudge sundaes wouldn't come close to easing this hunger.

EPILOGUE

Two weeks later.

"COME ON, POPS. WE'RE going to be late."

"Yeah, yeah. You've yet to tell me where we're going."

Adam winced. He hoped to delay this conversation until they were already on the road. He'd hired a driver and a luxury town car for the day. He didn't think there'd be enough room in the Batmobile for everyone to breathe during their first family outing in over a dozen years.

It had been a horrendous two weeks with hospitalizations, surgeries, moving his mother to a new care facility and wrapping up the Smith/Jayne case. The horrific videos of their torture and murder of young girls, made them two of the worst serial killers in U.S. history. Forty recordings had been found, but so far only thirty-four bodies had been unearthed on the property. Jayne had been the mastermind, the organized killer keeping Mason, the disorganized killer reined in enough for them to escape detection for almost eighteen years. It was beyond evil, and being exposed to it left a gaping hole in Adam's soul that even killing Jayne didn't fill.

No one had yet to fully recover from their injuries. His father had not only called 911 the second the van had crashed into Adam's car, but Vince had called Brad Warren and read him the license plate of the van. Instead of stopping immediately after impact, Jayne had driven on, leaving Vince to think it had been a hit and run accident. Jayne had then circled back after Vince had rushed down the embankment and taken Vince by surprise.

Had help not been close by, the bullet to Vince's spleen would have killed him. Cold rage and fear still grabbed at Adam's gut every time he thought about what happened. Vince had made a decent physical recovery from surgery, but spirit-wise, he wasn't doing too well. That he'd let himself get shot and a killer take off with Adam and Eva had demoralized Vince.

Adam couldn't get Vince to see how much he'd actually saved the day. Thanks to the information Vince had given 911 operators and the paramedics at the scene, State troopers and police were already scouring the rural area of the cabin after catching traffic cam footage of the van exiting Interstate 75 north of Atlanta. They'd arrived at the cabin minutes after Eva called from a phone she found in the van.

The damage to Adam's shoulder from the trauma of dislocating it to the bullet tearing through muscle and bone, meant a long recovery with physical therapy and at least one or more surgeries to go. Right now, he was dealing with the pain and how his injuries might affect his career in the FBI. He needed to get back on his feet and return to finding the Artist of Death. *A day at a time*, he told himself. His entire life had boiled down to the phrase.

Vince came into the living room. He was dressed but didn't look ready for this step. "What aren't you telling me, Adam? I really don't feel up to going anywhere yet."

"Shirley doesn't want to delay having her birthday celebration any longer. So Eva has helped her arrange a special night and everyone who helped rescue her is invited. You won't have to do much of anything except eat a good meal, listen to some music, and relax, okay?"

Vince frowned. "Maybe. You talk to Eva about Tony and his family's murderer yet?"

"Somewhat. I've told her you agree that Carlan wasn't the killer, but I didn't get into the crime scene and Melissa's doll yet or whom she interviewed. She isn't going to buy anything less than the truth and I don't want to lie to her, so I'm still working on an angle that won't compromise you or your cases at the GBI. But you can talk to her about your book you want to write. Have you put anything on paper yet?"

"No. Maybe it would be best if I just stayed here."

"Today we're celebrating life, Pops. And I'm asking you, son to father, to please come." Adam didn't tell his father that they'd be including his mother in the celebration. They'd make that step when the time came.

Vince sighed. "A father that almost got his son killed and may have ended his son's career."

Adam clenched his teeth. Every part of his life had been reduced to tiny steps. "We've been over it a dozen times. Your intervention saved the day. It gave me time to arm myself and Eva. Without the knife and the gun I hid, I don't know if we would have made it. Now will you please come?"

"Yeah, yeah. All right, but I'm taking a cab home if I want to."

"Okay." Adam was betting that once Vince got out among the living, he'd find it harder to crawl back into the hole he'd been digging for himself. That he didn't liven up even when they talked about Tony Hayden wasn't good.

Baby steps, Adam told himself again. It was that way with Eva, too. She'd been admitted to the hospital with him, for concussion observation. So she'd been there when he'd awoken from surgery and he'd seen her every day until he'd been released from the hospital. But he hadn't seen her since. They'd spoken on the phone and texted about the healing of those injured and about the case, but hadn't gotten personal, which left him in limbo. The amount that he missed her in relation to the time he'd known her was crazily disproportionate. A smart man would be back in D.C., putting some distance between him and her, and chilling out until he had a sane handle on what she made him feel.

He headed out to the waiting car, his pulse already kicking up a notch in anticipation of seeing Eva.

Eva ran her gaze over the festive balloons and Happy Birthday banner and drew a sigh of relief. She'd wanted everything to be just right. When Shirley declared she'd celebrate her birthday even if she was still in the hospital, Eva—with Shirley's permission—put together a special gathering for the amazing woman. The only flaw in Eva's plans was the beyond perfect birthday cake sitting front and center of the party. It was so decadently chocolate, she was sure she gained a pound every time she looked at it.

The informal atmosphere of Powell's Piano bar made a wonderful place for the casual gathering. Tracy, the owner, let Eva rent the entire place for a few hours. And at Shirley's request, Eva had hired a Grammy-worthy band from Texas to play, The Aaron Hendra Project. To Shirley, the band's songs were hope to her and for the world.

Today was as much about Shirley's courage, as it was about her birthday. Released from the hospital just yesterday, Shirley had made remarkable progress in recovering from the horror. Physical therapy had her mobile with a special boot for her maimed foot. The woman's resilience, and attitude over what she'd suffered, awed Eva. It even had Eva re-examining her own perspectives about tragedy. In Shirley's perspective, bad things were going to happen in a broken world, but conquering the bad with a spirit of life-affirming hope, broke any hold evil might have gained over her. She refused to let the bad rule her future. Shirley sat surrounded by friends, paler and thinner than before, but the smile on her face didn't waver.

Life wasn't as clear for Eva. In all honesty, what happened with Smith, Jayne, and Adam had shaken her to the core, and she'd yet to sift through the pieces. She'd started the investigation determined to see Smith get the death penalty, having delivered the punishment by her own hand left her with mixed emotions. She'd never killed a man before and she didn't regret the mortal blow she'd dealt Smith. There'd been no options for either her, or Adam. It was either kill, or be killed, but it still affected her. She felt as if she were on the outside of a snow-globe looking in.

While Jayne and Smith's deaths, and exposing their crimes had brought some measure of justice to Kaylee, it had left in Eva's mind a darkness of depravity unmatched by anything she'd known before. She thanked God, she didn't have to go back and face the cries of the victims again, to tell their story as she'd done for Kaylee. The tapes Jayne made of their crimes, said all that could be said.

Eva had mixed feelings about the case. Not about stopping the evil, or punishing its perpetrators, but all the wrongs that had contributed into making the monsters. Before publishing Kaylee's story, Eva felt as if she needed to reveal those wrongs as well. Jayne had been the driving force, and mastermind of the killing duo. Autopsy revealed the mutilation Jayne suffered as a young child had left her/

him physically dysfunctional as either male or female. Eva didn't know if the FBI would tell Mame Jayne about what Daisy had become. Part of Eva hoped not, but then another part of her wanted the world to know what factors in Daisy's early life, and later years, might have led her/him into becoming a killer. The same was true for Smith, and the environment he grew up in. Did Jayne or Smith ever have a chance at a healthy, normal life? Why shouldn't the Reverend Smith and his wife be made to face the music of their actions socially if not legally? Many experts believe that by the age of seven, a person's core schemas—the processes by which they relate to the world—are formed. On the other hand, she'd heard of children who'd suffered the unspeakable and had gone on to be towers of light and goodness in the world.

Eva didn't know whether Grace DuMond had been informed of her relationship to the twins beyond Jayne being her camerawoman. DuMond had taken a leave of absence from crime reporting, though. While the circumstances of why DuMond wouldn't be around were terrible, Eva wouldn't miss the woman at all.

Everyone in law enforcement and the dozen or so communities that made up the Atlanta area were shocked and horrified that these two monsters had lived among them killed for almost twenty years.

Unfortunately, there were still some late breaking facts without any answers that left a knot of worry inside Eva. The flat tire that had almost sent her and Paddy to their deaths, had been no accident. Mechanics found a .50 caliber bullet embedded in the wheel rim. The illegally purchased automatic rifles Smith and Jayne used to ambush Zeb and Hank, had been located in an equipment bin in Jayne's van, but no .50caliber weapon had been found. So, someone other than Jayne or Smith had been behind that attack. Then, fire inspectors discovered the St. Claire mansion had been bugged with high-tech audio devices hidden inside fake smoke detectors.

Apparently Saturday, just after she, Devin and Iris left for the charity auction, Cablecast had called Lannie. Said they were recalling some faulty equipment after reports of a possible fire hazard. Lannie had the option of bringing the equipment to the nearest store or letting their technician come and test the equipment.

Lannie opted for the tech to test the equipment. Driving an official Cablecast van and wearing a Cablecast uniform, the tech had apparently planted fake smoke detectors in each room he'd entered. The GSM devices were cell phone activated and could be accessed from anywhere in the world. Mason had still been in jail at that point and Eva had yet to interview him, giving him no reason to target her. Nor did the duo have any of the devices in their possession.

The bugging wasn't related to Smith or Jayne. So duo had inadvertently done the St. Claire's a favor by setting fire to the mansion.

Overall, apart from Shirley, everyone seemed to be walking the same paths as they were before the events—somewhat. Lannie fussed over Paddy's health like a mother hen. He wasn't the least bit interested in carrot sticks and coconut water—ever. Eva doubted a chicken wing or an ounce of single-malt whiskey would go to waste tonight.

Since arriving at the party with a reluctant Dr. Caro in tow, Iris's attempts to maneuver Dr. Caro and Devin into the same space had failed. But ironically, by giving up and turning her attention to the piano bar's usual piano player, a humorous Brit by the name Sir John, Iris may have succeeded after all. Though across the room, in conversation with Sheriff Doug and Brad Warren, Devin kept glancing at Dr. Caro as she and Iris laughed over something Sir John said.

The only people who had yet to arrive were her Aunt Zena, who moved through life on her own time table, and Adam. He'd texted that he'd be bringing his father and his mother. Eva knew from her phone conversations with Adam that this was a big step for all of the Frasiers. Making every excuse possible, Eva had avoided seeing Adam after his release from the hospital last week. She had needed some distance to gain a sane perspective on him. It hadn't helped. He was part of why she was such a hot mess inside.

Somehow, his brief intrusion into her life, had redefined her world. Instead of butterflies fluttering a storm in her stomach, she had albatrosses doing flips. The man had almost lost his life to keep her safe, and she had a hard time figuring out what to do about it. Add in the fact that Devin's premonition of a fiery serpent killing Adam had yet to rear its ugly head, and Eva was completely lost as to what to do about him. She'd argued with Devin several times already, but her brother was certain the threat still lay in her and Adam's future.

The door opened and Eva turned to see a grim-faced Adam walk in with his shell-shocked-looking father and clearly confused mother—a petite woman with graying auburn hair and misty blue eyes. Eva hurried over to the Frasiers as she motioned for Lannie. Adam had clued Eva in that Linda was a big *Downton Abbey* fan. So was Lannie. Eva hadn't watched the series before because she rarely watched anything other than certain news shows, but she took a few hours to binge-watch a few episodes in order to connect with Adam's mother. Surprisingly, Eva now felt compelled to go back and start at the beginning of the family's saga.

Lannie joined her.

"Adam, Vince, I am so glad you are here."

Adam nodded; his neck and smile were stiff as a board. "Eva, Lannie, this is my mother, Linda Frasier."

"I'm very happy to meet you." Eva shook Linda's tentative hand. The woman's lost expression pulled at Eva's heartstrings.

Lannie reached out to Linda with a big smile and immediately launched into something familiar for Linda. "I am so glad to have a fellow *Downton Abbey* fan at the party. I love Violet Crawley. Who is your favorite character on the show?"

Linda immediately brightened. "Edith. Oh, it's Edith. She found Marigold and fought everyone to keep her daughter at her side."

"Yes, Edith is wonderful," Lannie said.

Linda looked around. "Where are the little girls? This is a birthday party, right? I wonder if Jenna will be here."

Vince groaned.

Eva smiled. "It's a big girl birthday party. We'll have music and dinner. Adam mentioned that you like music."

Linda nodded. "I do, that would be lovely."

"Excellent."

"Are you sure Jenna's not here?"

"I haven't seen a little girl here. In just a bit you can tell me about her and then I'll be able to keep an eye out, too."

"You are so kind to help." She looked about, seemingly lost again.

Lannie took Linda's hand. "Why don't we go sit at a table and talk about *Downton Abbey*."

Linda launched into an avid response as Lannie led her toward a table.

Adam and Vince followed, hovering anxiously. Walking with them, Eva smiled at the men. "Vince, there's a pitcher of tea at the bar, why don't you bring Lannie and Linda a drink?"

The man blinked then brightened. "Great idea." He handed Lannie a canvass bag with red yarn spilling out and made a beeline to the men at the bar.

"No, hurry," Lannie told Vince.

Looking as fragile as a snowflake about to melt from embarrassment, Adam stuffed the yarn back into the bag. "Mom's making a sweater…for Jenna." He glanced at his father's retreating back. "Pop's still recovering."

Adam clearly regretted coming. Eva set her hand on his arm. "We *all* are recovering. Relax. Whatever it is, it's okay."

He met her gaze, his expression pained and troubled. "You don't know…I shouldn't have brought—"

Eva reached up and set her finger on his full mouth to still his words. His eyes widened and the never far away awareness arched between them. That he'd made such a Herculean effort for his mom and dad jerked her heart and drew her closer to him. "Yeah, you should have. And it will be just fine. I wish I could have my parents here, imperfections and all."

He caught her hand in his warm and firm grip then exhaled as he shook his head. "Hell. Nothing like perspective is there?"

She nodded, and they must have stood looking at each other for a moment because, Lannie interrupted by saying, "You two go find a sauna. Linda and I are going look at the sweater she's making. I've always wanted to crochet but never learned how."

Linda sat at the table next to Lannie, her blue eyes bright with interest. "Heaven's, it's easy to crochet. Let me show you."

"A Sauna?" Adam, still holding her hand, arched a brow as he pulled Eva to the side of the room. "Did I miss a conversation?"

Cheeks burning, Eva shook her head and pulled her hand from his. "Not that I recall."

Adam laughed. "I'll let it go—for now. But you do have to tell me the truth on this. Any more news on the bugs they found in your house or the bullet in your tire?"

"No. They're doing ballistics and trying to trace the high-tech equipment. I'll let you know if something turns up."

He shook his head. "Not good enough. We can't sit around and wait for the other shoe to drop. I feel as if we need to start searching for a motive and go hunting for the shark."

Eva blinked at Adam. The "we" thing made her pulse kick, even as she realized he was Sir Galahading his way right into Devin's death premonition. Yet, according to Devin, it was inevitable, and nothing she could do would stop it. She refused to believe that. "Hold that thought for another day. Tonight, we're taking a break. Remember? You're the one who said I have to breathe."

"Right, you are. In light of breathing, let's go back to that sauna then."

Eva was going to shoot Lannie. Adam was dogged enough to dig the truth out of her. Glancing out the window, she saw a tour bus pull into the parking lot. "Looks as if Aunt Zena is here."

Adam leaned down and narrowed his gaze at the tour bus. "ZENA KNOWS. LINK TO THE BEYOND TODAY!" He straightened and raked a hand through his hair. "This can't be happening. *She's your aunt?*" He was ghost white and board stiff. You'd have thought he'd seen the devil himself. He gulped in air then marched for the exit door.

Eva blinked at his visceral reaction and followed him. He'd gone from playful to majorly upset in a heartbeat. He hadn't met Aunt Zena before and Eva hadn't mentioned her aunt was a renowned medium in the psychic world. Eva tended to avoid that subject and it was costing Adam now. He'd handled serial killers with more calm than he was her aunt.

Once outside, she spoke up. "Yes, Zena Knows is my aunt. What's wrong?"

He squeezed his eyes shut, visibly grappling for control. "Shysters like her are part of why my mother's in an institution."

Eva arched her brows. She was immune to skeptics of the paranormal, even welcomed them because that made it easier for the St. Claires to hide. But Adam's heated antipathy felt like a personal blow. His tone all but called Zena a criminal. "Explain how," she demanded.

"My mother went to Zena years ago to speak to Jenna in the great beyond. Zena Knows told my mother that a connection to Jenna couldn't be made because Jenna wasn't dead. After that my mother went wild to find Jenna and when that didn't happen the downhill spiral was brutal." He paced away from her then quickly turned back. "We just need to go home. We just need to leave now, before my dad and my mother go off the deep end."

Eva could feel her temper escalating with the rise in Adam's. Part of it was with his seemingly overblown reaction, and part of it was irritation at her aunt, who knew Eva didn't want to go around flouting psychic anything—especially on the St. Clair's home turf. So what does her aunt do? Show up in her tour bus, which there'd be no out of the way place to park. Murphy's Law Karma at work again. "Take a breath and help me understand what is going on here. Your mother went to my aunt—"

"Not long after Jenna was taken."

"And my aunt said she couldn't help because Jenna was alive."

"That's what she swore to my mother."

"You sound as if you're certain Jenna is dead. Is she?"

"I don't know, but—"

"But you resent someone believing she's alive? A charlatan or con artists as you put it, would take someone's money and repeatedly bring them back to communicate to a lost loved one. Not send someone away."

He exhaled, clearly searching to express his thoughts. "What I resent is the pretense and the surety. No one should prey on the grief of others by pretending to connect to the dead. Your aunt doesn't know for sure that Jenna is alive. No one can. And she shouldn't have made my mother believe so strongly. You don't believe she can talk to the dead, do you?" He looked at her as if she'd been the one to suddenly grow horns, not him.

She narrowed her gaze. "You don't believe there is an afterlife? A spirit world?"

He frowned. "Well...yeah, of course I do."

"Have you ever communicated with a ghost?"

"No." He glared at her.

"Did Armstrong walk on the moon?"

"Yeah."

"Have you ever walked on the moon?"

"No."

She glared back at him. "So you don't have to experience everything in order to believe it. I've never spoken to ghosts, but then I can't say my aunt hasn't. I communicate with the spirit world every time I pray, though."

"But that's completely different—"

"Is it?" She shook her head, wondering why she was even having this conversation at all. It suited her purposes for no one to believe in psychic anything. Yet, when it came to his sister, how could she leave him completely in the dark? If Aunt Zena said Jenna was alive then she was at that time.

Adam seemed to count to ten before he answered her. "You have to understand, my father had to press criminal charges against a man who'd taken advantage of my mother's grief to the tune of tens of thousands of dollars. And the reason I had to move my mother to a different facility this week, is because she escaped her old one to go off searching for Jenna with another psychic, who had no compunction at picking an elderly woman up on the side of the road outside a nursing home."

Crap. Real psychics were crucified because there were so many fake ones out there. "I'm sorry those things happened. You do realize you're painting everything black with a single brush stroke, don't you?"

He frowned at her, as if he'd tell her it was already all black. No painting needed.

She spoke before he could discredit her point. "We need to talk more about this, but later. Right now, the bigger picture is for your family to be here to celebrate life with everyone else. Let me go intercept my aunt. She'll come to the party as just Aunt Zena. She'll leave Zena Knows in the bus, and send the bus back to our hotel. Will that work for now?"

Adam drew several breaths. "I don't mean to be an ass."

"You're not. I see a man who's trying to protect his family after an already difficult day. Anytime you forge a new path, it's not going to be easy."

"Understatement of the year. Okay, we'll try. Hopefully, it won't blow up in my face. Mention psychics and both my father and my mother go off the deep end. Opposite sides, though. He's ten times worse than me against and she's a million times for." His look said he was doing something against his better judgement to humor her.

Down the parking lot, she could see the bus had given up looking for a place to park and was headed back to the front of the piano bar. "I'd better cut Zena Knows off at the pass. Go back inside and sometime, when you can separate emotions from the mix ask yourself, if there is a spirit world, why would it be *impossible* to communicate with it?"

Adam opened his mouth then shut it and Eva left him standing there.

She waved Zena's driver down. He opened the bus doors to let her in.

Dressed in a shimmering caftan of gold lame, Zena appeared like an exotic queen from another world. The peacock feather in her gold turban waved delicately with her every move. She was a beautiful woman with luxurious hair and myste-rious green eyes. Her hair color changed with the wind. Tonight it was red-gold. Adam's sister had been taken twenty-eight years ago, so Zena Knows, while young looking, had changed a great deal since her early years.

Eva prayed the situation would work out. She hugged her aunt. "I'm glad you're here."

"But? You aren't out here chasing an old lady down because you're worried I was late. What's wrong?"

Eva winced. "I have a favor to ask."

"Anything, darling. You know that." Her glittering rings flashed.

"Can I have just my aunt tonight? No Zena Knows. No readings or spirit communications. No psychic anything. In fact, it would be best if Zena Knows didn't even get mentioned."

Zena arched a brow. "Who is he?"

"Who's who?"

"The man you're trying to hide your family from."

"I'm not doing that—"

Zena shook her head.

Eva sighed. "Fine. Maybe a little. Adam's not the entire reason. Devin, Iris, and I are still in the psychic closet, so to speak, and once the rumors fly it's hard to bring them back to ground. I did ask you to leave the bus at the hotel, if you remember. But you're right. It's more for Adam's mother and father's sake. I'll explain later, but psychics are a sore spot with the men, and the mother is too fragile for Zena Knows right now. She saw you years ago about her daughter, and things did not turn out well for the family."

"How so?"

"After learning her daughter was alive, the mother drove herself off the deep end trying to find her."

Zena sighed. "The double edged sword. Damned by knowing and not knowing. This Adam. He's the man who saved you from those beasts and Devin from serious burns? The one Lannie calls Superman?"

Eva rolled her eyes. "Yes."

"Well, if psychics are kryptonite for him and his family then he's in serious trouble with a St. Claire. But tonight we can pretend to be normal." Zena eased off her turban and unzipped the front of the caftan to slip it from her shoulders. Beneath, she wore a black cocktail dress that Eva doubted she'd have fit into—ever. "Gus," Zena called out to her driver in the front. "Take the bus back to the hotel, and take the night off." Zena picked up her purse, and caught Eva's arm. They exited the bus, heading for the piano bar. "Lead me to your fearless wonder. I'll go along for now, but realize that once you marry him, he'll have to deal with the real us."

Eva gritted her teeth. "Nobody is marrying anybody."

"And that's a problem with you and Devin. Both of you are afraid to live, love, or laugh. I may have a poor success rate, but that doesn't stop me from trying and having a fabulous time failing."

"Does that mean—"

"Unfortunately, yes. Rolando and I have parted ways. Though I think it was more his wife's fault than mine."

Eva nearly bit her tongue in shock. "Rolando was *married*. How could you—"

Zena waved her hand. "Sorry dear, that didn't come out right. Rolando was a widower. His wife died five years ago."

"Then how? I don't understand."

"Well darling, every time I opened the door into the beyond, she was there hounding me about Rolando. Made it very difficult for me to communicate with anyone else on the other side. It was like trying to have a civil conversation with a banshee screaming in my ear."

"That would be challenging."

"You're kind. It was a nightmare that I wasn't willing to live with for the rest of my life."

"I'm sorry. Where's Rolando now?" They entered the piano bar.

"Left him in Hawaii. He surfs. With all the bikini babes running up and down the beach, it won't be long before he replaces me—or at least *tries* to replace me.

But enough about my woes. This is a party, is it not?"

"That it is. You'll love the band." Eva's anxious glance about, showed Adam close to his mother, but in conversation with Brad Warren. Vince was still at the bar and had joined Sheriff Grant and Devin. The band was warming up to play. "The lead vocalist for the band is Aaron Hendra. He is from Australia, and is a complete surprise. I should have expected it, though, since Shirley praised him and the band."

"A surprise how? Is he married?"

Eva rolled her eyes. "Yes, he's married. His wife Tiffany is a beautiful woman who spends her life inspiring and building up other women through her Sanctuary of Style network. What I wanted to say about Aaron is he's not your typical 'rock star' musician. The man even goes over to Africa to minister to the victims of poverty and war."

Zena grabbed Eva's hand. "Providence at work again. I'll have to speak to him about Africa. I just found out the current charity I'm supporting only sends twenty-five cents out of every dollar to those in need."

"I'm sure he'd be glad to discuss the charity he works with."

"Eva, got a minute?" Tracy, the owner who was graciously playing bartender tonight waved at Eva.

"Go," Zena shooed her off. "I'll meet your Adam and the band later. I see Iris took my advice and made Caroline come. We've some plotting to do."

Eva hurried over to bar. *Poor Devin.* If Aunt Zena was getting into the matchmaking fray, Devin didn't stand a chance. Eva almost laughed until she realized she was in the same boat as Devin, now.

Tracy had Betty Grable hair and eyes paired with a Carol Burnett-like humor that Eva thoroughly enjoyed.

"Everything okay?" Eva asked, taking a seat at the bar.

"More than okay. I didn't know what Shirley—what all of you really—had been through when you booked this party. It had to be horrifying and it's amazing to see all of you here celebrating life."

Eva smiled. "That would be because of Shirley. Otherwise, I think we would all be hiding in our individual rabbit holes."

"I had a close friend who chose to end her life *after* surviving a violent crime.

So, what is happening here, is…important and close to my heart. I'd like to pro-
vide a champagne toast for everyone this evening. Then wondered if, sometime in
the future, you and Shirley would talk with me about holding fundraisers for the
National Victim's Assistance Program, and maybe even, events like this to celebrate
life here, free of charge?

Eva set her hand over Tracy's where it rested on the bar. "I'm deeply sorry about
your friend. And, yes, we will talk. A very interesting idea that I think Shirley would
love to consider. In fact, I am planning on fundraisers to add to the scholarship
fund I've established for the families of my security men who were killed. This
place would be perfect."

"Good. I've wanted to be a part of something that makes a difference in the
world around me. I think God sent you all my way for that reason. Do you want
to do the champagne after the buffet dinner?"

"Perfect and thank you."

Tracy shook her head. "No, thank you." She turned to fix some drinks.

Eva spied her aunt speaking to Adam and decided she needed to be around
for damage control.

When she made it to Adam's side, he and Zena were laughing about something.

"I'm glad you two have met," Eva said.

"I'm sorry," Adam held his hand out to her aunt. "I didn't introduce myself.
I'm Adam Frasier."

Zena smiled and took his hand. "Zena St. Claire, Eva's aunt."

Adam's jaw dropped.

"Nice to meet the man who saved my family. I owe you. I'll leave you and
Eva to chat while I go greet Devin." Zena left, parting the crowd like the Red Sea.

"She's *Zena Knows*? I didn't recognize her. She had black hair years ago. She
is so…so…"

"Tomorrow her hair could be blue. She changes it often, but the woman
remains the same. Savvy. Dynamic. Not a shyster?"

Adam winced. "Yes, so it seems."

"I should text Devin warning."

"Because?"

Eva explained the matchmaking plot.

He shook his head and laughed. "The perils of normal family shenanigans. I'd forgotten."

"*Normal?*" Eva cried before she could bite her tongue. *Her family was a universe away from normal.* Thankfully, Aaron Hendra interrupted. The band was ready. His Aussie accent rumbled through the room. "It's great to be in Atlanta and an honor to play for Shirley tonight. She's requested our first song be "Alive." It's from our debut album, *Octobersong*, and is very dear to my heart. I wrote this for my amazing wife, Tiffany.

The song began and Eva stood shocked as the words unfolded. *You make me feel like I'm alive.*

Adam caught her hand and pulled her with him. "Seems that Providence is speaking. Let's dance."

Eva shook her head. "It's been years, Frasier. I don't—"

"*Years?*" he asked, arching a brow. "You promised to breathe, Ms. Saint. So let's breathe for a few minutes. It's just a dance. I'll lead. You follow. Simple."

He pulled her into his arms, setting fire to her senses. For once, she leaned against him, letting her being feel the heat of his, letting her burdened soul rest in the strength of his presence for a brief moment in time. "Don't you know that nothing is ever simple, Frasier?" she whispered.

He didn't answer, just eased her closer to him.

But she could pretend for just a minute. Couldn't she? Before closing her eyes, Eva saw others dancing, and some who appeared about to dance…maybe. Lannie had hold of Paddy, and Vince stood with Linda, his arm at the small of her back. They were swaying to the music, smiling as if all the dark clouds of pain, trouble, illness, and tragedy in their lives had parted and the warmth of the sun touched their hearts.

You make me feel like I'm alive.

Eva closed her eyes and wondered if the impossible could ever be possible.

Coming in 2017
Exposed Case File 2: *Hayden's Hell*

Acknowledgements

This book is dedicated to those who fight against the many faces of evil that seek to destroy all things good. In a broken world with many wrongs, fighting the good fight, making life safer—one day at a time—takes dedication, courage, and heart. Each person matters.

My life has been greatly blessed with many amazing, caring, and talented people. They make my books possible in so many different ways. Their encouragement, support, inspiration. and love mean everything to me and make my life so very rich. Thank you.

To Beth and Doug thank you for your thoughts. To Dayna, Ashleigh, Ivy, Wendy, Tierney, Rita, Annette, Stephanie and Jacquie, huge thanks for helping to make the Exposed Series and Case File #1, KAYLEE'S JUSTICE possible.

And much appreciation to the creative people who bring good things to the hearts of others.

Remember everyday to dream, believe, create, inspire, love, and heal. Be kind and pay it forward.

FIND JENNI ONLINE:
www.jenniferstgiles.com
Twitter
Facebook
Tumblr

About the Author

USA Today Bestselling Author Jennifer St. Giles might have a split personality. Or as a nurse and mother of three, she knows how to multi-task. She writes in a number of genres from gothic historicals, paranormal thrillers, romantic suspense, and sexy contemporary romance. She has won a number of awards for writing excellence including, two National Reader's Choice Awards, two-time Maggie Award Winner, Daphne du Maurier Award winner, Romance Writers of America's Golden Heart Award, along with RT Book Club's Reviewer's Choice Award for Best Gothic/Mystery. She loves hearing from her readers via her website jenniferstgiles.com or you can find her on Facebook and Twitter @jenniferstgiles.

Made in the USA
Columbia, SC
19 August 2018